The
LONG
WAY HOME

ALSO BY ROBIN PILCHER

Starburst

An Ocean Apart

Starting Over

A Risk Worth Taking

ROBIN PILCHER

The LONG WAY HOME

**Doubleday Large Print
Home Library Edition**

THOMAS DUNNE BOOKS
St. Martin's Press
New York

THOMAS DUNNE BOOKS.
An imprint of St. Martin's Press.

ISBN 978-1-61664-136-8

First published in Great Britain under the title
A Matter of Trust by Sphere

For my father, Graham Pilcher
and my father-in-law, Robin McCall

who, in their youth, gave so much
and, thereafter, asked for very little

The
LONG
WAY HOME

1

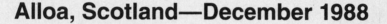

Alloa, Scotland—December 1988

As she left the driveway and ran down the narrow lane leading to the farm, the silence of that cold winter morning was absolute, save for the crunch of breaking ice as her Doc Martens stamped through the puddles that ran ribbon-like along the rutted track. Tears glistened on her rosy cheeks, but the broad smile on her face showed that they were due to the frigid air nipping at her brown eyes rather than from any feeling of unhappiness. In fact, Claire Barclay could not have been happier. The cold that penetrated her padded jacket and bit at her ears through the woolly hat she wore pulled over her short hennaed hair was counteracted by a tingling warmth flooding from deep within.

Because Claire Barclay was most definitely in love.

Actually, she had been in love with Jonas Fairweather, expert motor mechanic and budding champion rally driver, ever since she had first come to Scotland at the age of eleven, but even though she had spent nearly every day of the next seven years in his company, she had never told him. And he had never said anything to her. They had never even kissed.

So the question that had arisen on so many occasions in Claire's mind was when to broach this subject, and take their friendship from its present stage into one of deep and everlasting affection.

Today was the day, the time was right. She had finished with school and now had nine months to spend with Jonas before she went on to university at St. Andrews. And it was Christmas, the season of glad tidings. The previous evening, they had been together in the workshop, and they had talked and laughed while he worked on his car until well after eleven o'clock.

When she left, his farewell had not been the usual muffled goodbye called out from the depths of the car engine. He had walked with her to the door and stood close, spinning a spanner in his hand, catching her eye and smiling at her. She had sensed then that something was going to happen, but he had just slipped the spanner into the pocket of his coveralls, pushed the door open and said, "See you tomorrow then."

Yes, the time was definitely right.

She walked into the farm courtyard and went to the door of the workshop and slid it open. She realized immediately that things were not normal. There were no signs of activity, the bonnet of the Ford Escort was closed and the only sound came from the gas heater roaring away in the corner. She was about to turn and make her way over to the farmhouse when she caught sight of Jonas, dressed in his usual grease-stained coveralls, sitting on an old broken-backed chair by the closed tool chest. He was slumped forward, seemingly oblivious to her presence, resting his elbows on his knees and covering his face with his hands. She walked quietly towards him and, as she approached, began to hear the occasional unsteady intake of his breath.

"Jonas?" she asked concernedly. "What's wrong?"

"Go away," he replied without moving his hands from his face.

"What's happened?" she said, putting a hand on his shoulder.

He reacted to her touch as if he had been scalded. Violently pushing away her hand, he jumped to his feet and walked away from her and stood facing the rear of the workshop. "Just head off, will you. I don't want you to be here."

Claire shook her head incredulously. "No, I will not head off, not until I know . . ."

He turned and glared contemptuously at her. "For Christ's sakes, just get out. Get back to your big mansion house and stay there." He began to walk quickly over to the door. "You're not welcome here."

Tears welled up in Claire's eyes as she followed him out into the courtyard. "Jonas, what on earth has happened?" she cried after him. "Why are you being like this?"

He spun round but kept walking backwards towards the farmhouse. "Just leave me alone, will you?" He scythed his hands apart. "It's over . . . for good. I never want to see you again."

Claire stood in shock as she watched him turn and hurry off to the farmhouse. He entered and slammed the door behind him. She ran over to it and tried to turn the knob, but it was locked.

"Jonas!" she yelled out. "What are you doing? Please, Jonas, let me in." She laid her cheek against the cold wood of the door. "You can't do this," she said quietly. "I love you." She slumped onto the doorstep, brushing away the tears that fell freely down her cheeks with the back of her hand, ignoring the icy dampness that seeped through her denim skirt and thick black tights.

She stayed there for half an hour, only moving when the shivering in her body became so severe that she felt she might pass out with the cold. She got up and glanced back at the closed door before making her way stiffly across the courtyard and back out along the track.

It was the last time she would ever use it.

2

New York—May 2005

Pushing the set cutlery on the table to one side, Claire Barrington placed the menu and reservations book on the laundered white tablecloth and smoothed down the back of her black pencil skirt before sitting down on the velvet dining chair. She pulled it in and opened up the book, turning the pages to find that day's bookings. Every line was filled, both for lunchtime and the evening meal, and additionally six names and telephone numbers were written in red at the side of the page in case of cancellations. It wasn't a surprise or anything out of the ordinary. Since her husband Art had started the restaurant over sixteen years ago, Barrington's had steadily built up a reputation of being one of the best places to eat in the East Village.

Claire glanced over her shoulder towards the kitchen. There was no sign yet of the chef appearing. Pushing back her chair, she got up and walked over to the bar, taking out the small make-up case that she always kept on a shelf behind it. She had learned over the years to take opportunity of every downtime moment and she hadn't yet had the time to check her appearance since arriving that morning. She undid the zip of the case, extracted a lipstick and was in the process of applying a light red gloss to her mouth when the chef hurried through from the kitchen. She turned to him and smiled. "So, what happened to you, Jean-Pierre?"

"I am sorry, Claire, I was talking to the fruit supplier. He was not able to fill the order for the avocados."

Claire smacked her lips together and studied them in the mirror at the back of the bar. "What can we do about that, then?"

"There is another man I can try. I will phone him after."

Claire replaced the make-up case behind the bar and led the way back to the table. The chef followed close behind, wiping his hands uncertainly on his starched white apron. He had come over from France to work in the United States two years before as a sous-chef in one of the smart uptown hotels, and although quite happy in his work, he had seen the job advertised at Barrington's for a head chef and had decided to apply. As soon as he arrived at the little restaurant in the East Village, with its smart cream exterior and the green-striped awning with "Barrington's" in italic letters across it, giving shade to the small wrought-iron tables that were trellised off from the sidewalk, he knew that he wanted the job.

During the interview, his Gallic mindset had caused him to focus more on the owner's wife than on what was being said to him by the owner himself. He liked very much what he saw in front of him—the short dark hair, the brown eyes and the small nose with the hint of childish freckles across its bridge. They seemed to belie her age, which he would guess at being about mid-thirties. She remained standing behind her husband during the interview, and so he was able to take in her slim figure and maybe too-slender legs, but what he had not read was the steely assuredness of her character behind the elegant appearance.

"Excuse me," she said, breaking into her husband's explanation about the job's required duties, "but are you more concerned with staring at my body than hearing what this job entails?"

He had spluttered out an apology, his face reddening as he glanced from husband to wife. His credentials got him the job, but he had never dared to cross Claire Barrington again.

He now sat down on the chair opposite Claire. He took off his tall white hat and laid it on the table, and sliding a hand through his hair, he watched in silence as she studied the menu.

"Those avocados are important, Jean-Pierre," she said without lifting her eyes. "We need them for the cress salad to go with the fish."

"Don't worry. I will get them."

"What fish are you going to use?"

"Halibut. I have already had the delivery."

"How much did you get?"

"Enough for thirty covers."

Claire glanced across at the reservations book. "That should be about right. We're about sixty for lunch. What about steaks?"

"More than enough. The price was so good last week, I put in a big order. I shall get sufficient out of the deep freeze this morning."

"And the dessert?"

The chef smiled. "Liam has asked if he could make a pavlova, so I have given him the chance to shine."

Claire frowned dubiously at Jean-Pierre, knowing that the young sous-chef had yet to prove himself. "Then on your own head be it."

He nodded. "I will be watching him."

Claire closed the reservations book and placed the menu on top of it. "Okay, so we'll wait until Art gets back before we discuss what we'll do for dinner. Five o'clock all right for you?"

"Of course," Jean-Pierre replied, getting to his feet and replacing his hat. "When is Art coming in?"

"I'm not sure. He's gone to the bank."

The chef glanced out of the window at the teaming rain. It fell so heavily that it hazed the view of Tompkins Square Park, no more than a stone's throw on the other side of the road. "I hope he doesn't get caught in this, otherwise he will be *mouillé jusqu'aux os,* wet to the skin."

"Let's hope not."

As the chef made his way back to the kitchen, Claire sat straight in her chair and stretched out her back. The rain, thank goodness, had not started falling in earnest that morning until she had arrived at the restaurant, which was situated on the corner of East Tenth and Avenue B. When she left the apartment on Gramercy Park at eight-fifteen to walk Violet to school, the sky had not seemed unduly threatening, but by the time she had seen her daughter through the school gates on East Fourteenth, a thin film of rain was falling from the darkening skies, the kind that can effectively dispel even the merest evidence of effort from newly blown-dry hair in a matter of seconds. The cheap pack-away umbrella that she all too frequently left out of her handbag was therefore a godsend, its bright tartan canopy keeping her sufficiently protected as she strode the remaining four blocks to her place of work.

However, things had changed for the worst by the time Claire returned from hanging up her coat in the small office at the back of the restaurant. Great rivulets of water poured off the striped awning outside, and in Tompkins Square any form of leisurely movement had ceased. Pedestrians huddled in pairs under inadequate umbrellas as they scampered this way and that along the crossing paths; joggers sprinted off to their destinations, not bothering to stop on the sidewalk to wait for the traffic, but leaping over gushing storm drains and dodging precariously around spray-spurting cars. In the fenced-off dog exercise area, owners rounded up their charges, cutting short their pets' moments of wild abandonment for the day, while those who frequented the park day in, day out, and who had little place else to go, still grouped themselves forlornly under the relative protection of the wide-branched trees, their woolly-hatted heads bowed miserably and their hands pushed deep into the pockets of battered army-surplus jackets and ill-fitting overcoats.

Claire expected the weather to bring on a stream of telephone cancellations, but they never materialized, and at lunchtime every table was once again filled. Besides the steadfast custom of local residents and shop owners, a constant flow of taxis and town cars pulled up outside, their wipers on full bore, delivering businessmen and their clients from the financial district downtown. For the first hour of the session, Claire had to cope alone with front-of-house, helping customers divest themselves of sodden raincoats and dripping umbrellas before showing them to their tables. This was because Art had indeed got caught in the rain on the way back from the bank and had had to return to the apartment to shower and change into a dry set of clothes.

Nevertheless, Claire, as always, was equal to the challenge. She had helped Art run Barrington's for fifteen years now and in that time had learned to keep a cool head in the face of countless difficult situations while dealing with a full house. Even power cuts and sudden staff walk-outs did not faze her.

Nor did the long hours of routine work.

After lunchtime was finished, Claire and Art and their three staff set about clearing and resetting the twenty-three tables with laundered white cloths, gleaming cutlery and conically formed napkins for the evening influx of diners. While the staff then left for a couple of hours' respite, Art and Claire continued with their work, counting the lunchtime takings, checking stocks of wines and spirits and calling suppliers to arrange deliveries. Normally, one of them would have then gone to meet Violet at the school gates and walk her back to the apartment, but today, there being little respite in the weather and the extra cleaning in the restaurant resulting from it, Claire decided to ring Pilar, their housekeeper, and ask her to collect Violet in a taxi.

Six-thirty in the evening was always a low point, a time when Claire wondered if she was ever going to have sufficient energy to survive past midnight and witness the last customer leave the restaurant. As she stood at the lectern desk by the entrance door, consulting the reservations book and glancing around the tables to make sure they were all laid for the correct number of people, she felt her lids grow heavy and her vision start to swim in and out of focus. Exhaling a breath in a long whistle, she kicked off one of her flats and leaned down to give her aching foot a rub. When she felt the hand on her shoulder, she gave an involuntary jump and turned to find Art standing behind her, a frown of concern on his long angular face.

"You okay, angel?"

Claire smiled and reached up for his hand. "I'm fine. A bit exhausted, but I'll get my second wind in a moment."

"Good time then to go put your feet up," Art said, directing a thumb over his shoulder towards the office. "That's your step-father on the telephone."

Claire screwed up her eyes. "Oh, God, Leo. I forgot it was his night to call. How does he sound?"

"Great," Art replied, "and I'd say totally on the ball. He told me it's eleven-thirty in Scotland, and he's sitting in his bathrobe with a cup of hot chocolate, and he just wants to say goodnight to you before he heads off to bed."

Claire laughed. "That doesn't mean he won't want to speak to me for ever."

Art walked over to the coffee machine,

poured out a cup and handed it to her. "Go on, take as long as you want. We're all set up for the evening." He lightly brushed aside her hair and planted a kiss on her forehead and then watched as she made her way to the office, her tight black dress holding to the contours of her slim figure. "He's actually being quite funny," he called after her, "so maybe he'll give you the boost you need."

Claire closed the door of the office behind her and sat down in the high-backed swivel chair. She pulled herself into the desk and picked up the receiver. "Leo? Hullo, darling, how are you?"

Twenty minutes later, Art heard the door of the office open and turned to watch his wife walk back to the lectern desk, a new lightness in her step and a broad grin on her face. He went over to her. "What did I tell you? The old boy's in good form, isn't he?"

Claire laughed and shook her head. "Talking with Leo is like having a glass of champagne." She glanced outside at the continuing torrent. "He seems to be able to make the sun shine, even on a day like this." Dropping the pen down on the reservations book, she reached up and gave Art a long kiss. "Come on," she said, grabbing his hand and leading him towards the bar, "seeing I've mentioned it, let's for once break with tradition and have a glass of the real thing before the rush starts. I think today of all days we both deserve it."

3

West Sussex—June 1980

Claire had always thought the house to be the perfect size for the two of them. The others in the street were much larger, quite grand, in fact, and Claire knew from her friends at school who lived in these houses that nearly all their fathers worked in London. They would leave very early in the morning, long before Claire and her mother were awake, and cycle or drive their cars (if they were late, or the weather was bad, or they were just very lazy) the three miles to Haywards Heath, where they would catch a train to Waterloo Station.

Claire sometimes wondered why their

house had been built there at all. She had an idea that maybe the man who designed the original layout of the street had made a wrong calculation, and rather than re-draw his plans, he'd said to himself, Oh, I'll just stick a little house in there. No one will ever notice.

Or maybe he was just a very kind and thoughtful man and considered that the street should also have a house the right size for a young widowed mother (whose husband used to work in London) and her ten-year-old daughter.

Anyway, it was perfect for them. To the right of the narrow passage that led from the front door was the sitting room. It over-looked the street, but the car was always parked in the driveway and so it blocked most of the view. This was where Claire did her homework and, when she had fin-ished it, her mother allowed her to watch telly. Next week, it was going to be the sum-mer half-term, which meant she wouldn't have to do homework and she could watch telly for much longer.

Then, out of the sitting room, turn right in the passage and immediately right again, and into the kitchen, which was at the back

of the house. It had a door that led out into
the garden and a huge window behind
the sink, where Daphne—that was her
mother's name and Claire liked to call her
Daphne when she wasn't speaking directly to her—she would call her Mummy
then. And she had done exactly the same
with her father, David Barclay, but he had
died three years ago, just after her sev-
enth birthday. Anyway, Daphne liked to
stand at the sink and look out at her garden while she was doing the washing-up.
Actually, that wasn't right because Daphne
hated doing the washing-up, in fact she
hated doing housework in general, but
she did love gardening. Claire knew that
she was very good at it too, because
Daphne said it was very important to have
colour in the garden all the year round,
and she always managed to do just that.

Claire had also once overheard Mrs.
Paton from next door saying that Daphne
had green fingers. Claire had been really
upset about this because she had misun-
derstood what was said and thought
Daphne had caught a disease just like her
father, David, had, and that very soon she
would be left with no one to look after her.

But then Daphne had given her a kiss and wiped Claire's face with a hankie and told her it just meant she was a good gardener and could make plants grow.

Out of the kitchen and straight across the passage was the dining room. People never ate in there because Daphne never invited anyone to come to dine with them. She used to when they lived in London, but not any more. Actually, this year Daphne had used that room more than ever because she had been made chairman of the local horticultural society—she had told Claire that she hadn't wanted to do it, but they'd made her—and so now she used the dining room for her meetings. And then, because her mother was chairman, for one night next month they were going to have a man to stay. Daphne had told her he was an expert at growing exotic plants, which meant they had all come from other countries and were very difficult to grow in this country, and he was going to speak to Daphne's society to tell them how they could do it as well. Maybe they would dine in there when he was staying.

Along the passage to the front door, and

then make an about-turn and up the stairs. First on the left was Claire's own bedroom, which had a small double bed that was really too big for the room, but it was one of the few bits of furniture that Daphne had kept when they moved from the flat in London. Daphne also thought that if Claire wanted to have a friend to stay, they could share the bed, but Claire never really wanted that, because the bed was her territory and she liked to think of it still being in the London flat when it was the three of them—David, Daphne and herself. Next month, though, she was going to have to sleep with Daphne for one night, so that the man could have her room, because the house, after all, was only the perfect size for the two of them, and not for anybody else.

Then, straight across the small landing, was Daphne's bedroom. She had a much bigger bed than Claire's, but then the room was much larger than hers and could fit in other furniture as well. There was a chaise longue at the bottom of the bed, which was always a bit untidy with the clothes that Daphne had worn the day before, and a dressing table with a glass top which had some special photographs under it. There was one of Daphne and David on their wedding day; one of Claire when she was a little baby; one of Daphne's parents, who had both died because they had been quite old when Daphne was born; and then one of David's parents, wearing shorts and looking very brown on their farm in South Africa. If Claire wanted to see these photos clearly, she always had to push Daphne's make-up things to one side and blow away all the spilt face powder.

And then there was a big solid chest of drawers with brass handles. Top drawer—socks, tights and knickers; next one down—T-shirts and nighties; then it was shirts and blouses; and the bottom was jerseys. All Daphne's other clothes were stuffed into the fitted wardrobe.

And then, last of all, was the bathroom, which was up three more steps and overlooking the street again. There was a net curtain on the window so people couldn't look in and see you walking around without any clothes on. It had a bath with a shower hose that didn't really work because it leaked, a washbasin, and a loo with a horrid seat with a split in it. Claire knew she had to sit on it at a certain angle, otherwise her bottom got pinched. Claire thought it would be a good idea if her mother warned the man who was coming to stay next month about it.

And that was it. Oh, except the little grey Renault, which was a French car, parked in the driveway at the front of the house. Daphne always kept the rear seats tipped forward and the whole boot area covered in a sheet of plastic because she quite often helped other people with their gardens and she was always having to collect plants and shrubs and things from the garden centre. Daphne had got Mr. Paton from next door to help her put a heavy piece of wood across the drive so that when her front wheels touched it, it would stop her from hitting the house, and the back of the car would be just clear of the pavement.

So Daphne and Claire were the perfect number for the car, the car was the perfect length for the driveway of the house, and, as Claire had always thought, the house was the perfect size for the two of them.

4

Alloa—July 1989

Jonas Fairweather stood hidden in the bushes, breathing heavily after the half-mile run from the farm. As soon as he heard Claire was leaving that morning, he had rushed out to his car, only to find the starter motor jammed solid, so he had been left with no alternative other than to make it as fast as he could on foot along the pot-holed track to the house. One hundred and eighty-one days. He had counted every one that he not seen or spoken to her since the incident. He did not want to miss her now.

He pushed aside the dense foliage with

his hand, clearing a view for himself across
the lawn to the front of the house. The old
car was still there, sitting on the gravel
driveway at the bottom of the stone steps.
He pulled a grimy Casio watch from the
pocket of his jeans, its plastic fastener broken that morning when he had tried desperately to free the starter motor. It had just
gone eleven o'clock. Maybe she'd taken a
taxi instead. Maybe she'd already left.

He sighed with relief when he saw Claire's
stepfather in his familiar tweed jacket appear at the top of the steps. He descended
them slowly, struggling under the weight
of a suitcase, and went round the back of
the car and opened the boot. As he heaved
it in, Claire appeared with her mother and
walked arm-in-arm down the steps. They
spoke for a moment and then Daphne put
her arms around her daughter's neck and
held her tight. As the man clambered into
the driver's seat, Claire and her mother
exchanged kisses before both slowly meandered their way round to the passenger
door, talking as they went. Claire got into
the car and closed the door, her mother
leaning in through the open window for a

final kiss before the car rolled slowly forward. Jonas watched as hands waved from both windows and Daphne, left alone at the front steps, wiped the back of her hand below her left eye.

He broke from his hiding place and ran along the remaining stretch of track to where it joined the driveway, ducking into the bushes as the car swept past, now gathering speed. He saw only a glimpse of Claire, smiling excitedly at her stepfather beside her, and then he ran out onto the driveway and stood watching until the car disappeared behind the screen of rhododendron bushes.

Jonas bowed his head, thrusting his hands into the pockets of his jeans, and then he turned and ran towards a tree at the side of the driveway and kicked his foot out hard against its solid trunk. He headed off slowly back towards the farm, every now and again rushing to one side to kick out at some other form of immoveable object.

By the time he reached the end of the wood where the road opened out into the open fields of his father's property, he could not tell if the stinging tears in his eyes were due to the stabbing pain in his right foot or the unbearable, searing emptiness he felt deep within.

5

West Sussex—July 1980

Claire?" Daphne called out, lobbing her gardening gloves and secateurs into the wheelbarrow at the back door and prising off her muddy shoes on the doorstep. "Darling, are you there?"

There was no answer, only the low hum of the television coming from the sitting room. Daphne gave her hands a quick rinse under the sink tap and hurried through the kitchen, wiping her hands on a dishcloth as she went. She pushed open the door of the sitting room with her bottom and walked past her daughter, who was lying with her feet up the back of an armchair, her head lolling over the front of the seat, watching the television upside down.

"Darling, that is not good for you," Daphne said, pressing the "off" switch on the television.

Claire made no utterance of protest, but swung round through 180 degrees, stretched her arms above her head and let out a loud yawn.

"I'm not surprised you're like that," Daphne said. "It's like an oven in here." She walked across to the window and opened it up to let some fresh air into the stuffy room. "I thought you were going to play with Jessica this afternoon."

"I did for a bit, but her mum wanted to take her shopping, so I just came back."

"You should have come out into the garden to tell me, then."

Claire's mouth pouted and she hung her head miserably. "Sorry."

Daphne gave her a pat on the knee as she passed. "I'm not giving you a row, darling, so no need for that face. Listen, I'm going upstairs to get ready for the meeting. Paula will be here in a minute, so if I'm not down, will you tell her there's a shepherd's pie in the fridge? She can stick it in the oven for a couple of minutes."

"What time will you be back?"

"I'm not sure. Probably about eight-thirty."

"And is the man coming as well?"

"That's the idea, yes."

"Can I wait and eat with you two?"

"Darling, I don't think so. It's a bit late."

"Mummy, pleeease, it is half-term. I don't have to get up in the morning."

Daphne gave it some thought as she stood by the door. She smiled at Claire. "All right, why not?"

Claire jumped up from the chair and ran over to her mother and threw her arms around Daphne's soil-stained jeans. "Thank you."

"But you've got to be grown-up and not be a nuisance."

"I won't. I'll just listen to you two talking." She tilted her head back to look up at her mother. "Can we eat in the dining room?"

"Oh, no, Claire," she said, gently pushing her daughter away. "I really don't have time for that."

"But Paula and I could do it," Claire pleaded, as she watched her mother run up the stairs. "It wouldn't take us long to tidy it up and lay the table, and it would be much nicer for the man to eat in the dining room. The table in the kitchen is much too small for all three of us."

Daphne leaned her head over the banister. "Well then, maybe you should eat before us."

"Mummy, you said!"

Claire watched her mother shake her head resignedly before disappearing from sight. "All right," she called out from her bedroom, "but you must ask Paula nicely to give you a hand."

Claire didn't tell Paula about getting the dining room ready. She never really talked much to Paula anyway, because whenever she was babysitting for her, all Paula did was go into the sitting room and put on the telly. Claire waited until *Coronation Street* had started before getting up from her seat and leaving the room, because she knew Paula loved that programme and wouldn't want to stop watching telly for the next half-hour.

She went through to the dining room and began clearing all Daphne's books and bills and things off the table. She was going to put them all on the sideboard, but then thought that Daphne would want to serve the shepherd's pie from there, so she stacked them neatly on the floor beside it. The evening sun was now shining directly in through the window and Claire could see it was showing up a lot of dust on the table, so having found an aerosol can of furniture polish and a duster under the sink in the kitchen, she got up on a chair so she could lean right over and give the whole surface a good polish. The smell immediately reminded her of Mrs. Ishab, who used to come to help Daphne look after the flat in London. Mrs. Ishab was a very large lady and sometimes, when she was cleaning something very hard, her sari would slip and a big bit of brown flesh would suddenly appear and wobble away until Mrs. Ishab had stopped what she was doing and then got herself all tucked in again.

Claire opened the bottom drawer in the sideboard and took out three mats with pictures of birds on them. She thought at first she would put Daphne at one end of the table and the man at the other, but then that would make it very difficult for them to talk to each other, so she decided that the man should be at the head of the table and Daphne and Claire could sit on either side of him. That meant if the man did want to talk to her as well, then he could.

In the long middle drawer in the sideboard, Claire found plates and the bone-handled knives and forks. They weren't very shiny, so she gave them a quick polish with the duster, and then thought that it hadn't been a very good idea because it might make the shepherd's pie taste of furniture polish. She just laid them out beside the plates and hoped that it wouldn't.

The glasses took a lot longer to put on the table because Daphne kept them in a cupboard on the wall in the kitchen, and it meant that Claire had to climb up on a chair and then kneel on the work surface to reach the cupboard, and she could only manage one at a time because she had to hold on to the cupboard door with her other hand to get back down onto the chair again. And then it took even longer still because she suddenly thought that the table would look much smarter if Daphne and the man had wine glasses, even if they didn't have any wine to drink, and those glasses were kept so high in the cupboard that she had to stand up on the work surface to get them.

And it was while she was doing that when Paula called out, "What are you doing, Claire?"

Claire just stood stock-still, teetering on the edge of the work surface and gripping the stem of a wine glass. "Nothing."

She waited until she was sure that Paula wasn't going to come through to the kitchen before she got down onto the chair as quietly as she possibly could.

When the last wine glass was in place, Claire stood back and studied the table. It still looked very empty and not nearly special enough for them all to dine at. And then she had a really good idea. She pulled a chair over to the glass-fronted corner cabinet, got up onto it and unlocked the little key. She opened the door carefully and took out one of the three silver candlesticks. The candle in it was nearly all used up and there were dribbly bits down the sides, but it would have to do, and anyway, they wouldn't be sitting having dinner very long because it was only shepherd's pie, so it should last until they were finished.

Claire put the candlestick right in the middle of where they would all be sitting and then stood back once more to look at what she had done. Now, that was exactly what a proper dining room table should look like.

Only one more thing to do. Claire went back to the kitchen, unplugged Daphne's radio/cassette player, and took it through to the dining room. She put it on the very edge of the sideboard so it wouldn't be in Daphne's way when she was serving out the shepherd's pie, and then she got down on her hands and knees, pushed the plug into the socket and flicked the switch. She got up and pressed the "eject" button. The tape popped out and Claire read on it; "Sweet Baby James" by James Taylor. It was one of Daphne's favourites. She pushed it back in and closed the little window, hoping very much that the man would like it too.

She was just shutting the door of the dining room when she heard the whiny signature tune of *Coronation Street* start up. She hurried to the door of the sitting room and then slowed up as she walked in. Paula lay slumped in an armchair, her feet up on the low coffee table.

"What have you been doing?" Paula asked without taking her eyes off the television as she flicked through the programmes with the remote.

Claire beamed a grin of satisfaction that was never seen by the babysitter. "Nothing," she replied airily.

"Oh, darling, what a wonderful job you've done!" Daphne exclaimed when Claire opened the door of the dining room to allow her mother to carry in the steaming dish of shepherd's pie.

Claire skipped round the table. "I did it all by myself," she said, surveying her triumph with grinning pride. She knelt up on her chair and reached over to straighten up the wick of the candle. "I don't have any matches. Do you know where they are?"

"I'll get some in a moment," Daphne replied, hovering over the sideboard with the pie. "Darling, this is too hot to put down. Could you get another mat for me?"

"Oh, I forgot about that," Claire said rather gloomily. Sliding off the chair, she ducked below her mother's burdened hands, took another mat from the drawer and placed it on the sideboard.

Daphne put down the pie dish and, pulling off her oven gloves, turned to survey the table in greater detail. "Well, by my reckoning, it's the only thing you have forgotten. I think it all looks quite splendid."

The man appeared in the doorway, clutching a bottle of wine by its neck. "Aha, we're in here, are we?"

Daphne smiled at him. "Did you find everything you needed upstairs?"

"Absolutely. What a very comfortable house you have here." He placed the bottle on the table. "My word, this all looks rather smart." He fiddled with the open collar of his shirt. "I feel maybe I should have put on a tie."

"Oh, no," Daphne laughed. "This was all Claire's idea. She laid the table all by herself while we were at the meeting."

He stared down at Claire, his mouth open in surprise. "I can hardly believe that. It really looks as if it's been set by a professional waitress."

Claire grinned broadly at him, shrugging her shoulders in glee.

Daphne began to spoon the shepherd's pie onto a plate. "Claire, why don't you ask Mr. Harrison if he has a box of matches on him?"

"Leo, please!" the man exclaimed jovially, thumping the pockets of his crumpled tweed jacket. "Everyone calls me Leo, and look"—he took out a silver lighter and flicked the flame alight—"I can go one better." He leaned across the table and lit the candle.

Claire immediately ran round the table to the door and turned off the main light switch.

"No, darling, I think that's too much," Daphne said, putting down a plate on Claire's mat. "We won't be able to see what we're eating."

The man laughed. "And goodness, what a terrible waste of a good shepherd's pie that would be. We'd keep missing our mouths and it would all be down our fronts and piled up in little heaps around our chairs."

Daphne placed a plate at the head of the table. "Leo, if you'd like to sit yourself down there, I'll go and see if I can find a corkscrew for your lovely bottle of wine."

Claire had been really embarrassed when her mother had said that thing about turning the light switch back on, but she thought what the man had said—actually, his name was Leo and everyone called him that, so she was going to do it too—anyway, she thought what Leo had said was very funny and so by the time she had got back to her chair, she had forgotten all about being embarrassed. Daphne had found a corkscrew and Claire now watched Leo closely as he tried to get the cork out of the bottle. He puffed out his cheeks and frowned a lot and his face seemed to go quite red with the effort. This made him look even more like a happy circus clown, which had been Claire's first thought about him when he walked in the front door. That was because under his thick bushy eyebrows he had a pair of sparkly blue eyes that looked as if they were enjoying a good joke, and the top of his head was very bald and shiny but he had hair on either side that was very frizzy and unbrushed. And then his brown lace-up shoes seemed to be too big for his body, because he wasn't even as tall as Daphne, and he wore baggy green corduroy trousers and a blue shirt and a bright yellow cardigan under his tweed jacket. Claire thought that all he needed was one of those squirty flowers in the buttonhole of his jacket and then he would really be a clown. She also noticed that it probably wouldn't have mattered much if the lights had been left switched off because Leo's jersey had a few food stains on its front anyway. Claire decided that she really liked Leo.

"Well, cheers," Daphne said, holding up her glass of wine to Leo, "and thank you again for coming so far to speak to our little group. They really found it all quite stimulating."

Leo gulped down his mouthful of shepherd's pie before speaking. "I enjoyed it all tremendously myself, and I have to say I was most impressed by the knowledge of some of your members. There were a couple of extremely tricky questions asked, especially about plant propagation, and I'm not entirely convinced I answered them all that satisfactorily."

"Oh, I think you did," Daphne replied with a smile. "Everyone there was hanging on your every word. Your reputation on exotic plants goes before you."

Leo almost choked on his wine. "Oh dear, that makes me feel an awful old fraud." He wiped his mouth with a large red-spotted handkerchief. "To be quite honest, I've only been doing it for the past five years or so."

Daphne looked amazed. "Really? I thought it was your lifetime's work."

Leo laughed. "Heavens no, but it has, without doubt, become my passion."

"So what was it you did before?"

"Well, believe it or not, I was a brewer."

"A brewer! My word, you did have a change in direction."

"Yes, quite a considerable one, and I have to say it wasn't for the first time. In an even earlier part of my life, I worked as a chemist for a large Swiss pharmaceutical company."

"Goodness, you have led an interesting life," Daphne said, leaning her elbows comfortably on the table, her hands cupping her wine glass. "So, how did that lead to brewing?"

Leo quickly ate another mouthful of shepherd's pie. "We were living in Nottingham at the time"—he took a gulp of his wine—"and some colleagues of mine approached me and asked if I wanted to join them in purchasing a small privately owned brewery. I'd always had a great interest in the art of brewing—on a very small scale, I have to admit, having made my own home brew in the garage for some years—and I thought the opportunity was just too good to miss."

"Wasn't it rather a daunting prospect for you," Daphne asked, "going from producing a few bottles of beer in your garage to hundreds of barrels of the stuff?"

Leo laughed. "You'd think so, wouldn't you? Actually, it didn't prove difficult at all because we'd kept on most of the workforce, so I just kept my head down and learned about the mass-production side of things as I went along. My colleagues, however, were the ones who really had their work cut out. They had to sell the product, and therein lay the difficulty. The reason why the brewery had been put on the market in the first place was because the product had not been selling."

"And did they get it to sell?"

"Not at first, but then I suggested we increase the strength of the brew by about five per cent, and we took on a top London advertising agency who gave the beer a new identity that suited its more potent image, and sales thereafter just took off."

"So what was the reason you gave it all up?"

Leo finished his last mouthful of shepherd's pie and laid his fork down on the well-scraped plate with a clatter. "Thank you for that. It was absolutely delicious."

"There is more if you'd like," Daphne said.

Leo wiped his mouth with his hanky and held up a hand. "No, I'm absolutely full. Thank you." He stuffed the hanky back into the breast pocket of his jacket. "The reason I gave it all up was that Oakdene—that was the name of the beer—had become a bit of a 'cult' brand with the young, something that did not go unnoticed amongst a number of the big London corporate brewers. Anyway, in due course, one of them put an offer on the table that valued the business at an exorbitant sum of money." He laughed. "I think we must have given it all of two minutes' consideration before closing the deal."

"So that's when you moved up to Scotland?"

"Almost the next day. About the time that the sale of the brewery was being completed, I just happened to notice this extraordinary house being advertised in the *Sunday Times,* so I immediately jumped on a train to Scotland to have a look at it. It was all rather run-down and obviously in need of a good deal of money being spent on the fabric of the place, but it did have a sizeable piece of land with it and a wonderful garden with these most enormous greenhouses. Those were what really sold me on the place."

"So that's when you became involved with exotic plants?"

"On a grand scale, yes," Leo replied. "I had been growing a few in my garage alongside my amateur beer operation, a combination actually which nearly led to complete disaster. One winter, we were hit by a particularly cold snap of weather, so I had to increase the heat in the place to make sure all the plants would survive, and next thing I knew all my beer bottles started exploding." He grimaced. "It was rather awful, really. The garage sounded like a mini-war zone!"

Daphne burst out laughing. "Oh, my

goodness, what a mess there must have been!"

Leo slapped his hands to his head. "Absolutely, and what's more, over the following weeks it became quite apparent the plants did not appreciate the taste of my beer quite as much as I did!"

Up until that point, Claire had been rather bored, because she had done exactly what Daphne had asked her to do and that was to sit at the table and listen to her and Leo talking. But now Claire just grinned, shifting her gaze from her mother to the man. She had not seen Daphne laugh like that for ages. It was as if she was happy again, and there had certainly been no sign of that since David had died. And although she couldn't really understand what Leo was talking about when he was telling Daphne about his brewing company, she did think the story about the bottles exploding was very funny and she could imagine Leo's exotic plants being terrified by the noise, and she thought it would make a very good book with coloured pictures to show what was happening to the plants.

And now Daphne was asking Leo about

his family, and Claire stopped spinning the knife round on her mat and sat up in her chair and really listened. But then she saw that Leo's face had suddenly got very sad and that look of a happy circus clown had disappeared. He was telling Daphne that when he bought his new house and moved there with Anne, who was his wife, and Marcus and Charity, his children, Anne was very ill and Claire heard the name of the disease and knew it was the same one that David had got. Leo said that Anne had died six years ago, which was three years more than David, and Daphne bit at her lip and said to Leo that she knew how devastating it was because her husband had died, and they both looked very sad, which annoyed Claire because a moment ago they had both been so happy. So she thought for a moment and decided to say something to Leo.

"Leo," she said quite shyly because although Leo had said that everyone called him that, she actually hadn't said his name out loud.

"Yes, my dear," Leo replied, leaning towards her. Claire realized that he was smiling again, which pleased her.

"How old are you?"

Leo threw himself back in his chair with a loud guffaw, and that made Claire laugh as well, but then she saw that Daphne did not seem to find it as funny as she and Leo.

"Claire, you shouldn't really ask those kinds of questions," she said sternly and Claire could see that her mother's cheeks had gone quite pink.

"Oh, I think it's a very good question," Leo said, which made Claire feel quite relieved. "I am fifty-two years old, Claire. Now you've got to tell me how old you are."

"Ten," Claire replied, swinging her legs back and forth under the table.

"Well, I think you're very grown up for a ten-year-old, because I have never heard of a girl of your age who can lay a table as well as you."

But Claire wasn't really listening to him saying that because she was trying to do a sum in her head that was pretty difficult to do without paper.

"Leo," she said again, loving the way her mouth had to shape into an *o* at the end of the word.

"Yes, Claire," he said with a chuckle.

"That means you are"—she was almost there, counting out the difference on her fingers under the table—"fifteen years older than Mummy."

"Bravo!" Leo exclaimed, giving one thumping clap of his hands. "Well done, you, working that out. Not only a professional waitress, but a brilliant mathematician as well."

Daphne was covering her mouth with her hand and staring at Claire, but Claire could tell that Daphne's eyes weren't round and cross, but more slanty and smiley. She took her hand away and Claire saw that her cheeks were blushing even more.

"Darling, I really think it's time for bed. Would you like to say goodnight to Leo?"

Claire got off her chair and went to stand by Leo. "Goodnight, Leo."

And she was about to walk past him when he caught her up in his arms and gave her a long hug that nearly squeezed all the breath out of her and then gave her a noisy kiss on the top of her head. "Goodnight, my dear."

"On you go," Daphne said, giving Claire's bottom a pat as she ran past her to the door. "I'll be up in a moment to tuck you in and say goodnight."

And as Claire made her way up the stairs, she thought how lovely it was to be given a real hug from a man again, and Leo's clothes had not really smelt of old food, but he had actually smelt quite as she remembered David used to smell.

And that was another reason why she really liked Leo.

6

New York—February 1990

As it turned out, Leo had been quite right about Claire becoming a professional waitress, although it had never been part of her great plan in life. Before leaving on her gap year to work her way round the world, Claire had secured for herself a place at St. Andrews University to read History of Art, but then, after spending two months with her grandparents in South Africa, she moved on to Australia. There her final summer job before returning home, working in a restaurant in Sydney, stretched on into the New Year, thanks to her having an affair with a devastatingly good-looking young

Australian called Steve. She managed to defer her place at university for a year, but in the end it was hardly worth it. The relationship ended abruptly in late January, the morning after her twentieth birthday party, following a blazing row that showed Steve's character to be both nasty and paranoid, accusing her quite unjustly of making a pass at his best friend. Claire decided there and then that she did not want to fall victim again to the hurtful idiosyncrasies of one more member of the male species. She had had enough of both Steve and his country, and in a downtown café that afternoon she bought herself a plane ticket to New York with a three-day stopover in Los Angeles.

By the time she arrived in New York, her meagre finances were exhausted and she had to fall on the kindness of a young female photographer whom she had met on the flight from Los Angeles to put her up for the night in her small apartment in the East Village. By the end of the following day, having trudged around the letting agencies in the area, burdened by jet lag and the heavy rucksack that contained her life's belongings, she triumphantly clutched in her hand the keys for a shoebox of an apartment a block away from where she had spent the previous night. The rent advance had stretched the credit on her Visa card to its limit.

Pride, however, played a big part in Claire's not immediately calling up her mother and asking her to cable out more money. She had been self-sufficient for eight months now, and when she returned home at the end of the summer, she wanted to prove both to herself and to others in her extended family that she was quite able to cope financially on her own. Her priority now, therefore, was to find herself a job as quickly as possible.

She actually hadn't gone into the small restaurant on the north side of Tompkins Square seeking employment. She had just dumped her rucksack in the apartment and come out to explore her new surroundings and to celebrate the successes of her first day in New York by spending a couple of her last remaining dollars on something to eat. In fact, when she entered and saw how busy the place was, she almost turned to leave, but the tall young man with the long white apron tied around his waist approached her with such a warm smile and a genuinely welcoming greeting that she followed him to the corner table without giving it another thought.

She ordered the cheapest item on the menu, a small Caesar Salad, and sat eating it slowly as she watched the young man move quickly about the place. There were just over twenty tables in the restaurant, Claire's trained eye working out there was probably seating for eighty customers, and as he was the only one serving, he continuously searched round to see if a table needed to be cleared or if a diner was trying to attract his attention. It appeared that he was coping quite admirably, but there came a moment of truth when Claire saw from her vantage point in the corner as he went behind the wickerwork screen to pick up a couple of newly prepared orders that had been pushed through the hatch from the kitchen. Out of view from everyone but Claire, he clapped both hands on top of his head and mouthed a silent scream, as if mimicking impending insanity, and then, having shared his joke with someone on the other side of the hatch, he picked up the plates and reappeared with a grin of good humour on his face.

And, at that point, the large woman in the pink trouser suit who was dining with her diminutive husband at the table nearest to Claire felt the need to go to the restroom. Getting to her feet, she caught the edge of the table with her sizeable stomach, tipping it momentarily to an angle that proved too much for her full glass of red wine. Her husband let out a warning cry and grabbed at his own glass in time to save it, but the other toppled over, spreading a dark red stain over the surface of the white tablecloth. Claire immediately glanced in the direction of the young man. He spun round, the smile changing to a frown of exasperation. He came over to the table, dismissing the woman's apologies with a kindly remark that it couldn't matter less, and quickly set about clearing the table so that the stained cloth could be replaced.

Claire saw the hand go up at the far end of the restaurant. A group of dark-suited businessmen were preparing to leave, two of them already on their feet and shaking hands with each other. As the young man returned from fetching the new tablecloth, his ever-searching eyes caught this too, and for a moment he stood turning from one table to the other, not knowing whom to attend to first.

Claire immediately put down her knife and fork, placed her napkin on the table and got up and walked over to him. "Excuse me."

He was too distracted even to look at her. "If you could wait just a moment, I'll be with you as soon as I can."

"No, listen, why don't you let me reset this table for you? I know what to do."

Now turning to her, the young man gave her a forced smile and shook his head. "No, really, that's very kind of you, but . . ."

"I honestly don't mind," Claire said, pushing her hands into the back pockets of her jeans and looking around the restaurant, "and I do know from experience if you don't get a hand right now, you'll get out of sync with your other tables and you'll be chasing your tail for the rest of the night."

The young man cast a worried glance at the bare table where the large lady and her husband were sitting expectantly. He smiled at Claire and nodded. "You've just convinced me you know what you're talking about." He handed her the tablecloth. "Thanks, I really appreciate this," he said as he went off to deal with the businessmen.

Claire spread out the cloth, giving it a brisk smooth-out with her hand before replacing the cutlery and glasses. She noticed that the couple had been halfway through their main course when the incident with the wine glass happened. "Would you like me to take your plates back through to the kitchen and ask Chef to reheat them?"

"Oh, please don't bother," the large woman said with a flustered wave. "It was my own silly fault that the wine glass went over in the first place."

Claire smiled cheerily at her. "It's no bother at all. I'll be back in a couple of minutes."

Walking behind the screen, she slid the plates through the hatch and leaned over to peer through. The chef, a rotund Hispanic-looking man with a drooping moustache, caught sight of her. He pushed unceremoniously past his sous-chef and approached the hatch. "Who are you?" he askeld gruffly.

"I'm just helping out for a moment. Could you warm up these two main courses, please? A wine glass went over on one of the tables and it needed to be relaid."

Glaring suspiciously at her, the chef took the plates off and thrust them into the oven before returning to the hatch. "Where is Art?" he asked, his accent making it sound as if there were about four consecutive *r*'s in the name.

"If you mean the person who's working here, he's getting the bill ready for one of the tables."

The chef grinned at her, showing a gold tooth that glinted in the bright fluorescent light of the kitchen. "That person who is working here is also the owner, Art Barrington." He went back to the oven, and using his apron as an oven glove, he took out the two plates and brought them back to the hatch. "That is why this place is called Barrington's, right?"

Claire bit at her bottom lip. "Ah, I didn't really take any notice of the name . . ."

The chef lobbed a couple of clean napkins onto the hatch counter. "Those plates are very hot. Make sure you warn the customers."

Claire returned to the waiting couple. "Chef has warned that you'd best not touch the plates," she said, placing them on the table. "They're very hot."

"Thank you, my dear," the woman said, putting a hand on Claire's arm. "My husband and I were just remarking on what wonderful service you have here."

Claire was quite amazed that neither seemed to realize that, until a few moments ago, she had been sitting at the next table, nor did they notice that her faded jeans and crumpled white T-shirt in no way matched Art's smart uniform. But she smiled at them and couldn't resist saying, "Well, in that case, I do hope you'll come again."

Turning to walk back to her table, she almost bumped into the owner of the restaurant, who had been standing behind her.

"Thanks for doing that," he said quietly to her, "and for appeasing them so successfully."

"My pleasure," she replied. "I just know

what it's like when things get on top of you."

The entrance door to the restaurant opened and a young couple came in, scanning the place for a spare table. Art held up a hand to Claire and went over to them.

"Can I help you?"

"Have you got a table for two?" It was the girl who asked.

Art swept a hand across his dark hair. "I'm afraid I don't." He glanced across to the table recently vacated by the business-men. "I have a reservation for that one in fifteen minutes. I'm really sorry."

Hearing this, Claire approached Art. "Look, I'm actually just leaving, so they can have my table if it hasn't got a later booking."

Art smiled at the young couple. "Could you just give me a moment, please?" He took Claire's arm and guided her over to the screen. "You can't do that. You haven't finished your own meal."

"It doesn't matter. Actually, I'm not really that hungry."

Art gave a cursory glance around the tables. "Listen, I was hoping you would stick around until the place closes. You know, have a drink with me so I can thank you properly for what you did."

Claire gave it a moment's thought. "Okay, but there are conditions."

Art smiled at her. "What might they be?"

"You let that young couple have my table, you give me a long white apron like the one you're wearing and let me help out for the rest of the evening, and in return you give me my meal for free."

Art laughed. "That's not much of a bargain on your part. I was going to do that anyway."

Claire shrugged. "Take it or leave it."

Art turned and disappeared into the kitchen, returning a few moments later with a laundered white apron. "I'm Art Barrington, by the way," he said, handing it to her.

"And I'm Claire Barclay," she said, tying the apron round her waist.

Art gave her a wink. "Okay, Claire, let's go to work."

Three hours later, Art carried two large glasses of wine over to a table in the centre of the empty restaurant. Taking off their aprons, both he and Claire sat down exhausted on chairs opposite each other.

"Well, Claire Barclay, you are a true star," Art said, holding up his glass. "How much easier that was for me tonight!"

Claire raised her own glass and clinked it against his. "I enjoyed myself. The place runs really well." She took a sip of wine. "How long have you owned it?"

Art kicked off his loafers and leaned back in his chair. "Just over six months now."

"My word, that's not long. Judging from tonight, you seem to be doing really well."

Art waved a dismissive hand. "Yeah, well, it was hit and miss at the beginning, but then I began turning the corner about a month ago."

"Has it always been a restaurant?"

"Not like this. It was more of a fast-food café, really." He took a healthy slurp of wine. "Do you know anything about this neighbourhood?"

Claire laughed. "No, I know nothing about New York, let alone this area. I only arrived here yesterday evening."

"Where from?"

"Australia, via Los Angeles."

Art looked suitably horrified. "You don't say! Hell, you must be wiped out."

Claire nodded. "I have felt better, yes."

"Where are you staying?"

"Just round the corner. I've rented a small apartment."

"Right," Art said, slowly nodding his head as he gave this consideration.

"So what kind of neighbourhood have I just moved into?"

Art smiled. "Oh, it's okay now, it's on the up, but a few years ago this whole area was a real no-go zone." He pointed a finger out towards the darkened park on the other side of the street. "Tompkins Square over there was filled with drug pushers, addicts, pimps—you name any form of illegal activity and I bet it was being carried on out here. Even the police were afraid to venture down this way."

"So what changed it all?"

"A tough mayor called Ed Koch back in 1988. He was pretty ruthless in his means, but at the end of the day it worked. People started moving into the East Village and establishments like this began opening up."

"So you got in quite early."

"Yeah, I did."

"Had you run a restaurant before?"

Art laughed. "Hell, no, I was at Harvard studying law, but I realized after the first year it wasn't for me and just gave it up"—he frowned—"which did not go down too well with the old man."

"Is he a lawyer?"

"Yeah, he does corporate stuff in the financial district."

"And what does he think now?"

Art nodded slowly. "He's getting convinced. He sees I'm making a real go of it. He even brings his clients here on occasion, which is great because it spreads the word around with the guys who have the money." He drained his wine. "So tell me, what are your plans? If you've got yourself this apartment, how long are you aiming to stick around in the East Village?"

"I suppose for the next four months or so. I've got to be back in the U.K. in September to start university."

Art looked surprised. "You haven't started yet?"

"I should have, but I got caught up with

someone in Australia and deferred for a year."

Art nodded. "That sounds a good enough reason. So what are you going to do here?"

"Well, the priority is to find a job."

"Do you have a work visa?"

"A temporary one, yes."

"What kind of job are you after, then?"

Claire smiled. "Probably something similar to what I was doing tonight."

"And would you want to continue doing just that?"

She was so taken aback by the directness of Art's question that she didn't answer immediately.

"Do I take it from your silence that that's a no?" he asked.

"Yes—I mean no, it's not a no. It's a yes." Claire shook her head. "I'm sorry, it's just that . . ."

"What?"

"Well, to be honest, I can't quite believe I've just been offered a job within hours of arriving here."

"Well, fortune smiles on you," he said, rubbing a hand at the back of his neck, "and probably on me as well. I've been meaning to take someone else on for the last two months but just never seemed to find the time. I couldn't afford to pay you a fortune, but how about we start you on a hundred dollars a week and in addition you get to keep all the tips?"

Claire's eyes widened. "Wow, that sounds great. When would you want me to start?"

Art shrugged. "Seeing you've just arrived, best if you answer that question yourself."

Claire thought for a moment. "Well, maybe you could give me a couple of days to sleep off the jet lag and get settled into my apartment."

Art nodded. "Sounds good enough. Turn up here Friday then, say about eleven o'clock in the morning?" Reaching an arm behind him, he took a card from the lectern desk and gave it to her. "And if you do have second thoughts about it all, I'd appreciate it if you gave me a call."

Claire got to her feet and slipped the card into the pocket of her jeans. "Don't worry, I'll be here. Count on it."

Art remained seated as she began to make her way towards the door. She stopped for a moment beside him and bent down and gave him a quick kiss on the cheek. "Thank you for being a lifesaver."

Art smiled up at her, his eyes heavy with fatigue. "It's my pleasure." Reaching over, he took her hand and gave it a tight squeeze. "I think we'll do well together, Claire Barclay. I have a good feeling about this."

And the consequence of that "good feeling" was that Claire never went to St. Andrews University. Their working relationship was not the only one to flourish, and consequently she only kept the tenancy of her small apartment for three months before moving in with Art. And on the exact day in September when she should have been donning her red gown at the beginning of Fresher's Week, Art proposed to her and Claire gave only scant consideration for her tender years and the distance from her home country before accepting.

They were married on a wet, blustery December afternoon in New York, and closed the restaurant for only one evening for the reception. It was Leo who gave Claire away, as it was he who, quite aptly, should be the first to learn that Art's wedding present to his new wife was an equal partnership in Barrington's Restaurant. It was Leo, after all, who had foreseen her future.

7

West Sussex—March 1981

After Leo Harrison's one-night visit to the Barclays' house in West Sussex, it became his custom to phone up Daphne at exactly 7:25 every Tuesday evening, a time when he knew that she would have finished getting her daily fix of *The Archers* on the radio. Because he was so punctilious with his calls, Daphne always allowed Claire to answer the phone and chat briefly to Leo before eventually taking the receiver herself. During the first month of these calls, Claire would remain seated at the kitchen table, chin in hand, listening in to their conversation, but as Leo's opening remarks to

Daphne were always about her garden, it was never long before Claire would take herself off to the sitting room to watch television. Soon Claire did not even bother to answer the phone on a Tuesday evening, so she was never aware that, over the next five months, Leo's telephone calls became very much more frequent and eagerly awaited by Daphne, and that their main discussion point was considerably more involved than simply talking about horticultural matters.

When Leo invited them both up to Scotland to stay for the weekend, Daphne thought it best if she went alone. She knew what Leo wanted to discuss and she needed time by herself to judge whether there was any future in continuing this quite unorthodox relationship. So she told Claire that the sole purpose of her visit was to glean some useful advice from Leo on the growing of exotic plants. Her daughter, therefore, was quite happy to accept the alternative that was on offer, staying with her friend Jessica at her parents' house on the other side of the street.

When she returned on the Sunday evening, Daphne placed a boiled egg and

sliced toasted "soldiers" on the kitchen
table in front of her daughter and sat down
opposite her with a mug of tea. On the
way back in the plane, she had worked out
exactly how she was going to break the
news to Claire, but now she had her doubts
about whether this was the best time to
tell her. She pressed hard at a thumbnail
as she watched Claire push a slice of toast
deep into her egg, making the yolk ooze
up and over the sides.

"Don't make too much of a mess, darling. Just eat it."

Chin in hand, Claire continued to play
around with her egg. "Didn't you have a
nice time with Leo, Mummy?"

Daphne picked up her mug and took a
sip of tea. "I had a lovely time. What makes
you think I didn't?"

Claire held the toast above the egg and
watched the yolk drip off. "Because you
don't look as if you did."

Daphne paused for a moment. "Claire,
do you remember when Leo came to stay
and you very cleverly worked out how many
years were between us?"

"Yes, we were sitting in the dining room,
and the answer was fifteen."

Daphne smiled. "Absolutely right. Do you think that's a lot of years?"

Claire shrugged. "Quite a lot."

"But not a huge lot?" Daphne asked tentatively.

Claire put down her toast and thought about this. "Well, if I was fifteen years older than I am now, I'd be nearly . . . twenty-six."

"Oh, heavens," Daphne groaned, leaning an elbow on the table and rubbing her fingers against her forehead. "It does seem a lot when you put it like that." Her carefully planned approach had gone awry. With a shake of her head, she sat up straight and decisively slapped her hands down on the table. "Claire, what would you think if I told you Leo had asked me to marry him?"

Claire stared at her mother, astounded. She said nothing but a twitching frown intermittently wrinkled her brow as she tried to work this all out in her head.

"But you've only seen him twice, haven't you?" she said eventually. "Is that enough to get married?"

"Well, we have talked a lot on the phone and . . . we do get on very well together."

"Do you think that's enough for him to love you, though, like Daddy did?"

That caught Daphne totally unawares. Swallowing hard to halt the swell of emotion that rose in her throat, she glanced up at the ceiling, her eyes glistening.

"No, I don't think it's quite the same, but we are both very fond of each other."

"So are you going to say yes to him?"

"What would you feel about it if I did?"

Daphne waited for a reply as Claire studied the inside of her egg. "All right, I suppose."

Daphne tapped a finger on the table. "I'm really trying to think what's best for the both of us, Claire—you know, for the future. It would mean security in our lives."

Claire frowned. "I thought this house was secure. You always put the alarm on when we go out."

Her mother smiled. "Not quite what I'm talking about, darling. I'm meaning that Leo really wants to look after us and to share his home with us and he wants to be, well, a sort of father to you, although of course he could never replace your own father."

"That was David."

"Yes, David." Daphne paused. "Anyway, Leo also has a family—a boy and a girl not much older than you—and the way I see it is that they need someone to be their mother as much as you need Leo to be your father."

Claire wrinkled up the side of her nose. "If you married Leo, would that make them my brother and sister?"

"Stepbrother and -sister."

"How old are they?"

"Marcus is nearly fifteen and Charity is thirteen."

"Are they nice?"

"Well, with Leo being their father, I'm sure they're both very nice."

"Haven't you met them then?"

"No, I haven't because they're away at boarding school, but Leo showed me photos of them."

"Would I have to go away to boarding school as well?"

Daphne saw the worry in her daughter's dark-brown eyes. "No, darling, you wouldn't. Leo and I discussed this and we decided it would be best if you went to a local school. Of course we would have the money from selling this house and your father left you a small inheritance as well, but Leo thought it a much better idea if we kept that for when you were a little older."

Claire reached out and pushed her boiled egg to the centre of the table. "So if you and Leo have decided where I'm going to school, that means we are moving to Scotland and you are going to marry Leo."

Daphne nodded. "Yes, that's exactly what it means."

"And we have to sell this house."

"Yes, but you wait till you see Leo's house. It's very old and has big rooms and outside there are wonderful gardens and huge grass lawns. It's a perfect place to play, much better than here."

"Who will I play with, though? I won't have any of my friends, and Leo's children will be away at boarding school."

"They'll come back in the holidays, and I'm sure you'll make lots of friends at your new school."

Claire looked despondent for a moment but then suddenly her eyes brightened. "If we have to sell this house, maybe it could be to a woman who has just lost her husband and she has a daughter and they're looking for a perfect house for the two of them."

Daphne appeared relieved that her daughter had at last come out with a positive statement. "I think that could be a good selling point. I'll mention it to the estate agents."

"And they could buy the French Renault as well, because they might not have a car that fits into the parking place, and then the mother could do gardening jobs like you do for other people."

Her mother laughed. "I'm not sure if we could dictate their lives that much."

"All right, but we could tell them it's a good idea and that it was mine."

"Well, let's see, shall we?" Daphne said, pushing herself to her feet. "Now, do you want any more of that egg?"

Claire shook her head and slid off her chair. Daphne stroked her daughter's short dark hair and gently guided her towards the door. "In that case, let's get you upstairs to bed. We can talk lots more about this tomorrow."

8

❧

Between London and Edinburgh—June 1981

Sometime during the night, Claire was woken by a squeal of metal and a jolt that shifted her violently in her bed. She opened her eyes and looked around disorientated in the stuffy darkness of her surroundings. Outside, a door slammed shut and a tinny voice that was unintelligible to her blared from a loudspeaker. Still half-asleep, she kicked out a foot sideways to get rid of her covers, feeling hot and clammy in her pyjamas, and became aware of the strange narrowness of her bed when her heel banged noisily against the partition wall. She sat up, and as consciousness came to her and her eyes accustomed to the dark, she remembered that she was on the sleeper train heading up to Scotland and that in the bunk below her was Daphne.

She leaned over the edge as far as she could and looked down to see if her mother was sleeping. Daphne was facing inwards towards the partition, the sheet pulled up over her head so all that showed was her black curly hair on the pillow. Claire thought she looked like one of the Muppets.

She lay back on her bunk, nestling her head into the pillow, and stared up at the ceiling, only a couple of feet above her head. Boarding the train the previous evening had been one of the most exciting things she had ever done: arriving late in the taxi at King's Cross Station and moving through the hustle and bustle on the platform before they were shown to their compartment by the man in the maroon waistcoat. It certainly was a lot more fun and much easier than travelling by plane, when you had to sit around in an airport for hours and go through those horrible search places where the people who worked there never smiled. But now, lying on her bunk, she felt a nasty churning feeling in her stomach and it didn't seem at all exciting any more. It was like being kidnapped and taken away far from home, and knowing you could never, ever go back, and she thought it was like how the Lost Boys in *Peter Pan* must have felt when they were taken to Neverland; only it wasn't really the same for her because she had her mother sleeping in the bunk below.

A really worrying thought came to her. What if that wasn't Daphne down there but someone or something else that really did look like a Muppet, only not with a silly, funny face but with a cruel and ugly one?

A whistle blew outside the carriage and immediately the train gave a lurch and began to move on. Claire leaned over the edge of her bunk again and looked down at her mother.

"Mummy?" she whispered.

There was no movement from the figure in the bed. Claire began to breathe fast and she bit worriedly at her bottom lip. Of course, there wouldn't be any movement if that . . . thing down there didn't know its name was meant to be Mummy.

"Mummy!" she called out in a panicked voice.

The sheet was thrown back and Daphne sat up. She looked blindly around. "I'm here, darling." She got to her feet and her face was right beside Claire's. "What's up?"

Claire put out an arm and looped it round her mother's neck. "I just had some bad thoughts."

Climbing up the first few rungs of the ladder, Daphne leaned over and kissed her daughter on the cheek. "This is all a bit strange for us both, Claire," she said, gently stroking her forehead, "but it will be all right, I know it will."

Claire twirled her fingers in her mother's hair. "I wish we hadn't sold our house, though, because if we didn't like living in Scotland, we could have gone back to it."

Daphne laughed quietly. "I'm afraid that's what's called 'burning your bridges.'"

"What does that mean?"

"Well, I suppose . . ." Daphne paused, trying to get her mind awake enough to think of some near-upbeat explanation. ". . . it means we look forward to really happy times and forget all the sad ones we've had in the past."

Claire thought about this for a moment and smiled at her mother. "All right."

Daphne kissed her daughter again. "So try not to worry and get back to sleep, okay?" She descended the ladder and ducked down to get back into her bunk.

"Mummy?"

"Yes?"

"We don't need to forget all about David, though, do we?"

There was a pause in the darkness before Daphne replied. "No, darling, we will never forget David."

9

Edinburgh—June 1981

While waiting for the train to arrive, Leo just happened to glance down and notice the egg stain on the lapel of his dark-green tweed suit. Murmuring a quiet oath to himself, he gave the encrusted blob a hard rub with a fingernail, which led him to notice that that too was not in the most pristine condition either. He held up his splayed hands, hoping that the nail was a one-off case, but then realized to his horror that the dirt did not end at his fingertips, but at the white cuffs of his shirt—or they had been white when he put it on that morning. He groaned. This, of all days, was one when he should have avoided making an early visit to the greenhouses. Once there, he always forgot about all other things he was meant to be doing.

He turned and looked back down the platform, searching out a sign for the gents' loo. He saw one in the distance above the mass of travellers who thronged the main concourse of Waverley Station, but at that moment the loudspeaker above his head announced the imminent arrival of the overnight sleeper service from London Euston. He turned again just as the slant-fronted engine came adjacent to the farthest point of the platform.

Swallowing nervously, Leo wiped his hands on the sides of his jacket and watched as the carriages drew slowly past him, peering in through the windows to see if he could catch a glimpse of his new bride and her daughter. He felt apprehensive about seeing Daphne, wondering how she would react in person to the news he'd broken to her on the telephone only the previous day.

Of course it was his own silly fault for not looking carefully enough at the letter that had arrived from the registry office. He thought there was exactly a month in hand before the appointed date of their wedding, but then it wasn't the first time he'd got in a mix-up about events happening in June and July. He had tried to change the date, but the registry office couldn't come up with anything suitable until September. And Leo felt that that intervening three-month period might give too much time for second thoughts. He had managed to get a beautiful, intelligent younger woman, whose interests were perfectly matched with his own, to agree to marry him, and he didn't want anything to stand in the way of that going wrong.

And my word, she was beautiful. His heart gave a leap when he saw her descend from the train, dumping her heavy suitcase down on the platform before turning to help her daughter. The image he held of Daphne, and one of which he had a daily reminder from the photograph that sat on top of the chest of drawers in his bedroom, was of a woman dressed for mucky labour in the garden—Wellington boots, jeans and an oversized sweater. It was certainly not this apparition that he saw now in the floral tea dress with bright red splashes

and the white linen jacket. He stood transfixed as she looked along the platform towards him, pushing her dark hair away from
her face. She caught sight of him and her
mouth broadened into a happy smile, and
Leo knew in that instant that all was well.
He moved towards her, quickening his pace
as he went as if being drawn helplessly into
the core of her own personal magnetic field.

"You're here," he said, making it sound
as if he was quite astounded that she was.
He felt awkward in front of Claire, not
knowing how demonstrative he should be
with the greeting he gave her mother. It
was Daphne who came forward and gave
him a kiss on both cheeks.

"Leo, how lovely to see you." She turned
round to her daughter. "And look who we
have here."

Leo bent down, his hands on his knees.
"Hullo, my dear, how are you? Do I get a
kiss?"

Claire came forward and gave him a
peck on the cheek, and then immediately
retreated behind her mother. Leo glanced
at Daphne, his bushy eyebrows hooded in
concern.

Daphne smiled reassuringly at him.

"She's all right," she said quietly. "Just a bit disorientated."

"I'm sorry. Maybe it would have been best if . . ."

Daphne shook her head. "No, don't mention it. As it turns out, I think the excitement of the day will be just what she needs."

Leo smiled at her. "Exactly what I'm thinking for myself." He reached out and gave her arm an affectionate squeeze before walking over to retrieve the suitcase. "Your other stuff arrived yesterday in the removal van," he said, pulling out the retractable handle on the suitcase. "I've just left it all in one room in the house." He began wheeling the suitcase down the platform and Daphne and Claire fell into step beside him, Claire clutching tight to her mother's hand. "Thought it best if I left it up to you to work out where everything should go."

Daphne linked her arm through his as they walked and, after a few paces, turned to him. "I'm excited too, you know," she said.

Leo caught her look and saw from the sparkle in her dark-brown eyes that she meant what she said. He straightened his back, happiness and pride seeming to elevate him from the platform, and he lengthened his stride to that much more befitting a man fifteen years his junior. "Come on, I've just got a huge appetite. Let's go and have a slap-up breakfast."

Daphne laughed. "Well, before that takes place, Leo, my dear, I hope very much you might think about washing your hands."

10

Do you think the man will mind?"

Daphne had been chatting away non-stop to Leo during breakfast, so these were really the first words that Claire had uttered since arriving in Scotland. Not that she minded. She had been quite content to sit eating her Shreddies and poached egg on toast and staring at all the other people who were seated in the vast dining room of the Balmoral Hotel.

Both Daphne and Leo turned to look at her, Leo with a heaped forkful of egg, bacon and sausage poised before his open mouth. This was the second surprising thing that Leo had done that morning, ordering a full English breakfast in Scotland.

"Which man is that, darling?" Daphne asked.

"The man whose car it was that Leo put his parking ticket on."

Daphne turned her attention back to Leo. She leaned on the table, a querying smile on her face as she rested chin on upturned hand. "Yes, Leo, I wondered that myself."

Leo swallowed his mouthful at speed, waving his linen napkin as if already dismissing the question as being nothing to worry about. "Seeing he owns a Porsche, I'm sure he has got quite enough money to pay for a parking ticket. Anyway, he was as illegally parked as I was."

"Have you done it before, then?" Claire asked.

She saw Leo glance at Daphne, who continued to study him closely. Claire knew from the look on her mother's face that she was trying hard not to laugh.

"Well," Leo replied, "I suppose I have—from time to time."

"And did nobody ever find out what you'd done?" Claire continued.

Carefully scraping his plate clean, Leo set his knife and fork together and wiped his face with his napkin. Claire could see by the faint smile on his face that he was hoping that this time gap would allow him not to answer the question. But she was intrigued and wanted to know.

"Did they?"

Leo now drank from his coffee cup—a little more time—before fixing Claire with an expression of both humour and guilt. "Er, yes, that has been the case once in the past."

Claire's eyes widened. "What happened?"

"I was visited at home by two policemen. Two rather angry policemen, actually."

"And were you arrested?"

"No—not quite, but I was made to pay rather a hefty fine."

Claire giggled. "Was it more than if you had just paid for the parking ticket?"

Leo scratched his thick greying hair with his fingers and screwed his eyes tightly shut. "Yes, I'm afraid it was a lot more."

Daphne slowly shook her head. "Well,

wouldn't you say it's about time you stopped doing it, then?"

Leo's mouth drooped like a naughty schoolboy's who had been given a strict telling-off, but when he sneaked a glance at Claire, she noticed there was a wicked twinkle in his eye. She grinned at him and decided in that very moment that Daphne had done exactly the right thing in agreeing to marry him. Life with Leo, she thought, was going to be rather good fun.

11

The wedding took place, by a matter of seconds, at 10:30 A.M. in Edinburgh's main registry office on George IV Bridge. This time, though, it had nothing to do with Leo's haphazard organization. They had parked his ancient Humber in a nearby car-park and were standing outside the registry office with twenty minutes in hand, but there they remained for the next sixteen minutes until a filthy Land Rover with bright-orange baler twine dangling out of the back door bounced a wheel up onto the pavement in front of them and came to an abrupt halt. The door was thrown open with a screech of unoiled hinges and a man stepped out, sweeping a hand over his grey stubble of hair before pulling a dirty tweed cap firmly down on his head. He was of no great height, but as broad as he was tall, and wore an old grey flannel suit with a green knitted tie that failed in its attempt to close the gap left by the missing top button of his shirt. He walked towards Leo with a huge gnarled hand outstretched.

"Right then, lad, how's our bridegroom this morning?" he boomed out in a Scottish accent so guttural that Daphne thought he had to be furious with Leo for some reason.

Leo shook his hand. "Fine, fine, Bert," he replied hastily, conscious of time slipping ever faster towards the half-hour. "Have you brought Agnes?"

Bert flicked a thumb over his shoulder. "Aye, she'll be trying to get herself out of the vehicle," he said, beaming a grin at Daphne so broad that his top dentures momentarily dislodged before being reset with a dexterous movement of his jaw.

"Ah, there you are, Agnes," Leo called out. "Come on, as quick as you can."

Daphne shifted her gaze to the tiny woman who came round the side of the Land Rover. She was dressed in a dark-green overcoat that, despite the warmth of the morning, was buttoned to the neck, and on her head she wore a pink woolly hat that looked more suitable for warming a teapot. Over her arm was looped an enormous brown plastic handbag while in her hand she bore a bunch of roses, their stems wrapped in tinfoil.

"Well done, you remembered the bouquet," Leo said, taking the flowers from the woman and thrusting them into Daphne's hand. "Only time for a quick introduction, I'm afraid. This is Daphne and her daughter Claire—and this is Bert Fairweather, my best man and my neighbour, and Agnes Smith, who helps me in the house and has kindly consented to act as the other witness." He moved towards the entrance door, glancing at his watch. "And now we must get a move on, otherwise we'll miss our slot."

Daphne did not move. "Leo," she said.

Leo turned. "Yes?" There was a distinct note of concern in his voice as if concluding that, at this late stage, Daphne had indeed had second thoughts.

"Where are your children? I thought they were coming with Bert."

Leo slapped his hand against his forehead. "Oh, yes, I'm sorry, I forgot to tell you. They're not coming."

Daphne slowly shook her head. "Oh, Leo, this is not right, then."

"Oh, no, no!" Leo exclaimed, hurrying back to her and giving her arm a reassuring squeeze. "It's nothing like that. Of course they would have been here if I'd not made such a stupid mistake with the dates, but Marcus had an end-of-term cricket match that he desperately wanted to play in, and Charity has . . . well, she's going straight down to London from school to stay with a friend."

Daphne lowered her head and picked at the petals of her bouquet. "Those sound like excuses, Leo." She looked at him. "They don't want me to marry you, do they?"

"Of course they do. They're as happy as cows in clover that I'm getting married again. They said so, I promise you."

She studied his face, which now seemed pale with worry, and saw in it no sign of deception. "Cross your heart, Leo?"

Leo exuberantly made a cross on his chest. "There." He smiled at her hopefully. "Are you convinced?"

She weighed this up, her mouth twisted to one side, her eyes narrowed. "Probably," she replied at length, her voice expressing humorous doubt.

"Good," Leo said, looping his arm. "Are you ready to become Mrs. Harrison, then?"

Smiling, Daphne slipped her arm through his. "I think so—probably."

12

Alloa—June 1981

Leo said it would take just over an hour to do the journey back to his house. Before they left Edinburgh, he handed over an old AA map with curling pages to Claire in the back seat and pointed out the route they would be taking. Along the M9 towards Stirling, over the river Forth at the Kincardine Bridge, and then Alloa was no more than five miles on from there.

Claire, however, did not study the map for very long. She was much more interested to see how different Scotland was to England and peered out of the window of the car while they trailed through the outskirts of Edinburgh. When they hit the motorway, her first thought was that there seemed to be much fewer cars on the road, and then she thought that the towns and villages they passed were rather dull and ugly and it looked as if the people who lived there couldn't have very much money. There were green fields as well, of course, but they seemed flat and characterless compared with the small rolling paddocks, enclosed by copses of tall leafy trees and dense hawthorn hedges, which had surrounded their village in West Sussex. She began to feel that it was all rather disappointing.

And it got no better when they reached the Kincardine Bridge. When the teacher at her school in Haywards Heath had heard that Claire was moving to Scotland, she had shown Claire a picture in a geography book of the two huge bridges that crossed the river Forth, and this was definitely not one of them. It was just a normal old iron bridge, not very high and not very long, with square concrete arches at either end. She leaned forward between the front seats and asked Leo about it and he explained to her that the road bridge she

THE LONG WAY HOME 99
was talking about was much farther down

was talking about was much farther down the river. So Claire just sat back on the worn red leather seat and thought to herself that it would have been much more exciting if they'd been able to use that one.

And when Leo eventually announced, "Nearly there," Claire really wished that they weren't. The town they were approaching was even more ugly than those she had seen at the side of the motorway. The row of dark-slated houses that fronted the road seemed unkempt and gloomy and the few gardens that she saw were just a mass of weeds or filled with things like an old dishwasher or a discarded carpet.

"It's not a very beautiful place," she said to no one in particular.

Leo glanced round at her. "No, you're right, but you see, Alloa was at one time a big coal-mining centre, and all around here there were huge coal pits, and these houses we're passing were where the miners used to live. They weren't very rich, I'm afraid, so there was never very much spare money for doing up their houses."

"Aren't they still living here?"

"Not any more. All the mines are closed

now and new industries have been brought in to give people new jobs."

"They still don't look as if they have enough money to do up their houses," Claire murmured glumly.

Leo sidled a glance at his new bride, trying hard to suppress a smile. "No, I think that's a fair observation."

Passing two large factories with tall stainless-steel chimneys that had plumes of white smoke coming out of them, Claire now saw that they were driving through a new housing development where some of the houses weren't even finished and those that were didn't even have grass outside them, just brown earth. She really was beginning to think that maybe Daphne had been making it all up about Leo's house just so Claire wouldn't say no about her getting married to Leo. But then he turned the car to the right up a freshly tar-macked road between a row of these new houses and they drove through two stone pillars that had a pair of sculptured eagles on them with their wings outstretched, and it was as if they had just gone into another world. The road immediately became a gravel driveway that was so full of potholes that the car began lurching from side to side, and it all went rather dark and gloomy because they were enclosed by rhododendron bushes that grew out so far that they nearly touched the sides of the car. But then suddenly they were through them and the light came back, and Claire caught her breath because there, on either side, were the lawns that Daphne had told her about. A huge beech trees grew in the centre of each, with enormous branches that spanned out, drooping so near to the ground that Claire knew they would be perfect for climbing and making brilliant dens in. And then, once clear of the trees, Claire saw the sloping glass roofs of the greenhouses away over to her left, set against a high stone wall that appeared to run right round the property. She could tell they were not very well cared for because only in places were the wooden window frames still white, but that didn't matter at all. They were so much bigger than the little greenhouse that had been in their old garden, and she could imagine the smell of warm earth and growing plants, which she loved, being at least ten times more delicious in these ones.

She had her head still turned, wondering what all the exotic plants that Leo grew in the greenhouses looked like, when Daphne said, "What do you think of that, darling?" From where she sat, she could only see the back of Daphne's seat, so she pushed herself forward and stood up, looping her arms around her mother's neck, and all she could say was "Wow!"

The driveway began now to loop round a circular lawn with a bubbling fountain in its centre, and on the far side of this stood the house, a vast stone-built rectangular building with a mass of chimney pots at either end and a flat roof with castle-like battlements. Wide stone steps, narrowing as they rose, led up to a central front door and, on either side of it, the tall windows on each of the three floors were a mirror image of one another. There were no plants growing up the front wall and Claire thought at first the house looked rather bare without them. But then it occurred to her that actually the house was quite like a miniature version of Buckingham Palace where the Queen lived, and she instantly felt rather proud and grand, if not a little nervous, that this was where she and

Daphne—and Leo, of course—were going to live from now on.

Leo rolled the car to a halt at the bottom of the steps and Claire pushed open the back door, got out and stood looking up at the house. She heard a scrunch of gravel and turned to find Leo standing beside her. Putting his hands in the small of his back, he stretched out his spine as he too surveyed the house, and for the first time Claire had the astonishing thought that this was her new stepfather, this was the person she was going to see every morning, day and night.

He looked down at her. "Do you like it?" he asked.

Claire smiled at him. "Yes, it's very big and very lovely."

Leo nodded. "An excellent description, my dear, that's exactly what I think." He held out his hand to Daphne, who had come to stand beside him. "Come on, let's leave the luggage. I'll get that in a moment. There's something much more important to be done."

Claire followed them up the steps and watched as Leo pulled a huge key from his jacket pocket and proceeded to unlock the heavy wooden door. He pushed it open and then turned to Daphne with a broad smile on his face. "Welcome home, Mrs. Harrison," he said and Claire's mother let out a cry of surprise as Leo scooped her up effortlessly in his arms and carried her into the house.

"Leo, for goodness' sakes, watch your back!" she laughed.

"Don't worry," he replied, placing her down on her feet again. "Nothing wrong with that. I'm used to carrying much heavier things than you."

Claire did notice him grimace slightly when he turned away from Daphne and headed back outside to collect the luggage, but she didn't say anything because she was transfixed completely by what she saw before her. The hallway was enormous, a wood-panelled cavern that Claire knew had to be the full height of the house because way above her head was a huge round window that she could see blue sky through. Around where she stood, there were old sofas and armchairs with faded loose covers, some rubbed away to holes around the edges, and against the walls was placed an odd assortment of furniture.

There were dark-wooded antique book-cases with ornate glass doors that were crammed with books and a couple of modern desks with metal legs and plastic handles on the drawers. In the centre of the hall was a scrubbed pine kitchen table that was laden with piles of newspapers, unopened mail, two balls of twine, three cases of wine, a pair of gardening gloves and a white Panama hat—and right behind that was a wide blue-carpeted staircase that led straight up to a banistered landing. The walls were hung with pictures, some gilt-framed portraits of serious-looking men wearing wigs and others just splashes of bright colours that really made no sense at all to Claire.

It could have seemed to her a strange and quite frightening place to be, but the whole area was filled with the homely smell of fresh lilies and furniture polish and Claire decided that she was completely comfortable with it all.

Leo reappeared, puffing slightly with the burden of the suitcase, and dumped it down on the bare polished floorboards.

"How many rooms are there in the house?" Claire asked.

Leo scratched at his head. "You know, Claire, I've never counted. I suppose, including those in the basement, I would say about . . . twenty-three?"

"Wow!" Claire exclaimed in amazement. "Can I go and explore a bit?"

"What an excellent idea," Leo replied, clapping his hands together so forcefully that the sound echoed around the hall. "You head off and count up all the rooms you can find, and if it's more than twenty-three, then I shall give you"—he twisted up the corner of his mouth as he contemplated this—"fifty pence. How does that sound?"

"And if it's less than twenty-three?"

Leo shrugged his shoulders. "Then I'm still wrong and the deal still stands." He pointed to the stairs. "Start up there first and work your way down, and if you get lost, just shout out 'Cooee' and I'll come and find you."

With an excited glint in her eye, Claire ran round the table and began climbing the stairs. "Don't worry," she called out, "I won't get lost."

13

Buffeted by the slipstream of passing lorries, Daphne sat in the front seat of Leo's Humber on the hard shoulder of the M9 motorway and stared ahead at the raised bonnet of the car. Through the small gap at the bottom of the windscreen, she could see Leo's hands become increasingly covered in oil as he tinkered with various parts of the engine. She turned around and smiled patiently at the three children in the back seat, conscious that hardly a word had passed between them since they had picked up Marcus and Charity from the station in Edinburgh. Claire returned the smile, but it was a wary one and she glanced either side at her new stepsiblings who were turned away from her, staring vacantly out of the windows with their Sony Walkman earphones plugged firmly into their ears.

Daphne felt an immediate swell of protection for her daughter, realizing that up until now she had never had reason to compare closely her stage in life with that of other children. Charity was only two years older than Claire, but at thirteen, she seemed like a young fledgling of a woman next to her. Besides the pink T-shirt with the Adam Ant image that she wore over her budding chest, she was dressed in a Levi's combo of jacket and jeans, white Reebok trainers, and on each of her hands she sported two small silver rings. Daphne could tell she had obviously visited a good hair stylist during her visit to London because her short blonde hair, which looked thick and lustrous, perfectly framed her pretty round face with its button nose and eyes as blue as those of her father. It was the mouth, though, that gave Daphne cause for concern. It was small and tight with determination, even with the ongoing action of chewing gum, and Daphne had a worrying notion that it spoke of a certain meanness in the girl's character.

As for Marcus, Daphne realized that she was more worried for herself rather than for Claire, and she wondered how on earth she was ever going to start to form a relationship with him. Girls she was used to, but not a young man whose body was flowing with the first surges of testosterone and who had already shown an alarming disrespect for his father when the car had broken down. From what Daphne had witnessed so far, he seemed quite unlike Leo in both looks and character. He was tall with dark hair that flopped across a strong-boned face and wore an open-necked shirt with the sleeves rolled up, a pair of jeans with a wide leather belt and Timberland sailing shoes with no socks. It was quite apparent to Daphne that he possessed the typical air of a public schoolboy, self-confidence bordering on arrogance. He was only fifteen, but there was no doubt in Daphne's mind that, in a couple of years' time, he would be a serial heartbreaker.

Without a word, Daphne turned to the front, mulling over the frightening uncertainties of this new phenomenon called "stepmotherhood" and guiltily wishing that the easy, harmonious way of life that she, Leo and Claire had become used to over the past week could go on forever.

It was Claire who eventually broke the silence. She turned to Marcus and stated proudly, "There are twenty-five rooms in the house."

Marcus looked round at her, pulling on a wire to dislodge one of his earphones. "What?"

"There are twenty-five rooms in the house."

Daphne turned again to see Marcus furrowing his brow and shaking his head as if he thought it hardly worth his while to make any comment on the subject. "So?"

Claire's face went pink and she stuck her hands between her knees and rubbed them together, glancing nervously at her mother.

Daphne's immediate wish was to jump to the defence of her daughter by saying something like "She's just making conversation, you rude little devil," but she turned away, biting hard on her lip. Oh, my word, she thought to herself, so this is going to be the way of things, is it?

She saw with relief that Leo had shut the bonnet and was waiting for a lorry to sail past before returning to the driver's door.

"That should be it now," he declared as he got in and slammed the door shut. He wiped his hands on a now-oily handkerchief and threw it down into the footwell before turning the ignition key and cranking up the engine. After three wheezing attempts, it eventually spluttered to life. "Aha! Bravo, old girl!" He flicked up his indicator and pulled out onto the motorway, turning to Daphne with a sheepish smile. "Sorry about that. It's in need of a service, I think. I'll give Bert Fairweather a call when I get home and see if he can't send young Jonas over for it tomorrow."

"Is Jonas his son?" Daphne asked.

"Yes, a fine young lad. He's not even as old as Marcus or Charity, but by golly, he can drive a car as well as you or me."

Daphne was bewildered. "He doesn't drive on the road, does he?"

"Oh gosh, no. He comes down that track next to the greenhouses. Bert's farm is part of my grand estate. He's my trusty

tenant, and I have to say, a wonderful mechanic."

"He's a lousy farmer, though," Marcus's
voice called out from the back seat.

Leo glanced at his son in the rear-view
mirror. "He's not that bad, Marcus."

"He's crap, Dad, and you know it. The
whole farm is just a mass of weeds and
the courtyard looks like a car dump."

Leo shrugged. "Yes, granted, it's a bit of
a mess, but I still maintain he's a first-class
mechanic." He slapped a hand down on
the steering wheel. "He keeps this old lady
on the road, at any rate."

"I don't know why the hell you can't just
buy another car," Marcus said. "This one's
had it."

"Not at all," Leo exclaimed, sounding as
if his son had just suggested that they put
down a faithful old dog. "Plenty of life in
her yet."

"Well, as long as you don't ever bring it
back to school again. It's a real embarrassment."

Leo smirked at Daphne.

"By the way, Dad," Marcus continued.
"Toby Winston's parents are going over to
Paris on business for a couple of days next

week, so I've asked him to come and stay. He's arriving the day after tomorrow at Stirling Station."

"Toby Winston?" Charity suddenly piped up.

"Yeah," said Marcus, "so don't you go pestering him like you did the last time. He doesn't fancy you, you know."

"And I don't fancy him, either," Charity replied indignantly.

"Like hell you don't."

Leo cleared his throat. "Come on, you two, less of that." He glanced in the mirror again. "Actually, Marcus, I think it might be a good idea in future if you consulted first with either Daphne or myself before you go inviting people to stay, okay?"

Marcus gave no reply to his father, but after a few seconds he leaned forward in his seat and peered at Daphne. "You don't mind, do you, Daphne?"

Daphne turned and stared impassively at him, realizing that only two hours had passed since she had met the boy and here he was already putting her to the test. She was well aware that whatever answer she gave would probably set the trend for the way he treated her in the future. She wondered whether to be a viper or a doormat, and decided on splitting the difference.

"Well, as I'm the one who's going to be cooking for you all from now on and no doubt making up the beds for your guests, then a bit of warning would certainly be appreciated."

Marcus did not move. "You could get Agnes to make up the beds."

Daphne smiled coldly at him. "But I don't choose to do that, Marcus."

Marcus flicked his head to the side as if he couldn't care less one way or the other and slumped back into his seat and plugged in his earphone again. Daphne glanced across at Leo, who seemed to have shrunk slightly into his seat, as if ducking to avoid the barbed vibes that were flying around the interior of the car.

And in that moment, Daphne understood that "stepmotherhood" was going to be like walking on hot coals, and that any authority she had in the house might well be undermined by the manipulation of family loyalties.

14

Like mother, like daughter. Almost from the moment that Marcus and Charity set foot in the house, Claire began to wish too that it could have just remained being Leo, Daphne and herself in the house for always. During the past week, she had had the full run of the place, exploring every inch of it from the dusty cluttered attic to the dark, dank cellar. But now that her step-siblings had arrived, it was as if cuckoos had taken over her nest. Her favourite place of all was the old playroom upstairs because it had huge sagging sofas with big cushions that you could flump down into

to watch television, but it was almost the
first place that Marcus and Charity went
to on their return, and when Claire had
plucked up enough courage to enter the
room, they glared at her in such an un-
friendly way that she just turned round and
left. As she walked dejectedly along the
landing, she felt for the first time since Leo
and Daphne had got married an empty,
sad longing to be back in their little house
in West Sussex, where her space was her
own and she didn't have to share it with
anyone.

She thought about going into her bedroom to read, but when she opened the
door the afternoon sun was streaming
through the window, and feeling it was
wrong to waste such weather, she decided
instead to go outside to see what Daphne
was doing.

She actually hadn't been to the greenhouses yet. Leo and Daphne had spent
much of the last week together, either
there or in the garden. At times, when she
had been doing her exploring, she would
look out of the window of a particular
room, because that always helped her to
work out what part of the house she was

in, and she would more often than not see her mother and Leo chatting away together whilst they weeded a flower bed or studied some aspect of the garden. She even caught sight of them once, through the fugged-up windows of the nearest greenhouse, with their arms around each other, and it was then that she realized that this was a very special time for both of them, before Marcus and Charity came home, and would be about as much of a honeymoon as they were going to get. And so Claire decided to leave them to enjoy it.

But now she felt the need to speak to her mother. She descended the main staircase and made her way across the hall to the heavy front door. She opened it, glancing furtively back up the stairs when it creaked on its unoiled hinges, and then closed it quietly behind her. She ran across the gravel onto the lawn, and then sprinted over to the greenhouses.

From the moment she entered, the nostalgic smell of warm, sweet vegetation seemed to calm her troubled mind, but she could see that it was only Leo who was there, working away at the far end of the greenhouse. He was in his shirtsleeves,

his tweed jacket hanging on a propped-up
spade, and he was bent over, studying one
of the plants on the raised shelves that ran
each side of the central paved path. She
walked towards him, studying as she went
the hundreds of little flowerpots that housed
Leo's strange-looking plants.

She announced herself quite nonchalantly. "Hullo, Leo."

He straightened quickly and looked
round at her. "Oh, Claire!" He patted the
breast pocket of his shirt, making a hollow
drumming sound on his empty spectacle
case. "That was a bit of a fright you gave
me."

"Sorry," Claire replied quietly. "I was just
looking for Mummy."

"Ah," Leo said, wiping a bead of sweat
off his forehead with the back of a soil-
stained hand. "I think she's in the kitchen—or
maybe her bedroom, I'm not actually sure
where." He immediately resumed his work,
pushing in soil with his fingers round the
spindly base of a plant with spiky dark-
green leaves. "So what brings you out
here?"

Claire shrugged. "Nothing, really."

"Where are Marcus and Charity?"

"In the playroom, I think."

Leo looked round at her and nodded slowly, his mouth screwed up to one side. "Your territory, hmm?" He pulled at one of his ear lobes in thought. "It's . . . maybe going to be a bit awkward to begin with, Claire, you know, all of us living together. I suppose Marcus and Charity have got used to it being just the three of us . . . and now there's you and your mother as well. In time, everyone will find their place, believe me."

Claire let out a sigh. "I don't mind, really, if Marcus and Charity want to do things without me. I always used to play by myself when Mummy and I lived in England."

Leo smiled at her. "Actually, that's rather like me. I really enjoy being in my own company, especially out here."

"This is the first time I've seen you here without Mummy."

Leo pointed a finger at her. "Yes, absolutely right. Very astute of you. And the reason for that is"—he dragged the words out so that again he could give himself time to think—"well, I'm afraid your mother wasn't all that pleased with me when I didn't give her my full support over that little stand-off she had with Marcus in the car. She probably has very good reason, but you see, Claire, I don't think the time's quite right yet for taking sides. At this early stage, it just wouldn't be fair."

So things have already begun to change, Claire thought to herself.

"Have you and Mummy had a row, then?"

"Not at all!" Leo exclaimed. "We're just giving each other a little space to work out how things are going to be." He picked up a small plastic spray bottle, unscrewed the top and handed it to Claire. "Seeing you're here, I could do with a hand. That needs filled up from the water barrel just outside the door."

Claire eyed the green hose that hung in a coil on the tap behind Leo. "Why don't you use the water from there?"

"Much better to use rainwater for these plants," replied Leo, running a hand lightly up one of the sharp leaves. "Helps them to thrive."

When Claire returned with the filled bottle, Leo had turned to work on the other side of the path, tamping in earth around the base of another of the spiky-leaved plants, and it was then that Claire realized that the shelves at the top end of the greenhouse were laden with pots containing the same plant.

"Thank you, my dear," Leo said, taking the container from her. He screwed on the spray nozzle and handed it back to her. "Now, if you could just mist the leaves of each of these plants with water, that would be wonderful. It'll save me a lot of work."

"You've got a lot of these, haven't you," she said, already starting on her task.

Leo turned and surveyed both shelves. "Yes, I suppose I have. I rather have a soft spot for them."

"What are they called?"

"Well, the proper name is *Dracaena marginata,* but it's more often called a Madagascar Dragon Tree." He brushed the back of his hand almost affectionately against the leaves of one of the plants. "Actually, I think it's a bit of a cheat calling something that size a tree, so I just call it a Dragon Plant."

"What a lovely name. Is it very . . . exotic?"

Leo laughed. "Not as exotic as some of the plants in here, but it is one of my favourites." He leaned a hand on the shelf, the other on his hip, watching as his stepdaughter carefully sprayed the leaves of the plants. "Do you know, I don't think in all the time we've been here that either Marcus or Charity have ever set foot in these greenhouses. They certainly have never shown the remotest interest in my plants. It's rather a joy for me to have a young under-gardener." He resumed his work. "And listen, Claire, going back to what we were saying about, well, settling in, I want you to know that this house and its surroundings are just as much yours and your mother's as it is ours—for the foreseeable future, at any rate—so you must treat it as such, okay?"

Claire nodded. She didn't really take in everything that he was saying. Leo did have a habit of waffling quite a lot. "What's the house called?"

Leo turned and stared at her, surprised. "My word, have I never told you that?"

"No. I've just always called it 'the house.'"

Leo frowned and gave his head a quick shake. "Very remiss of me, I'm sorry. It will be rectified immediately. The name of the house is Croich."

Claire burst out laughing. "What?"

"Croich." He spelled it out. "C-R-O-I-C-H. It's an old Scottish name, I think."

"It's not a very nice one," Claire remarked, the sides of her mouth downturned in disgust. "It sounds like you're being sick."

Leo repeated the word, this time with much greater emphasis on the last two letters. He nodded decisively. "Agreed, it's revolting. You and I should think of a new name immediately."

Claire stopped her spraying and looked around the greenhouse for inspiration. "What about . . ." She looked momentarily thoughtful before her eyes suddenly brightened at the idea that had come into her head, ". . . the Dragon Plant House!"

"Hmm," Leo murmured, giving Claire's suggestion an exaggerated amount of consideration. "Yes, that is a superb name! From now on, you and I shall stop sounding as if we're being sick and call it the Dragon Plant House." He glared fiercely at her. "Maybe it'll change into a very special house now that breathes fire and eats people!"

Claire stared at him with wide eyes. That was not at all how she wanted to think of the house. "But only if they're evil and nasty," she said hopefully.

Leo frowned. "Yes, of course," he replied, taking the spray from Claire's grasp and using it at random on his plants, "that was what I meant to say. Only if they're evil and nasty. Quite."

At that moment, a young boy appeared outside the greenhouse and stood looking in at them. He was dressed in a pair of dirty coveralls that hung loosely on his small frame, their oversized legs tucked into Wellington boots, and his hands were pushed deep into the pockets.

"Leo, there's someone outside," Claire said quietly.

Leo turned and peered through the smeared glass. "Ah, it's Jonas Fairweather," he said, giving the boy a wave. He dusted his hands together, picked up his jacket and slung it over his shoulder and walked past Claire along the path. "He's here to collect the car. Come and meet him."

Claire watched as the boy walked parallel to them as they made their way to the door. He was not much taller than she and had long black hair that swept across his forehead and down the side of his face, and he saved it from obscuring his right eye with a constant flicking back of his head.

He was standing in front of them when they appeared out through the door.

"Hullo there, Jonas," Leo said jovially. "How are things going, lad?"

"Fine," the boy replied sullenly, his head bowed as he kicked a small stone off the lawn and into the flower bed.

"Jonas, this is my stepdaughter, Claire Barclay."

Jonas looked up and acknowledged her with a brief nod of his head.

"I think you and Claire must be about the same age," Leo continued. "How old are you now?"

"Twelve," Jonas replied quietly.

Leo frowned at Claire. "Is that about your age?"

"I'm eleven," Claire said, feeling her cheeks glow hot with embarrassment.

"Jolly good, near enough," Leo called out as he strode off across the lawn to-wards the house. Jonas and Claire fol-lowed after him, not looking at each other. "Could you tell your father I think it's the distributor cap that's needing replaced, and while he's at it, he may as well change the oil?"

"When d'you want it back?" Jonas asked. It was the first time Claire had heard him string together a sentence and he spoke with the same thick Scots accent as his father, whom Claire remembered meeting when he acted as Leo's best man at the wedding.

"Soon as you can. What about tomorrow?"

"Dad's not back till tomorrow evening. I could do the work if you wanted."

Leo stopped by the old Humber, parked at the front of the house on the gravel driveway. "That's fine by me," he said, opening the driver's door. "I'm sure you'll manage quite perfectly. What about getting spares?"

Jonas almost smiled, the side of his mouth curling up a fraction. "Dad's got most things."

Leo laughed. "Of course he has. Silly question." He took his jacket off his shoulder, folded it and put it on the driver's seat. "There, that should give you a bit of extra height." He stood back and gestured a hand towards the open door. "It's all yours. Take it away."

Jonas walked over to the door and then turned, glancing first at Claire and then at Leo. "If she came too, she could bring your jacket back."

Leo nodded. "What a good idea. Would you like to go, Claire?"

Claire looked apprehensively at Leo. It wasn't that she was frightened to be driven by someone who was almost the same age as herself, but more because it was Jonas who had suggested she should go and she wasn't quite sure what she would say to him when they were alone in the car together.

Leo came over and put a hand on her shoulder and guided her round to the other side of the car. "Go on, it'll be an adventure for you, and I trust Jonas's driving skills implicitly." He opened the passenger door. "The farm is only about half a mile away, so you can just walk back whenever you want."

Claire climbed warily into the passenger seat and Leo closed the door behind her. She did up her seat belt and glanced across at Jonas, an anxious smile on her face, and she thought then that he did look awfully small to be driving such a big car. He turned on the ignition and started the engine and then selected a gear by pulling down on the lever that stuck out beside the steering wheel. Sliding down in his seat a fraction, he pressed one of the two floor pedals with a fully outstretched foot and they set off smoothly down the drive with Jonas peering over the top of the steering wheel.

Jonas's speed never exceeded more than a fast walking pace, but nevertheless his concentration did not waver for a moment, and he certainly did not appear to want to speak, much to Claire's relief. Some way down the drive, he turned right along a track that ran behind the greenhouses. It was dark and damp-looking, the sunlight cut out by the tall trees that hemmed them in on either side, providing an impenetrable canopy above. But it only lasted for about a hundred yards before they were out in the sun again, driving between two unfenced fields of ripening barley topped with a sea of red poppies, towards a cluster of buildings at the far side.

Having not been out of the policies of

the house since arriving, Claire was quite amazed they were in this open country-side, knowing that the main driveway led straight out into the suburbs of Alloa. But then she saw that the urban sprawl ex-tended out on both sides of the fields, and she thought that Leo's property was rather like being on an island of coloured beauty in the middle of a cold grey con-crete sea.

As the car made its way slowly down the rutted road, Claire began to see what Marcus had meant, during their journey back from Edinburgh that morning, about the place being in a terrible state. The fields gave way to a scrubby area of land that was littered with old cars, some with no doors or windows, others wheel-less and resting up on blocks of wood. Most had their bonnets raised, which made them look as if they had just broken down, one after the other, and then left to rot.

Jonas pulled into the courtyard of the farm, scattering aside a few scrawny hens that squawked with indignation at their treatment. He spun the steering wheel round, narrowly missing a stack of rusting oil drums, and came to a halt in front of a drab stone-built farmhouse, the doors and windows of which were in dire need of a paint.

"Is that your house?"

"Aye, Dad and I live there."

"What about your mother?"

"She's away," Jonas said flatly. "Lives with another man in Kirkcaldy."

"Oh, I see," Claire replied, now feeling a bit stupid for asking the question in the first place.

Jonas clicked the gearshift and began reversing the car through the open doors of the shed behind them, glancing in his wing mirrors as he went. Claire could tell that he had done this many times before because he did it all without stopping once, and when the car was in the shed there was no more than a couple of feet clearance on either side.

Jonas pulled on the handbrake and turned off the engine.

"You're quite a good driver," Claire said shyly as she unbuckled her seat belt.

Jonas shrugged. "I get a lot of practice about here with Dad's old cars." He opened the door carefully so that it wouldn't thump against the workbench and squeezed out, taking Leo's jacket with him. "Better come out this side," he said. "There's more room."

Claire clambered over the seat and got out. She slid past him so that he could shut the door, and in that instance she breathed in the metallic smell of oil and grease that permeated his coveralls.

"Are you going to do some work on the car now?"

"No, I'll leave it to the morn," Jonas replied, closing the door and edging round to the front of the Humber. "If it's a faulty distributor cap, I'll have to work out where to get another, maybe from that old Sunbeam Rapier round the back of the steading." He handed her Leo's jacket.

"So . . . I'd better just walk back to the house, then."

"Aye."

Claire folded Leo's jacket over her arm and took a few steps towards the track. She turned. "Bye then. I might see you when you bring the car back."

Jonas stuck his hands into the pockets of the coveralls and walked past her. "I'm coming with you."

"It's all right. I think I can find my own way back."

Jonas glanced round as he continued towards the track. "I'm coming with you."

Claire ran to catch up with him and they walked side by side in silence down the track.

"Leo told us you were from England," Jonas said eventually.

"Yes, I lived in West Sussex with my mother."

"Scotland's pretty different, eh?"

"Yes, it is."

Jonas aimed a solid kick at a stone in the middle of the track and it spun off into the barley. "D'you like it, though?"

"I think so. I've only been here a week."

They covered the next twenty yards in silence.

"I suppose you'll be heading away to school after the holidays, like Marcus and Charity," Jonas said.

"No, I'm not. I'm going to school some-where around here."

Jonas glanced at her and Claire saw a sparkle edge his dark eyes. "Maybe you'll end up in the same place as me, then."

"I might do. Where do you go?"

"I'll be starting at Clackmannanshire Secondary in Alloa next term."

"So you'll be moving to a new school as well."

"Aye, I am. I suppose we're a bit the same, then."

Claire smiled at him. "I suppose."

They had reached the far side of the barley fields and were now walking in the shelter of the trees. The dense foliage obscured the sun and the air had suddenly lost its warmth. Claire, dressed only in a T-shirt and jeans, felt a shiver go through her body. Jonas noticed it.

"You should put on Leo's jacket."

"It's all right."

"Go on."

"It's far too big for me. I'd look stupid."

Jonas laughed and pulled out the sides of his coveralls. "How d'you think I feel, then, wearing one of my dad's boiler suits?"

Claire looked at the jacket slung over her arm. "Okay, then." She put it on as they continued to walk, and it wasn't until she glanced at him to see why their conversation had dried up that she realized that he was trying to stop himself from laughing.

"What's so funny?" she asked almost indignantly.

Jonas grinned at her. "You are. That jacket makes you look like a monkey."

Claire was open-mouthed at the insult. "And you look like a . . . balloon man."

Jonas adopted a strongman pose, bowing his knees and flexing the muscles in his thin arms. "Balloon Man and Monkey Girl, the new Superhero team," he said, mimicking an American accent, "conquering the evil forces of the world."

Claire immediately caught the spirit of the game, and flapping the long arms of Leo's jacket away from her body, she galloped off down the lane making the kind of screeching noises that she thought a monkey would make. Jonas gave chase, holding out the legs of his coveralls, and yelling out "Boing! Boing!" as he went.

They didn't stop running until they came to the lawn, where they collapsed in fits of laughter on the newly mown grass. Eventually, their laughter subsided and they lay on their backs in silence and looked up at the high powdery clouds that drifted slowly across the blue sky.

It was Claire who spoke first. "Do you

want some orange juice?" she asked, sitting up and leaning back on her hands.

"Got some with you, have you?"

"No, but there's some in the kitchen. We could go there."

Jonas propped himself up on an elbow and plucked at the grass. "Nah, I'm fine without."

Claire studied his face, seeing the sullenness return to his features. "If I did have it with me, would you want some?"

Jonas shrugged. "Might have done."

"Don't you like going into the house?"

He shot her a look under his dark eyebrows that told her he didn't want to give an answer.

"Why not?" she asked anyway.

Again he shrugged. "I just keep clear of the place during the holidays."

Claire thought for a moment. "Is it because of Marcus and Charity?"

Jonas answered with a smile and a flick of his head.

"Do you not get on with them?"

"Nah," Jonas replied, falling back onto the grass again.

Claire looked towards the house. "I don't think I do either."

"They're stuck-up."

Claire frowned. "Are they? What are they stuck up?"

Jonas laughed and Claire was glad that he had become light-hearted again, even though she didn't see what was so funny. "Up themselves, mostly," he chuckled.

"What does that mean?"

"You know, they think they're better than other people."

"What? Like you and me?"

"Aye, exactly."

"They're not, though, are they?"

"No way." He now plucked forcefully at the grass with both hands as if he was angry that it was growing around him. "Anyway, I'm going to be famous when I'm older."

"Doing what?"

"Not sure yet. Probably something with cars." He turned and looked at her. "That's what I'm good at."

"Will you race them?"

Jonas grinned broadly, his eyes gleaming brightly, and Claire knew she had probably just worked out his dream.

"Aye, like Jackie Stewart."

"Who's he?"

"A racing driver from Scotland. He was the best."

"Why not any more?"

"He retired about eight years ago. He was world champion."

"And has no one taken his place?"

"Sure they have, but not from Scotland."

"So maybe you'll be the next Scottish world champion, then?"

"Maybe. I've already won a couple of races."

"You have not!"

"I have too!"

"Driving a car?"

"No, you numpty, I can't do that. I race go-karts."

"Whereabouts?"

"On the circuit up at Knockhill. It's about fifteen miles from here."

"Do you have your own go-kart?"

"Aye, Dad bought me a beat-up one about a year ago. We've done work on it together, though, so it's a real mean machine now." He picked up the small pile of grass that he'd been pulling out of the lawn and threw it up into the air, watching as it scattered in the light breeze. "I'll show it to you if you want."

"Really?" Claire asked excitedly. "When?"

"Tomorrow afternoon sometime?"

"Okay, I'll walk over to the farm."

"Leo's car will be ready by then, so I'll bring you back."

Claire pushed herself to her feet. "I'd better get back to the house. My mum will be wondering where I am."

"Marcus and Charity will probably have told her."

"They don't know I'm here."

"Aye, they do. They've been watching us from the playroom window for the past ten minutes."

Claire turned to look at the house and just caught a glimpse of a figure ducking away from the window. She knew it was Charity.

"Marcus has a friend coming to stay tomorrow," she said, still looking up at the window. "His name's Toby."

"Oh, him," Jonas groaned. "He's a pain in the butt. Charity'll be drooling over him all the time he's here."

"That's what Marcus said." She turned to Jonas. "How did you know that was the playroom window?"

Jonas smiled. "I only said I didn't go into the house during the holidays."

"Right. So when Marcus and Charity are away at school . . . ?"

"I'm there most days. I do odd jobs for Leo around the place, filling log baskets and the like." He got to his feet. "Of course that'll probably change now with you and your mother being here."

"It doesn't have to," Claire replied, "especially if you and me are friends." Her cheeks coloured immediately, realizing what she had just said. "Well, we are, sort of, aren't we?"

Jonas stuck his hands into the pockets of his coveralls and gave his usual non-committal shrug. "Aye, I suppose."

Claire smiled at him and held up a hand. "Bye, then."

"See you tomorrow."

She walked back towards the house, passing close to the greenhouse. She looked in and saw the rows of spiky-leaved plants on the shelf. Her memory jogged, she turned round to see if Jonas was still there. He hadn't moved, still standing in the centre of the lawn with his hands in his pockets, watching her. She ran back to him.

"I forgot to tell you," she said, panting slightly. "Leo and I have come up with a new name for the house."

"Oh, aye?"

"We're going to call it the Dragon Plant House."

Jonas nodded. "After his plants."

"Yes. Do you like it?"

Jonas shrugged once more. "It's all right. I doubt Dad'll want to change the name of the farm, though."

"Why should he do that?"

"Because it's called Croich too. I don't think he'll go for the Dragon Plant Farm."

Claire looked flustered. "Oh, the name's not really changing. It's just, well, Leo and me who will call it that."

Jonas smiled at her. "It's a good name, then."

Claire was relieved. "I'll see you tomorrow."

She ran off towards the house.

"Claire!" Jonas called after her.

She turned round. "What?"

"Don't bother telling Marcus and Charity about the name."

Claire stood still as she gave this some thought. He was right. They would just think she was being really stupid. "Okay."

And she turned and continued running.

15

It was Leo's idea to have the evening meal in the dining room. He said to Daphne he thought everyone was in need of a bit of a "bonding session" and one that he and Daphne could subtly orchestrate through conversation. Also, with the arrival of Toby Winston that day, it would set a certain standard for the week that Marcus's friend was to be with them, and Leo was adamant that the young shouldn't be allowed to "veg out" in front of the television whenever they wanted. A bit of effort, he reasoned, was required from all parties.

Not least, Daphne. When it had just been

she and Claire in the little house in West Sussex, there had seldom been any requirement for her to test her culinary skills. Then it had been more a case of finding time between her gardening commitments to make a quick dash to the supermarket or just rustling up something from what happened to be lurking in the fridge at the time. Now, with six mouths to feed—raise that to eight with the eating capabilities of Marcus and Toby—three times a day, and despite Agnes the housekeeper's constant help as sous-chef, Daphne seemed to be permanently standing over a row of battered pots bubbling away on the old gas cooker in the kitchen.

What was more, the problems were not only confined to food preparation. When they arrived back at the house the previous day from Edinburgh, it had seemed a good idea then to tackle the issue of "mutual support" that had arisen with Marcus in the car, and she had guided Leo aside to ask if they might have a quiet word about it. But his reaction had been simply to raise a hand and say, "Now is not the right time," and he had disappeared off to the greenhouse. And then she had felt like kicking herself because she realized he was absolutely right. Any attempt to force a discussion on the subject might well prove divisive in the long term, and she really did not want that to happen. They had been getting on so well together.

However, later, when Leo eventually reappeared in the kitchen, where Daphne had been juggling her time between preparing the evening meal and still clearing cupboards to make way for her own belongings, and he told her that he had allowed Claire to go off with a twelve-year-old boy in the car, she could not hide her irritation. She told him quite forcefully that, through his actions, he had not only shown scant regard for Claire's safety, but had also taken it upon himself to make a decision about her daughter without consultation when he had so adamantly declined to discuss his own offspring.

Give him his due, Leo did not try to argue the point. He apologized for his lack of consideration and said that it had only come about because he thought that Jonas and Claire would get on rather well together. And then, of his own volition, he did broach the subject that Daphne had wished to discuss earlier that afternoon.

It did not take long to clear the air. Neither wanted to fall out with the other, and it ended with Leo giving her a long hug and promising that, from now on, they would never wittingly avoid any discussion regarding the children. And it was later, when all was settled between them and Daphne was standing peeling potatoes at the kitchen sink, she saw through the window Claire and the boy, Jonas, lying about on the lawn, talking and laughing with each other. As she watched them, she realized that Leo had shown more understanding of her daughter than she had given him credit for. Claire was a solitary player, a free spirit, and much less sophisticated than either Marcus or Charity, and Jonas, the young neighbour, was the perfect foil for her. By letting Claire go in the car with him, Leo had cleverly directed the creation of a friendship without forcing the issue.

When Leo called Marcus, Charity and Toby downstairs for supper that evening, there was the inevitable grumbling rebellion as the television was switched off in

the playroom and the remote thrown forcefully onto one of the sofas. They traipsed
into the dining room, where Claire, who
had been with Daphne in the kitchen since
coming in from the garden, was giving her
mother a hand to serve out. Daphne noticed resentful eyes being narrowed at her
daughter and, understanding this wordless innuendo, thought it best if Claire
stopped what she was doing and went to
sit down at the table.

Leo entered the room clutching a bottle
of red wine and a corkscrew. "I thought
we'd all have a dash of the good stuff," he
said, picking away the foil from the top of
the bottle, "seeing this is going to be a more
formal occasion."

"Can me and Toby have a lager instead?" Marcus asked.

Leo looked disappointed. "Oh, all right,
you heathens, if that's what you want." He
poured a dash of wine into a glass at the
head of the table, picked it up and nosed it
before swallowing it down in one. "You don't
know what you're missing, though." He re-
filled his glass. "Right, seeing Claire is already sitting at this side of the table, how
about you, Charity, going on the other side

with Toby, and Marcus can come round here."

Charity beamed an infatuated smile at Toby, delighted with her father's seating plan, but it was not an emotion shared by Marcus when he returned with the two cans of lager. "Oh, come on, Dad, that's ridiculous. Why can't I sit next to Toby?"

"Because I want to have these two lovely girls beside me, as I'm sure Daphne wants to have the company of two handsome young men."

"But . . ." Marcus moaned, pushing back the flop of hair from his face, "why can't you, Daphne and Claire sit up this end and we'll go down the other?"

"Please, Marcus, just do it," Leo replied. "It's not going to kill you." He poured a small quantity of wine into Charity's glass and filled it up with water.

"Oh, Dad," Charity moaned, "that's not fair. Why are they allowed to have a full can of beer each?"

"Perhaps because they're at least two years older than you," Leo said, sitting down at the head of the table and unfolding his napkin. "Anyway, there's nothing wrong with what you've got. Rich Man's

Ribena, that's what it's called." Daphne placed a plate of stew, potatoes and carrots in front of him. He gave her a smile. "Thank you, my dear, that looks delicious." Taking a mouthful immediately, he laid down his knife and fork and sat back in his chair. "So, Toby, how long are your parents going to be in Paris?"

The conversation warmed up during the meal and Daphne breathed an inward sigh of relief as she noted the near harmony that seemed to be settling on the occasion. Leo cleverly involved Claire in the interchange, and at one point, when she was being asked by Charity about her previous school, he caught Daphne's eye and gave her an almost too obvious sign of hope by rubbing crossed fingers down the side of his cheek. However, it was not to last. During a brief lull in the flow of conversation, a moment when watches might be consulted to see if angels were passing overhead, Toby Winston displayed noteworthy manners by trying to bridge the silence.

"Are you really going to change the name of the house, Leo?" he asked.

Leo had a spoonful of summer pudding

half-way to his mouth. "What?" he asked, puzzled by Toby's question. He happened to glance at Claire as he said it, cream dripping slowly from the spoon onto his plate. Daphne saw her daughter's cheeks go red, her eyes darting around the table.

"I didn't tell anyone," she said to Leo, a tremor in her voice. "Only Jonas, and we've just been calling the house that between us."

"What's all this about?" Marcus asked, frowning at his father.

"Oh, I see!" Leo exclaimed, suddenly understanding what Toby was referring to. "That was nothing, just something Claire and I had been discussing in the greenhouse."

Marcus glared at his sister. "What, changing the name of the house? Jeez." He threw his napkin down on the table and got up and stalked off towards the door.

"For goodness' sakes, Marcus," Leo exclaimed. "Just sit down and stop being so dramatic."

Marcus spun round. "Dramatic! Dad, they've only been here a week and they're already trying to change the name of the house. Can't you see what's happening? It's a damned takeover bid."

Daphne pressed her fingers to her forehead as she watched Leo hold up a hand to try to pacify his son. "Marcus, stop being ridiculous. You're blowing this whole thing out of proportion."

"I don't think so," Marcus replied and stormed out of the room.

The sound of the door slamming was followed by an uneasy silence that was eventually broken by Charity. "So, what is this new name?" she asked, directing her question to Claire.

"The Dragon Plant House," Claire replied, "but it's only a pretend name."

Leo leaned across and patted Claire on the arm. "Of course it is, my dear."

"And I really didn't tell anyone—except Jonas." Claire happened to glance across at Charity to see her sarcastically mouthing Claire's last words. Being witnessed at least made the girl's pudgy cheeks glow with embarrassment.

"Ah, well," Leo continued, "maybe Jonas told Toby, then." He looked over at Marcus's friend. "Is that what happened?"

Toby looked embarrassed. "Yeah, I suppose," he replied with a shrug.

Leo nodded slowly. "Well, let's try putting this rather idiotic episode behind us. Toby and Charity, you'd better head off and join Marcus, wherever he is, and tell him that Croich will remain Croich and that no other name is being considered, okay?"

Toby and Charity got up from the table and left the room. As the door closed, both Leo and Daphne gave simultaneous sighs of relief. Leo looked at Claire. "Do you want to go too?"

"Maybe best not just now," Daphne said quickly, smiling at her daughter. "We'll just let the air clear a bit, shall we?"

"Jonas told me not to tell Marcus and Charity about the name," Claire said quietly. "I didn't think he'd tell Toby."

Leo wagged a finger at her. "I'm pretty sure he didn't."

"Why do you say that?" Daphne asked.

"Because Jonas keeps his distance when the children are at home. He wouldn't have spoken to them."

"So who else would have told Toby?"

"Ah, I reckon that's down to a good old case of eavesdropping. Toby has stayed here a couple of times with Marcus and I have observed him to be a clandestine smoker. One of his favourite haunts is in the bushes behind the greenhouses, so it would be my guess he just happened to overhear Claire and Jonas talking together after they brought the car back."

"Are we supposed to say anything to him?" Daphne asked.

"What, to Jonas?"

"No, to Toby, about his smoking." She shook her head. "I'm afraid I haven't had any experience of this yet."

"Well, it's a tricky one, but under present circumstances, I think we have enough to consider other than Toby puffing away on a few cigarettes." He laughed. "I feel a bit sorry for the lad, though. He was trying his level best to make conversation and damned near blew his cover." He leaned back in his chair, his face becoming serious as he gazed to one side out of the window. "It is going to take time, isn't it?" He turned to look at Daphne at the other end of the table. "I hadn't quite envisaged all this taking place."

Getting up from her chair, Daphne walked the length of the table and leaned

THE LONG WAY HOME

over her husband, putting her arms around his neck. "It's early days, my love," she said, planting a kiss on the top of his head. "It'll all work out, you'll see." She took his empty plate and began moving round the table clearing the places. "Claire, maybe you could give me a hand, darling?"

Later that night, when Claire was lying on her bed in her pyjamas reading a book, her mother came into the room to say goodnight.

"Come on, you, time for sleep." She walked over to the window and pushed it up to get some air into the stuffy room before drawing the curtains.

Dropping her book to the floor, Claire drew up her feet and slid them below the sheet. She lay looking up at the ceiling as her mother sat down beside her.

"Are you all right?" Daphne asked quietly.

Claire nodded her head on the pillow. "I knew that Jonas wouldn't tell."

Daphne smiled. "He's already a friend, then?"

Claire looked pleased. "Yes, and he's very clever too. He knows everything about cars and things."

Daphne stroked her daughter's forehead, pushing a strand of hair gently to one side. "That's what Leo said."

Claire sat up, leaning on her elbows. "Mummy, Jonas goes to school very close to here and he asked if I was going to the same one. Do you think I could?"

"Well, we'll have to start thinking about all that quite soon, won't we? I'll have a word with Leo and see what he says."

Claire flumped her head down onto the pillow. "I'm glad I'm going to school near here. I don't think Charity would want me to go with her." She looked at her mother. "She and Marcus don't like us, do they?"

Daphne patted her hand. "You have to understand that it is quite difficult for them, darling. They did live in this house with their mother as well as Leo and it's a big change for them with us being here now. As Leo said, it will take time, but if you and I just keep being normal and friendly, then things will eventually settle down and we'll all just slide smoothly into one big happy family." She leaned over and gave Claire a kiss on the forehead. "But you remember, darling, that you are my own, very special girl and, whatever happens in the meantime, I am right here for you and always will be. Understood?"

Reaching up, Claire put her arms around her mother's neck and gave her a tight hug. She did not relinquish her hold and so Daphne remained, bent over her, until her daughter's arms eventually fell away and she drifted off to sleep.

16

New York—September 2004

In all her life, Claire had never given one moment's consideration to the idea that her mother might not be around forever. When Daphne called her at the restaurant to tell her that she was going into hospital for an operation—purely routine, she said, just a little female service—Claire had treated it like any other call with her mother and had got on with her work, the phone clamped between shoulder and ear. There was nothing, not even the faintest shiver of uncertainty and trepidation, that could have forewarned Claire that it would be the last time she would ever speak to Daphne.

Leo called her two days later to break the news, his voice tremulous and devoid of its usual jovial inflection, an empty shell now, bereft of its cornucopia of laughter and good spirits. Daphne's heart had suddenly stopped beating while she was under anaesthetic, he told her, and even though she was in one of the top hospitals in Edinburgh, with every state-of-the-art piece of equipment, they could do nothing for her. And then Leo lost his thread completely and Claire just listened to him sobbing at the other end of the line, repeating the same phrases over and over again—"It was only meant to be a routine operation" and "Nothing serious at all, just routine . . ."

It was just as well Claire happened to be in the office when she took the call, otherwise Art and all those who were enjoying their evening meal in the restaurant would have thought she'd had a stroke. Even after Leo had ended the call, she sat motionless with the receiver still held to her ear, staring at the wall above the desk. The noise from the restaurant sounded as if it were coming to her through a tube, or maybe it was just her brain screaming a warning to her that it couldn't take the overload of information that she was asking it to absorb. Her mother, her only parent, her friend, her confidante, her one true link with the past and with David, was . . . gone. Just like that, changing her life in no more than a click of fingers. And Daphne was only sixty-one.

After five minutes, when reality had begun to break through to her senses, her emotions spluttered to the surface and she wept long and uncontrollably.

Claire and Art flew over to Scotland the following day for the funeral. They left their return journey open-ended, but were estimating their time away to be no more than four days, so they decided to leave Violet in the capable hands of Pilar. Art meantime arranged for a friend to come into the restaurant, simply to make sure that the chef and head waiter didn't try to top-dog each other over the running of the place.

When they arrived at the house, Claire was surprised by the appearance of the place, not having been there since Christmas two years previously. Every window at the front sparkled with fresh paint, the heavy oak front door was revarnished, and the garden immaculately kept. But despite this, the old house seemed to sag under an immense pressure of melancholy. The shutters in every window were closed to the brightness of the morning and on every second step leading up to the front door was a flowerpot containing one single black poppy. Their heads were bent over in the light breeze, as if they too were respecting the mourning of the household.

"Hey, the place is looking really good," Art remarked, leaning his tall frame forward over the steering wheel to peer out of the window of the hire car.

"Yes, I suppose it is," Claire answered distantly.

When they entered the house, Claire stood for a moment taking in the all-too-familiar smell of the vast hall, a strange cocktail of dusty decay and sweet-scented flowers, and she was immediately hit by a devastating blow of nostalgia that truly brought home to her the seismic void left in her life by her mother's death.

"Oh, Art," she sobbed quietly, covering her face with her hands. She felt Art encircle her with his arms and hold her tight to his chest.

"I know, my angel," he whispered in her ear. "You just let it all out. I'm right here for you."

As they stood there entwined, a door creaked open at one side of the hall and Agnes Smith, the housekeeper, made a shuffling appearance, her eyes set in concentration on the laden tray she was carrying. Suddenly aware of their presence, she stopped and screwed up her eyes to see who was standing by the entrance door.

"Oh, my wee girl, it's yourself," she exclaimed, placing the tray on top of a glass-fronted bookcase that stood in a darkened recess. She approached them, wiping her hands on her apron before holding out her arms. Claire disentangled herself from Art's embrace and gave the little housekeeper a tight hug. "I'm so sorry about your mother, lass. She was a wonderful person and I was that fond of her."

"I know you were," Claire replied, giving Agnes a brave smile as she wiped away her tears with the back of her hand, "and I also know that the feeling was mutual."

The housekeeper wore a dowdy brown

housecoat below her apron and her head was adorned with a black felt hat pulled down over her ears, despite the warmth of the late summer's day. Claire could only think that this was Agnes's equivalent to a black armband. She hadn't really seemed to have aged that much over the years, but then Claire had always thought Agnes had borne a certain air of antiquity about her ever since first meeting her at Leo and Daphne's wedding.

Claire exhaled a long breath to steady her emotions. "How is Leo, Agnes?"

"Hit bad, he is," Agnes replied sadly. "Never ventured out of the sitting room these past two days, not even to go over to his greenhouses." She made her way across the hall to collect the tray. She picked it up and studied forlornly the untouched food on the plate. "Lost his appetite and all." She continued on to the kitchen. "You should away and see him, lass. Maybe your being here might bring a wee glint to his eye."

Art put an arm around Claire's shoulders and gave her a reassuring squeeze. "Are you okay to do this?"

"I think so." She smiled at him. "Would you mind if I went in alone?"

"No, not at all. It's better that way. I'll bring the bags in from the car and take them up-stairs to our bedroom. I'll be around if you need me, though."

Claire reached up and gave him a kiss on the cheek. "Thank you."

The sitting room was in darkness, other than a bright beam of sunlight that edged its way through one of the shutters that hadn't been fully closed. At first, Claire thought Leo must have gone off somewhere after Agnes took away his tray, because the silence in the room was absolute, but as she made her way behind the sofa, she saw him sitting in his armchair, staring blankly at the unlit fire. She took in a star-tled breath, seeing now how much Daph-ne's death had already taken out of him. He was seventy-six years old, but it looked as if the events of the past two days had added ten years to his age. Everything about him seemed to have shrunk. His spindly legs stuck out below his faded cor-duroy trousers; his shirt collar, still worn with a tie, barely made contact with his loose-skinned neck; and the frizzy hair that once grew in abundance at the sides of his bald pate was now reduced to a few grey wisps. The only thing about him that had retained its size was his tweed jacket, which seemed to sit apart from his body, accentuating the hollow crust of emptiness that now existed deep within him.

Claire walked quietly over to him and bent down and gave him a kiss on his cheek. "Hullo, Leo."

He started, as if woken from a deep sleep, and looked up at her. "Oh, Claire, my dear." He pushed himself to his feet and put his arms around her and Claire breathed in the nostalgic whiff of old tweed. She had thought she had reached the depth of her mourning over the past two days, but the smell and physical contact with this man, who had loved her mother so much, broke through any resilience and she began to cry. And then Leo too started to cry and they held each other, now both sensing their loss more acutely than before.

"Where is she?" Claire eventually asked, wiping the tears from her eyes with the back of her hand.

Leo gave her a kiss on the cheek and sat down again on his chair. "At the undertaker's. I thought it best. Do you mind?"

"In what way?"

"I wondered if I should have had her here."

"No, I don't think Daphne would have thought it was that important. Have you managed to do anything about the funeral yet?"

"Yes, it's all arranged for tomorrow. There's a service in St. John's at eleven-thirty A.M. and then we go on to the crematorium in Falkirk."

"Is that what she wanted?"

"Yes, it was in her will. She wanted her ashes to be spread around the garden here."

Claire was somewhat bewildered that Leo seemed to have everything so well organized, especially after what Agnes had told her about him never leaving the sitting room. "Have you made all these arrangements yourself?" she asked, sitting down on the sofa next to his armchair.

Leo shook his head. "I've been pretty hopeless, I'm afraid. John Venables, the solicitor, has been doing all the legal stuff. The damned thing is everything was geared to me stepping off the mortal coil first. I never thought in a million years that it would be Daphne"—he tailed off for a moment, rubbing a hand to his forehead as if to assuage a nagging pain—"so I suppose it's all got to be sorted out over again."

"I'm sure it will be. I wouldn't worry too much about it now." She paused, clasping her hands together, not really wishing to ask the question. "When are Marcus and Charity coming up?"

"Last time I heard it was first thing tomorrow morning. Lots to do down there, you know, lots to organize with the children and all that stuff."

"Yes, of course." She sighed deeply. "I thought one of them might have been able to come up a bit earlier to give you some help and support."

Leo shrugged. "There was talk of one of them staying up for a bit, but they didn't want to get involved, seeing that Daphne wasn't . . ."

He stopped and waved a hand at Claire, realizing he was about to say something he hadn't meant to mention.

"That Daphne wasn't their mother?"

Leo shook his head. "I didn't mean to say that. Look, it's probably for the best

I've been by myself since it happened." He looked at Claire. "And I really don't want there to be any reason for contention between you lot. We have enough to get through without having to deal with that."

Claire reached out and patted his hand. "Of course there won't be. I'm here only for you and Daphne, my darling, no one else." She glanced around the bare room. "So, is there anything I can do? What about flowers?"

"Coming tomorrow morning, I think." He turned and took a sheet of A4 paper from the table beside his chair and handed it to Claire. "That's the running order Jonas has made up. I don't think he's missed out on anything."

Claire stared at him, the sheet held limply in her hand. "Jonas Fairweather?"

For once, a faint smile broke the solemnity of his features. "Do you know another Jonas?"

"He's done all the arrangements?"

"Everything, from getting the death certificate right through to organizing the caterers for the wake."

"I thought he was away from the farm," she said distantly.

THE LONG WAY HOME   167

"He was, but he's come back."

"Did he succeed in becoming a rally driver, then?"

"No, he never found a sponsor for that. He's been financially successful, though."

"Doing what?"

"He got himself a position as a mechanic with one of the big Formula One teams. Always an absolute magician with engines, was Jonas. He travelled the world for a good number of years."

"I wouldn't have thought that would have brought him great riches."

"No, you're right, but then he came up with some bright idea on how to make his team's car more fuel-efficient without affecting its performance. It all remains completely incomprehensible to me, but nevertheless, it was regarded as being quite revolutionary in the industry. Anyway, he went into partnership with one of his fellow mechanics who happened to be business-minded, and the two of them went on to develop the concept for high-performance production cars. And then, about a year and a half ago, they sold the patent to one of the big German manufacturers for a fair whack of money."

"So he came back here to live."

"Yes, not long before the death of his father."

"Bert Fairweather has died?"

"Yes, I'm afraid so, of a heart attack. Sorry, I should have told you that. An oversight on my part." He glanced at her. "Actually, that's not true. I just didn't think you'd be very interested in knowing about the Fairweather family, what with you and Jonas not . . . well, you know what I mean."

Claire shook her head dismissively. "It's all water under the bridge now." She paused. "So does he do anything with himself?"

"Oh, certainly. As soon as he came back, he bought the controlling share of a sports-car franchise in Glasgow and then he bought the farm from me."

"You sold him the farm?"

"For a jolly good price, too. You might have noticed there's been a fair bit of work done to the house."

"Both Art and I were saying how good it was looking with everything painted."

"That's only what you can see. The whole roof has been releaded as well. For once, we don't have to rush around the top floor with buckets every time it rains."

"That must have cost you a fortune."

"Yes, but I was able to afford it, thanks to Jonas."

"So, where is he living? Surely not in that tumbledown farmhouse?"

Leo's smile was almost light-hearted. "You wouldn't recognize the place, my dear. He's completely renovated it, with a brand-new extension on the back and a conservatory on the front. It all looks very smart. And then, of course, the old cars and weedy fields are a thing of the past as well. He's started to grow strawberries for all the big supermarkets, so every square metre of the farm is covered in white poly-tunnels, and then behind the old steading— you know, where Bert used to fix his cars—there's this bizarre village of cara-vans and mobile homes where all his pick-ers stay, usually young Czech or Polish students." He slanted his head. "No, young Jonas is doing very well for himself."

"Is he . . . single?" Claire asked, her sup-posed nonchalance sounding a little too blatant.

"No, he's married to Liv. She's a wonderful girl, from Sweden, I think, and very attractive. They have two beautiful Nordic children, Rory and Asrun, who come over here quite often to give me a hand in the greenhouses, just like you used to do." He smiled at her. "They even call this place the Dragon Plant House."

Claire found herself experiencing a stupidly immature sense of hurt, wanting to keep every private memory of the place for herself at that precise moment. "Really? I didn't think that name would become common knowledge."

"Oh, I didn't tell them. That would have been Jonas's doing."

Claire was surprised. "I can't believe he would remember that."

"Nothing much gets past Jonas Fairweather, I can tell you."

Claire glanced back at the A4 sheet of paper she still held in her hand. "Well, that all seems pretty evident. He hasn't missed out on anything, has he?" She placed the sheet on the sofa beside her. "I suppose he'll be at the funeral tomorrow, then."

"No, unfortunately he can't be. He has to fly down to Manchester tonight to see a man about a possible business link-up. It was a meeting he couldn't put off."

Claire felt almost light-headed with relief. "That's a pity." She got to her feet and walked over to the shuttered window. She turned to her stepfather. "You know, Leo, I really don't think Daphne would like to have seen the house looking so sad and closed up. She was always such a bright, happy person. Don't you think we should make the house reflect that?"

Leo smiled weakly at her. "I wanted you to make that decision. As her daughter, I felt that was your right."

"In that case, let's get these open straight-away." She folded back the shutters on the first window and the sun shone into the room, its rays not only dispersing the air of mournful sadness with immediate effect, but also showing up a thick layer of dust on every piece of furniture. Claire wiped a finger over the top of the desk that stood by the window and held up the dark smudge to Leo. "Aha, I think I've just found employment for myself," she said, making her way across to the door and leaving the room.

As she walked across the hall towards

the kitchen, Art struggled to his feet from the sagging sofa next to the stairs and discarded the newspaper he had been reading onto the pine table. "How is he?"

Claire came towards him and gave him a tight hug. "He's all right. Probably better now we've spoken. Tomorrow is going to be hard for him, though."

"I'm sure of it. What about arrangements for the funeral?"

"All done."

Art gave her a kiss on the top of her head. "That's sounds pretty positive. Obviously Agnes was kind of wrong with her assessment of Leo's state of mind."

"Looks like it," Claire replied, not wishing to mention anything about Jonas Fairweather or his involvement.

Art walked to the centre of the hall and looked up to survey the high corniced ceiling and the cupola above it. "You know, I'd forgotten what a fantastic place this is." He looked at Claire. "What d'you think Leo will do with it now?"

"What do you mean?"

Art shrugged. "Well, it's just that with Marcus and Charity being based in London, I doubt they'll want to move up here, and you must have some pretty wonderful memories of this house."

Claire furrowed her brow. "I'm not following you."

Art smiled sadly at her. "Hey, I shouldn't have mentioned it. It was just that, well, when we arrived here, I could tell how much this place means to you and I just got to thinking . . ." He shook his head. "Listen, forget it, it's an inappropriate idea. My head's just running away with me."

Claire approached him and put a hand on his arm. "Go on, what were you going to say?"

Art paused for a moment. "Okay, so I'm not talking about the immediate future, but if, in time, Leo finds the place too much to handle, well, all I was thinking was that if neither Marcus nor Charity wanted to take it on, it would be a hell of a pity for it to be sold out of the family." He glanced around the hall. "And it just occurred to me that the place has every potential to be turned into something like a top-class conference centre, especially with all the industry around here, and being pretty close to both Edinburgh and Glasgow airports as well. . . ."

"It's a very sweet thought, Art," Claire cut in, "but I'm afraid you're forgetting one very important issue."

"What's that?"

"My only connection with this house was through Daphne. That was severed when she died. It has nothing to do with me now."

"Oh, I understand that entirely, but surely we could buy it. You know I've been looking for something new to invest in. We'd set up a restaurant on the same lines as the one back home, and I'd get a good management team in here to run that and the conference centre, and then we'd come over here every now and again on business expenses to see how it's going. You never know, I might even get time to play some golf."

Despite feeling drained of both emotion and energy, Claire could not help being amused by this ulterior motive. Art had "discovered" golf only three years before, but his passion for the game had become as strong as his enthusiasm for his business. He had even suggested that he might bring his golf clubs on this trip, but her frosty reaction had put pay to that.

She smiled wryly at him. "Ah, I'm beginning to understand your reasoning now."

Art laughed. "Well, do you blame me? This is Scotland, after all, home of some of the best courses in the world." He became serious. "And that does have a big part to play in my idea on this house, but of course, angel, what is most important is that you wouldn't have to sever your connection with the place and you'd still be able to see Leo."

"And where would he fit into this great plan of yours?"

"Well, we . . . could replace one of the greenhouses with a small condo for him"—he laughed—"and then we'd put in a connecting door leading from the bedroom to the greenhouse so that he could happily tend to all his weird plants wearing his pyjamas." He smiled at Claire. "Hey, listen, please don't think I'm being inconsiderate or hard-hearted mentioning this right now. As I said, I just know how much this house means to you—and to Leo. I'm just thinking of the future."

Claire sighed. "The only problem with your idea, Art, is that Marcus and Charity would have the biggest say in the matter, and I think they'd sell their souls to the devil rather than let me have anything to do with the house."

"Yeah, but money talks, if the price is right," Art said. "Would you let me at least mention this to Leo—at the right time, I mean?"

Claire considered this for a moment. "Okay, but now is not the right time."

17

Through both services, at the funeral and the crematorium, Claire stood next to Leo, with Charity and Marcus and their respective partners on his other side. Despite her own personal grief, Claire felt Leo was the one who needed greater support throughout the whole ordeal and constantly cast a watery eye at him. He seemed to cope well, standing upright and proud, focusing his eyes on some point directly in front of him rather than on Daphne's coffin, but as the curtains closed about it and the priest voiced the last words of the committal, his head bowed and his shoulders began to heave and he reached out a hand—his right, not his left—towards Claire. She took it and squeezed it reassuringly and as she looked at him with love and overwhelming sadness, she happened to catch the tight-lipped look on Charity's face as she stared down at their joined hands.

Of the seventy or so who attended the two services, only about half of them returned to the house for the wake, most of those being relations of Leo and friends whom he and Daphne had made during their twenty-three years of marriage. Claire's last remaining grandparent had died three years before and she had lost touch with her cousins on David's side of the family, so she was surprised when a portly, well-dressed man in his mid-seventies introduced himself as a second cousin of her mother.

Brian Knight was a retired solicitor from Hampshire, never married, who had always kept tabs on the extended family. Having read Daphne's obituary in the *Daily Telegraph,* he had flown up for the day to pay his respects. During her short discourse with him, it was brought home to Claire how few relations she had left on

both sides of her family and that Leo was
now really the only link she had left with
her youth.

Even though the house could accom-
modate quite easily all who returned there
for the wake, tables and chairs had been
set out on the side lawn next to the greenhouses, just in case the late-summer
weather continued to be kind. The day was
blustery but warm, high clouds scudding fast
across a pale blue sky, and therefore the
decision was made to serve lunch outside.
Claire and Art sat at the table next to Leo's,
his being resolutely bagged by Charity for
members of the Harrison family. Claire, however, had neither the time nor the inclination
to reflect on this. During the meal, she was
constantly getting to her feet to kiss or shake
hands with those who wished to offer their
condolences. By mid-afternoon, the repeti-
tion of stock answers to well-meant plati-
tudes had drained her energy reserves and
she longed for nothing more than a moment's solitary contemplation.

Her opportunity came when she was
carrying a tray stacked with dirty plates
and cutlery back to the house and was
relieved of her load at the front steps by

Agnes. Claire did not return to her table but skirted the lawn purposefully, avoiding any possible eye contact, and made her way towards the nearest greenhouse, where she had spent so much time with Leo and Daphne.

She cried the moment she entered the warm, humid interior, the heavily scented air immediately bringing back memories of her mother, not only here but in Daphne's small greenhouse at their home in West Sussex. She leaned her bottom against one of the plant shelves and covered her face with her hands, gulping in air to try to control her emotions, knowing that it would not be long before Art would see that she was not around and come looking for her. She reached out and brushed a hand up the tall spindly leaf of one of the dragon plants, saying silent words to Daphne that seemed to bring immediate comfort. She now felt her mother's presence more than ever, and in her head words seemed to take shape without any form of mental prompting. "Look after yourself and your family, my darling, and keep an eye on Leo."

She took a few steps across the central paved path, picking up an old rag from the plant shelf and rubbing it against one of the smeared panes. This gave her clear vision of Leo, sitting at his table in the dappled shade of the tree in the centre of the lawn. He was talking with Marcus and Charity, now both standing beside him, and while Charity led the conversation with her father, Marcus kept looking round, distracted by something taking place at the front of the house. Charity bent down and gave Leo a kiss on the cheek, after which Marcus patted his father's shoulder and shook his hand. He and his sister then began walking towards the house. They did not turn again, so they never saw Leo's final wave to them. But Claire did, and she also saw how he visibly slumped in the chair when his hand came down and how his head then bowed so low that his chin rested on his chest.

By the time Claire came out of the greenhouse, Marcus and Charity had disappeared around the front of the house. She hurried across the lawn and onto the gravelled driveway. One of the large black Mercedes, hired to ferry the family around during the day, was sitting at the front steps, and Harry Thomson, Charity's husband, was getting into the back seat. She approached the car, forcing a friendly smile.

"Harry?" she asked. "What's happening?"

"Ah, Claire, there you are," Charity's husband said, getting out of the car again. "We were all looking for you."

"Are you going somewhere?"

"Back to the airport. Our plane leaves at seven."

Claire found herself lost for words. She looked into the back seat, where Marcus's wife was already ensconced. She gave Claire a thin smile and a little wave.

"So, it's just you and Sarah going," Claire stated hopefully.

Harry cast a furtive glance towards the front door. "No, actually, we've all got to get back. Marcus and Charity are just saying goodbye to Agnes."

Without waiting to hear more, Claire turned and ran up the steps and entered the hall just as her stepsiblings were coming out of the kitchen, calling out their final farewells to the housekeeper.

"You can't go yet," she said forcefully.

Charity approached her. She still had the same round face of her youth, though her rosy cheeks were kept dulled by make-up. She had never lost her plumpness, however, and her dark wool suit strained across her full bosom and broad hips.

"I'm sorry?" Charity said.

"You can't leave. What about Leo?"

"What about him?"

Claire shook her head in disbelief. "Well, there's so much to organize, isn't there? Who's going to look after him now that Daphne's gone?"

Charity's look was one of sweet incomprehension. "I'm not sure quite what you mean, Claire. Aren't you forgetting the fact that our father lived here quite happily by himself for six years after our mother died and before he married your mother?"

"But that was over twenty years ago!" Claire blurted out, ignoring Charity's barbed tone. "Leo is an old man now, and whether you like to admit it or not, he's been devastated by Daphne's death."

Charity sighed. "Well, in that case, maybe all this is for you to sort out."

Claire gasped. "For heaven's sakes, Charity, you make it sound as if my mother died on purpose!"

"Oh, come on, Claire," Marcus said, stepping forward in defence of his sister. "That's a childish thing to say."

"Childish!" Claire exclaimed. "Have you heard what your sister's just said?"

"I think we should go now, Marcus," Charity said huffily, picking up her handbag from the pine table. "I knew you'd come on the drama queen today, Claire. You always had to be the centre of attention, didn't you?"

Claire thought that to convey hatred in a smile was an impossible thing to do, yet Charity passed the test with flying colours just before she stalked off towards the front door. And then she turned.

"Oh, by the way, Claire, you can tell your friend, Jonas, he did a very good job organizing everything today." She held up a warning finger. "But I'd just watch him, if I were you. Both Marcus and I dealt with him when Dad sold him the farm, and I tell you I wouldn't trust one hair on his head, not even for a second."

"It's just as well I've no plans to see him then, isn't it?" Claire replied curtly.

"Hmm," Charity responded before swinging round on her heel and clipping her way down the steps.

At least Marcus's smile was a little warmer when he said goodbye. He even deigned to give Claire a peck on the cheek before following after his sister.

"Marcus?"

He turned at the front door.

"Is there no way you could stay for a bit? I really can't organize all this by myself."

Marcus dragged a hand across his head, revealing now the incipient hair loss above his temples. Unlike Charity, he had not inherited his father's fuller figure, yet his tall, elegant manner and the narrow set of his sharp eyes seemed to reflect a constant disdain for others.

"I can't help out, Claire, sorry. I have a big deal going on right now with a property in the East End. Tomorrow's the crunch meeting. I can't miss it."

"But Art and I have got to get back to the States, sooner rather than later. Violet's

there by herself and we have our own business to run as well, you know."

Marcus shrugged. "As I said, I'm sorry.
Say cheerio to Art for me." He gave her a
cursory wave and left the house.

18

Alloa—April 1986

Claire stood at the kitchen table, nodding in time to the sound of Madonna's "Like a Virgin" pumping into her head through the earphones of her Walkman. She waved the plastic spatula around in time with the beat before plunging it into the bowl of creamy lemon icing and unceremoniously delivering a healthy splodge onto the freshly baked birthday cake that sat on the plate in front of her. And then her head twitched to the side as one of the earphones was forcefully pulled out, and she turned to find Agnes scowling at her.

"I said be careful, lass," the housekeeper

said sternly. "I haven't wasted three hours cooking that lovely cake for you to go ruining it with your heavy hand."

Claire grinned at her and stood back from the table to admire her work. "It looks quite good. Rather like a Picasso painting. I think Charity will appreciate it."

"I'll give you Picasso if you don't watch it," Agnes replied with a hint of humour in her tone before returning to her job on the opposite side of the table, moulding beefburgers out of an enormous pile of minced meat with floury hands.

The door of the kitchen flew open and Daphne walked in, hurriedly pulling on a quilted jacket. "Has anyone seen my handbag?"

Agnes pointed a white finger over to the cluttered sideboard. "It's over there next to the telephone."

"Thank goodness!" Daphne replied, scooping up the bag. "I thought I must have left it in the supermarket this morning."

"Where are you off to?" Claire asked casually.

"Leo and I are collecting some of Charity's friends from the station, but before that, we need to go to the garden centre to pick up some charcoal for the barbeque. We forgot to get it this morning."

"Sounds like a good excuse," Claire said with a smile.

Daphne approached her daughter and gave her a quick kiss on the cheek. "You know what he's like. Any opportunity to buy more plants."

A young man's voice cried out from the hall, followed by a resounding thump. Daphne gave Agnes a long-suffering look. "I do hope they don't break anything."

"Are you meaning limbs or furniture?" Agnes asked.

Daphne laughed. "I don't think we need worry too much about the latter in this household." She turned, her head held high as she sniffed the air, and then walked quickly over to the door. "Please don't smoke in the house!" she called out at the top of her voice. She sighed anxiously. "Agnes, could you possibly see that no one goes into the dining room? I don't want the boys getting stuck into the beer before at least seven o'clock, otherwise they'll be legless by the time the party starts."

Agnes gave a shrug. "I'll do my best, but I'm no policeman."

"No, quite. Maybe that's a tall order." Daphne gave a wave. "I'll see you later."

"Och, kids growing up these days," Agnes mumbled as she went over to the sink and washed her hands under the tap. "It was all a lot easier when birthday parties were just a few scones, a plateful of jelly and then everyone was taken home by their parents."

"I don't think Charity would appreciate that very much," Claire said, licking the last of the icing off the spatula.

"No, I doubt she would," Agnes replied, drying her hands on her apron. "So, what will you be doing with yourself tonight? Are you sticking around for the party?"

Claire shook her head. "That wouldn't be appreciated either. I'm going over to the farm. Bert's taking us up to the forestry track in Jonas's car."

"Well, you be careful, my girl. You'll be in more danger careering around in that car than you'll ever be braving the goings-on of tonight."

"I never go in the car, Agnes. My job is timekeeping, so I just sit at the side of the road and get covered in dust when Jonas zooms past."

Agnes let out a long breath and shook her head resignedly. "I canna understand why his father allows him to do it. He'll kill himself one of these days."

Claire laughed. "Don't be such a doom monger, Agnes. Jonas is a really good driver."

"Aye, and so was Jim Clark, and look what happened to him."

Claire was just about to question Agnes further on her knowledge of the famous Scottish racing driver when a floppy-haired youth dressed in jeans and a red polo shirt, his face red with exertion, walked into the kitchen.

"Excuse me, would there be any chance of a drink?"

"No," Agnes replied vehemently. "You'll have to wait. Those were my orders."

The boy looked taken aback. "I meant water, actually."

With a snigger, Claire went over to the sink and took a glass from the draining board and filled it up from the tap. She handed it to the boy and he finished it in one long draught.

"Thanks," he said, smiling at her as he handed back the glass. He turned and left the kitchen at speed.

"Who was that?" Agnes asked.

"Charity's boyfriend, I think," Claire replied quietly.

"Ah, well," Agnes sighed, taking the roasting pan piled with beefburgers from the kitchen table and placing it on the sideboard, "at least one of them has a few manners to speak of."

"I think you'll find—"

Claire was cut short in her admonishment of Agnes's curt remark by the re-entrance of the young man.

"Hi," he said, grinning at Claire.

"Hullo," Claire replied, casting an uncertain look at Agnes.

"Listen, a whole load of us are playing football on the front lawn. Do you want to join us?"

Claire again glanced round at Agnes, whose little face looked as if it was about to burst with intrigue. She turned back to the boy and smiled. "Thanks, but I'm, er, busy here."

He eyed the empty bowl of icing on the table. "Looks like you're finished."

"Yes, well . . ."

Charity's high-pitched squeal of joyous laughter echoed around the hall, and a moment later she came running into the kitchen, her blonde curls bouncing around on top of her head. She exhaled a long exhausted breath and then the pudgy smile slid from her face.

"Daniel, what's the matter?" she trilled. "Why aren't you coming?"

The boy smiled at Charity and then at Claire. "I was just asking your sister if she wanted to come and play football with us."

Charity's eyes darted from Claire to the boy and then back again, and then her face broke into an unexpectedly broad grin. "Why not? Come on, Claire, come and join us. What team shall we put her in?"

"She can play on our side."

Charity gave a short, almost manic, laugh. "Of course she can." She quickly appraised Claire's white T-shirt. "You can't wear that, though. We're playing in red."

"I've got a—" Claire began.

"No, come on, I've got something for you up in my bedroom." She grabbed Claire's hand, the first time Claire could ever remember having physical contact

with her stepsister, and dragged her towards the kitchen door. Claire only had time
hurriedly to unclip her Walkman from the
waistband of her skirt and discard it with an
ominous clatter on the kitchen table before
being pulled out into the hall.

"You go on out, Daniel," Charity said excitedly to her young beau. "We'll join you
in a moment."

Claire hurried up the stairs after Charity,
disconcerted by her stepsister's unprece-
dented friendliness towards her and wondering if it wasn't just an excuse for Charity
to give her yet another earful about keeping well clear of herself and her friends.
But Charity was still all giggles of sisterly
affection and mutual conspiracy when she
threw open the door of her bedroom and
hurried over to the chest of drawers.

"Do you want a pair of jeans as well,"
she asked, pulling open the top drawer
and delving into it, "or are you all right in
that skirt?"

"Don't worry," Claire replied, still thrown
by this sudden flood of bonhomie as she
looked down at her short flared skirt. "This'll
do."

"Dammit, I know I have a T-shirt here

somewhere." Charity slammed the drawer shut and pulled open the next and began throwing clothes carelessly out onto the floor. "Claire, you try the cupboard. There's a T-shirt just like mine, but it has a little yellow Ferrari logo on the front."

Claire walked over to the huge built-in cupboard and entered, squinting in the dark at the rows of clothes that hung on either side. "Where would it be?" she asked, turning back to Charity, who was now riffling through the lower drawer.

"On the shelf above the dresses. There's a small stool you can stand on."

"Is there a light in here?"

"No. I'm afraid not. The bulb's blown."

Claire groped out her hand and came across the stool at the back of the cupboard. She placed it below the shelf, climbed up onto it and began pushing the piles of clothes aside to look for the T-shirt. Suddenly she found herself in pitch-dark as the cupboard door was slammed shut and she heard the key turning in the lock.

"Charity? What are you doing?"

There was no answer.

"Charity?" she called out louder as she clambered down quickly and made for the door, banging her leg painfully on the edge of the stool in the process.

"Ow," she cried out as she limped forward, feeling for the door. "Charity, let me out, will you? This is stupid."

She pressed her ear to the door and listened, but she could hear nothing. The inky blackness of the cupboard began to close around her and the suffocating smell of Charity's clothes impregnated with the smell of her perfume was overpowering in its airless confines. Claire felt the first adrenalin waves of panic pump into her head as it slowly dawned on her that there was no one around to help her. Marcus was away with a couple of mates in his newly acquired car, Daphne and Leo had gone off for an indeterminable period, and there was no way for Agnes to know that she wasn't out on the lawn playing football with the rest of Charity's friends.

"Charity, please let me out."

She leaned down to rub the throbbing pain in her leg, and as the first tear rolled down her cheek she balled her fist and banged repeatedly on the door. After ten minutes she gave up and slumped crying to the floor, once again wincing with pain as one of Charity's upturned stiletto heels jabbed deep into her buttock.

She had no knowledge of how long she sat there on the floor of the cupboard, hunched up with her tear-stained face resting on her knees. She may even have slept for a bit. Eventually, however, her ears were so keenly attuned to the silence that she heard the distinct click of the door handle being turned at the far end of Charity's bedroom. She put out a hand to the door and leaned against it, straining to hear if someone had entered. And then she heard the softest of footsteps slowly crossing the room.

"Charity?" she called out. "Is that you?"

"Claire? Where are you?"

It was Jonas's voice, and the sheer relief Claire felt in hearing it made her burst into tears again. She clambered to her feet and banged on the door. "In here. I'm in the cupboard."

She heard the key turn in the lock and the door opened, and she fell out with force against the tall thin body of a very surprised Jonas. She threw her arms around his neck and held on to him tight, blinking her tear-filled eyes as they became accustomed to the blinding light that flooded in from the window.

"Thank God you came. I didn't think I'd ever get out of there." She relinquished her hold and stood back from him. "What are you doing here, though? You never come when they're around."

With a bashful flick of his hair, Jonas shrugged his shoulders and slid his hands into the back pockets of his jeans. "Dad and I were waiting for you at the farm, but you didn't turn up, so I decided to come over to get you. I came in the basement door so I wouldn't be seen, and then I bumped into Agnes in the kitchen. She said you were out front playing football with Charity and her friends, and I didn't think that sounded right, so I went and had a look out the hall window and you weren't there." Jonas glanced down and saw the trickle of blood on Claire's shin. "Here, you've cut your leg."

Claire went over to sit on the edge of Charity's unmade bed and pulled up her leg and began studying her wound. "It's all right." She gave it a rub. "Just really sore." She looked up at Jonas. "How did you know I'd be in here?"

"I didn't. I tried most of the other rooms first. I knew you wouldn't be away from the house, though."

From outside, a muffled cheer rang out from the football game on the lawn. Claire turned her head and looked towards the window. "It was Charity, you know."

"Who else," Jonas replied quietly. "What was the reason behind it?"

Claire sighed. "Probably because that boyfriend of hers asked me if I'd like to play football with them."

"Probably!" Jonas exclaimed with a laugh. "Claire, there's absolutely no doubt about it! It's a physical impossibility for Charity to go sharing any of her possessions around, especially when it involves a boyfriend and especially if it's with you."

"But I don't even know him! And anyway, I'm not nearly grown up enough for someone like him, being at private school and all. He wouldn't be interested in his girlfriend's fifteen-year-old stepsister."

Jonas was silent for a moment. "Why not?"

Claire held out her hands as if weighing up the jumbled explanation in her head. "Well . . . just because."

"Because you're not pretty enough or because you'll be running off to play with your dollies?"

She picked up one of Charity's ageing teddy bears from the bed and threw it at him. "Shut up, Jonas, you know damned well I never play with dollies."

He caught the cuddly missile effortlessly. "Then it must be your looks." He chuckled. "You don't need to worry too much about that."

She stared at him during the five seconds it took to understand the meaning of his remark. "Don't I?" she asked quietly.

Jonas gave no answer but walked over to the window and stood to the side of one of the heavy-draped curtains and peered down onto the front lawn. "Looks like the game's just finishing up." He hurried over to the door. "Come on, we'd better get out of here."

Claire got up from the bed and went to stand beside him as he opened the door and listened intently for any sound.

"Did you mean what you said just then?" she asked.

But again Jonas did not answer her question. He just grabbed her hand and together they made their way as fast as possible down through the house and out of the back door, never stopping until they had passed the rear of the greenhouses and had come out onto the track that led to the farm.

They both leaned against a tree to catch their breath, and Jonas turned to find Claire staring at him with sparkling eyes.

"Okay, what's the big grin for?" he asked.

"Not telling," Claire replied, giving his light frame a hefty shove that nearly sent him into the undergrowth at the side of the track. She turned and ran off towards the farm. "Come on, I'll race you."

19

Alloa—September 2004

After the car had left, Claire stood rooted
to the spot in the hall, completely dumb-
founded by the vitriolic attitude of Charity
and the premature departure of both her
and Marcus. Eventually, with a resigned
shake of the head, she turned and slowly
walked back out of the house to rejoin
the others on the lawn. She immediately
searched out Art, seeing him amidst the
gathering, talking to a small stocky lady
with wisps of grey hair breaking loose from
an untidy bun at the back of her head. He
caught Claire's eye and immediately ex-
cused himself from the woman and came

across the lawn towards her, a look of concern on his face.

"Hey, are you okay? You're looking washed out."

Claire forestalled an elderly couple's approach with a friendly smile and took Art by the arm, leading him to the far side of the beech tree so that they were hidden from the majority of those on the lawn.

"What's going on?" Art asked, perplexed.

"Marcus and Charity have left."

"Oh? Where've they gone?"

"Back to London."

"What?" he exclaimed, spinning round as if to search them out. "When?"

"About five minutes ago in one of the Mercedes."

"Hell, are they coming back?"

Claire shook her head.

"So, what's going to happen with Leo?" he asked.

"Charity thinks he'll be fine with Agnes."

"You think that too?"

Again Claire shook her head.

Art pulled a hand across the top of his head. "Claire, we can't stay on here much longer. We gotta get back for Violet, for Chrissakes, and for the business."

"I told them that, but they wouldn't listen. Charity was downright rude to me."

Art kicked angrily at the grass. "Jesus, this damned family of yours."

"It is not my family!" Claire exclaimed, her voice faltering as emotion welled in her throat. "My family was my mother, Art, and she has just died."

Art pressed a hand to his face. "Yeah," he said, steadying his voice. He put his arms around her and held her in a tight hug. "Sorry, I shouldn't have said that."

"I miss her so much," Claire sobbed against his shoulder.

"I know you do," he said, giving her a kiss on the top of her head. "I guess we'll just have to work something out."

Claire looked up at him. "You know I'm going to have to stay on here for a bit. There's no alternative."

Art heaved out a sigh. "I guess so." He let go of her. "Listen, I think I'll go make a few phone calls. No time like the present, as they say."

"Will you have to go back?"

"We'll see. If Pilar says Violet's quite

happy and the restaurant is running smoothly, then maybe we can stretch our time here to a week. I might even give this idea of the conference centre more thought if you'd let me speak to Leo."

Claire snuffled out a laugh. "Well, Marcus and Charity have made it blatantly clear that it's up to us now to organize his affairs, so I don't see why not."

"Right." He gave her arm a squeeze. "I'm going to head back to the house. You coming?"

"Not yet. I don't think I can engage in one more word of small talk. I might just get lost for a bit until the coast is clear."

Art nodded. "Okay, you do that. I'll be looking out for you."

He gave her a reassuring wink before turning and loping off towards the house.

Claire walked to the far end of the lawn, keeping the beech tree in line with her passage so that there was the least possibility of being seen, and then joined the driveway for fifty yards before turning off down the farm track. She had not set foot on that part of the property for nearly sixteen years, ever since those freezing Christmas holidays

when her friendship with Jonas had ended
so abruptly. Nevertheless, the sun glinting
through the canopy of trees and the smell
of damp undergrowth took her back to
those countless days when she and Jonas
had walked back together from the farm.
And as she walked now, she could almost
define the years of her upbringing by the
games they'd played and by the conver-
sations that had passed between them.
Early on, they had torn up and down the
road playing Monkey Girl and Balloon Man,
and then, when both started to attend
Clackmannanshire Secondary School, they
would just saunter the half mile, discussing
homework or which of their friends the other
one liked; later still, when both were in their
mid-teens and studying for their imminent
Standard Grades, there had been one of
the few disagreements between them when
Claire tried to persuade Jonas not to bunk
off school, telling him he'd be better to concentrate on getting his exams, rather than
spend every moment working on the old
car his father had given him; and then,
when the school had finally run out of pa-
tience with Jonas, and Claire was left to
continue on to Alevels without her best

friend being around, they talked only of the technique required to drive a car at break-neck speed up a forestry track and how, one day, he was going to be famous.

Yet never, during those late-evening walks, had there been any physical contact between them—not one brush of hands, not one secret, experimental kiss. They walked adjacent to each other but always on their respective sides of the track, the grass that grew in its centre, untouched by car or tractor wheel, seeming to act as a threshold that effectively kept in check any possible outward display of affection.

The emotional upheaval of the day and the abrupt departure of Marcus and Charity seemed to draw Claire like a magnet towards the farm. It had always been her refuge when her stepsiblings had been at home during the holidays, a place where she would go to escape their constant taunting or hurtful rejection. No matter how low and unhappy she had felt, as soon as she entered the mucky little courtyard with the scrawny hens scratching around the discarded pieces of machinery, her spirits had risen at the sounds emanating from the workshop: the chat between Jonas

and his father, the ringing clash of span-
ners, the high revving of an engine, and,
during the very occasional moment of silence, the thumping beat of pop music
coming from the old greasy-dialled tran-
sistor on the shelf above the workbench.
The old decrepit farm meant as much
home to her as either her mother's little
place in West Sussex or the Dragon Plant
House.

But then it had all ended on that day during the Christmas holidays so long ago.
She had never found out why there had
been such a devastating change in Jonas's
behaviour towards her. She had gone over
it all time and time again in her mind, trying
to work out what she had said, what she
had done. She had tried to call him, but he
would always just hang up the phone; or if it
was his father, Bert, who answered, he
would just mumble some excuse about Jonas being too busy to talk or that he had
gone away for the day. Eventually, she had
given up calling, and over the heart-breaking
months that followed, the unexplained loss
of Jonas's friendship manifested itself in
her mind as an emotional and resentful fusion of betrayal and distrust, a time bomb

of irrational anger that continually blew up
in the face of anyone in the Croich household
who happened to say the wrong thing at
the wrong time. But then she had left to
travel abroad, and in the course of time this
feeling had become controlled and eventually subdued. And then the happiness of
being married to Art and having Violet
closed around the last vestiges of pain and
misery, sealing them away in a vault of sad
remembrance deep within her that she
hoped would remain untouched forever.

She had never returned to the farm
again.

Claire now came to a halt at the slight
bend in the lane just before it broke free of
the trees and crossed the open fields to the
farm. The memories had broken the spell,
and she did not want to venture farther.
The flaming ball of the setting sun was now
shining directly into her eyes, and she put
her hand up to shield them, at the same
time hearing a noise, no more than a rustle
of branches, to her left—a deer, maybe,
clandestinely making its way through the
thick undergrowth. Suddenly feeling un-
comfortably alone, she decided to turn
back, but as she dropped her hand to her

side she saw a figure step out onto the
track by the old wooden gate that led into
the fields. She put up her hand again but
couldn't work out who it was, the figure being no more than a silhouette against the
blinding light. She knew from the height,
though, that it was a man. He stood looking
at her for a moment, his legs apart, strad-
dling the short tufted grass in the centre of
the track. He turned and walked off down
the road towards the farm, and it was then
Claire knew for certain his identity, recog-
nizing immediately the long stride and self-
assured sway of the shoulders she had
known since her youth.

She hurried back along the track, wishing to put distance between herself and the
departing figure, but as she went, a thin
toxic vapour of embittered thought seemed
to leak its way into her brain and she began
wondering whether there had ever been
this "meeting" in Manchester that Leo had
told her about. If not, and Jonas had taken
all that trouble to arrange every last detail
for Daphne's funeral, why had he not both-
ered to attend? It couldn't still be because
he didn't like going near the house when
Marcus and Charity were around. Surely

the affection he held for Daphne and his own undoubted success in life would have overridden such an aversion?

It wasn't until she was back on the now-deserted lawn, idling her way between the empty tables and chairs towards the house, that it came to her. Of course Marcus and Charity weren't the reason. Daphne had been her own mother and he would have known that she would be coming back from New York for the funeral. It could only be herself that Jonas was still continuing to avoid.

20

Alloa—June 1987

It was no more than five miles from the farm to the gate at the bottom of the forestry road, but Claire was always glad when they had reached it. The old Ford Escort had been stripped right down by Jonas and his father, the back seat removed to make room for the high-backed Corbeau rally seats and the cumbersome roll bar which Bert himself had welded up and fitted to the car in the farm workshop. With Jonas and his father occupying the front seats, Claire had to contort herself into the back. The springs of the car were rock-hard and, even on the smoothest of roads she felt every jarring bump through the inadequacy of her small foam cushion, the boom of the straight-through exhaust reverberating around the unpadded interior only heightening her discomfort.

Yet she would never have missed it for the world. Jonas's excitement at the prospect of another stone-spitting, side-skidding, high-speed dash was hers as well. She would wait at the top of the road, her finger hovering over the stopwatch button, waiting for the far-off blare of the horn which signalled their start. She would press the button and then watch for the clouds of dust floating above the young spruce trees, knowing instinctively at every point during the run whether Jonas was on time or behind, catching up or losing precious seconds. And then the car would appear around the final bend, its rear end slewed round, and she would watch as Jonas battled with the small leather-padded steering wheel, applying throttle so that the front-wheel drive of the car bit hard into the road, swinging it straight and the Escort would rocket up the final section. As it roared past, she would press the button on the stopwatch and, with eyes closed, fall back onto the cushiony heather, lying supine to avoid the cloud of dust and the stones that flew out from behind the wheels.

And then Jonas would be out of the car like a flash, pulling off his helmet as he ran towards her. He would stop in front of her, looking up to where she sat high on the bank.

"Well?" he would ask, his dark eyes darting with the adrenalin of the drive and the expectation of the result.

And Claire would make him wait, her brow furrowed as she pretended to study the clock, until Bert, the navigator, incongruously dressed in a dirty pair of dungarees and a gleaming white helmet with red flashes, had ambled down the road from the car.

"Good or bad?" Bert would ask, his stubbly cheeks pushed out by the helmet's padding.

And only then did Claire give her verdict.

Because of the noise in the car, they rarely spoke during the ten-minute journey, and on this occasion Claire was glad of it. Her stomach churned with nervous anticipation at the thought of what Bert had planned for her that afternoon, not so much because she doubted her ability, but more what Jonas's reaction would be when his father suggested it. Four months before, she had walked across to the farm after school and had found Bert alone in the workshop. It was the perfect opportunity to ask him.

From the moment Jonas had made the move from go-kart racing to rally driving a proper car, Claire wanted to be part of it as well. They were a team, and had been throughout their schooldays, and she didn't want to break that up. Timekeeping was fun and, in a way, quite exciting, but Claire wanted to share the same exhilaration as Jonas, to be part of his every moment of achievement. She wanted to be there in the car with him, she dependent on him, and he on her.

And this desire was not wholly driven by the infatuation with which Jonas embraced his sport. It was more to do with the infatuation she had for Jonas himself. She was nearly seventeen years old, no longer a girl but a young woman, and she wanted nothing more than for their relationship to develop into something much deeper. She dreamed of that moment when the barrier between friendship and love would crumble away, when he would put out a hand to touch her, and then an arm slide around her shoulders, followed by that first, long-awaited kiss.

All she just needed was the catalyst to allow it to happen.

So, that was the reason she had asked Bert if she could learn to co-drive for Jonas. She wanted to be his navigator, calling out the bends in the roads and the distances between them, so that Jonas could act on her instructions, shaving those precious seconds off his time, and then she would be indispensable to him—in life.

Bert took off his old tweed cap and scratched at his head as he pondered her strange request. "You've got to have a cool head for that, lass. You've got to think fast, act quick, and have nerves of steel because you'll be travelling at an awful rate. Do you think you're up to it?"

Claire swallowed hard and nodded.

Bert smiled at her, showing off a gleaming set of dentures. "In that case, aye, I'll give you a hand"—he tapped a secretive finger at the side of his nose—"but this one has to be between ourselves, lassie. Jonas is awful serious about what he wants to achieve in the sport, so he'll not tolerate anyone just playing around. Not a word to him then until I give the nod."

That evening, Bert phoned Leo and asked hlm to discuss the idea with Daphne, making it clear that he would not allow Claire to go near the car until he was certain she was up to the task. "Caution and ability will be the winners," he always said, "recklessness and stupidity the losers."

There was a great deal of discussion behind closed doors over the subject, Leo for once being as reticent as Daphne to grant permission, but they eventually came to the decision to put their trust in Bert. They knew of his deep fondness for Claire and that he would never allow anything to happen that would put her life at risk.

When the go-ahead was given, Bert sprang into action, making a special trip to the new book superstore in Dunfermline. He returned with a book on rally navigation and a video that featured the current WRC champion, Juha Kankkunen, voicing-over every event in which he had competed the previous year.

The subterfuge between Bert and Claire thereafter had been intense. Every night, after she had finished her Higher Grade studies, she would devour the information in the book and the video over and over again. Whenever possible, usually on the pretext of "getting some shopping in," Bert would pick up Claire from school in his battered Land Rover and they would go up to the forestry road for an hour, where he would drive slowly up and down the road, helping Claire to take down notes on distances and the angle of bends. "Cut down the yardage a fraction on this one, lass," he would say, "and you'll get Jonas to take the corner a bit earlier. That'll save him a few seconds in time."

And when Claire knew that road like the back of her hand, Bert then took her off onto another part of the forestry estate where she knew that Jonas had never been before. This new road interlinked with the other, but meandered its way for more than a mile round the back of the hill. Bert took Claire up and down the road, going through the same meticulous preparation until she could almost call out the instructions with her eyes closed.

And then, just the day before, when Bert had closed the gate that led out onto the main road, he got back into the Land Rover and thumped his hands on the steering wheel. "Right, lass, I reckon you're ready. You'll get your first run with Jonas tomorrow."

At the top of the forestry road, Jonas swung the car round the tight turning circle and came to a halt. Bert threw open the passenger door and pulled himself awkwardly out of the seat before propping it forward for Claire to squeeze out. He stood stretching out his back, and then shot an encouraging wink at Claire as he handed her his helmet.

"What's going on?" Jonas asked, peering up at them from the driver's seat.

"I'm timekeeping today," Bert replied.

"You're joking," Jonas said incredulously.

"No, I'm not, lad," Bert laughed. "You're always complaining about how I give instructions too late, so I'm going on strike." He leaned into the car, opening up the glove compartment and taking out the thick pad on which Claire had written her navigation notes. He handed it to her. "See if Claire can do any better."

"But she has no idea!" Jonas exclaimed, the side of his mouth twisted up in disdain.

Bert smiled knowingly at Claire. "Aye, she does, lad—aye, she does."

"What's been going on with you two?" Jonas asked, looking distrustfully from one to the other.

Taking the helmet from Claire, Bert slid it carefully onto her head and began adjusting the chinstrap. "Just wait and see."

With a resigned shake of his head, Jonas forcefully pulled on his own helmet. Bert took Claire's arm and guided her to the passenger door. "Keep your wits about you, lass. You know the road now like the back of your hand, but this time you'll be going at one hell of a speed. Just keep up with him." He gave her arm a reassuring squeeze as Claire got into the car.

"Slight change of plan to the run, lad," Bert said to Jonas as he leaned in to help her do up the complicated safety harness. "You know the road that comes in from the right half way down to the gate?"

"Aye," Jonas replied doubtfully.

"Well, head up there. It's exactly one and a half miles to the top, which means once you've started, your run will be two and a half exact. That's a good bit longer than you've done before, so keep your concentration and don't overcook it."

"But I've never driven that road before."

Bert shook his head. "You can't expect to win medals driving on the same bit of road all the time, lad."

"But I don't know it."

"Maybe you don't, but Claire does." He stood up and slammed the door shut. "And that's all that matters," he called in through the closed window.

"How will you know when we've started?" Jonas yelled out at his father.

"Just blow the horn," Claire said to him quietly. "He can hear it from where we start."

Jonas glanced worriedly at her and started the engine and took off down the road.

"Slow down, Jonas," she said, her head bowed as she looked through her notes. "We're not racing yet."

"Are you telling me what to do?"

She turned to him, smiling. "Yes, I am, so get used to it."

They drove in silence, Jonas only coming out with the occasional expletive as he

steered his way slowly round some of the
sharper bends on the new road. Claire
saw him bite hard on his bottom lip and
realized that he was as nervous about
what his father was asking him to do as
she was.

When they turned at the top of the road,
Jonas let out a steadying breath and revved
up the engine of the Escort. "Are you ready,
then?"

"No, not yet."

"Oh, for God's sake," Jonas muttered.

Claire threw her notebook onto the dashboard and turned to him. "Jonas, are you
angry?"

Jonas did not reply but looked straight
ahead, his breathing shallow.

"Because if you are, then we're not going to start until you calm down. This is a
really difficult stretch of road and you've
got to be rock-solid on it. I'll do the calling,
but you're going to have to listen to me,
okay?"

She said it with so much authority that
Jonas looked round at her and smiled.
"You sound like a real navigator."

Claire nodded. "I am. Are you ready
now?"

Jonas laughed and gripped hard on the steering wheel. "Aye, captain, never more so."

Claire retrieved her notes from the dashboard and gave her safety harness a final check-over. "Okay, then, let's do it."

Jonas slipped forward the short stubby gear lever and revved up the engine. He let out the clutch until it engaged a fraction and then gave a loud blast on the air horn, and with that, Claire felt the power of the car press her back into the seat as they took off down the road.

All the snail-paced practising that she had done with Bert could never have prepared Claire for the speed at which Jonas drove, and she had to stop herself mentally from just holding hard to her safety harness and staring like a mesmerized rabbit out of the windscreen. She gabbled out the two first instructions, not really understanding what she had said herself, but Jonas acted upon them and took the corners at exactly the right angle. Then there was the straight with the slight rise in the road and Claire was so busy getting ready for the next corner, she forgot to mention it. The car flew over the hump, airborne for

a second before it came down with a jarring thump that Claire felt right up her
spine.

"One hundred yards, ninety degrees
right," she yelled out, knowing the moment
she said it that there was less than sixty
yards to the corner. "I mean sixty yards!"

Jonas swung the steering wheel hard to
the right and the car skidded broadside
towards the corner. The back of the Escort
kept swinging outwards and Claire turned
to see the edge of the road dropping away
into the trees. Jonas pressed his foot to
the floor, throwing the steering wheel in
counterlock, and the front end of the car
caught a solid footing on the dirt track and
straightened.

"Sorry about that!" Claire cried out, her
heart pounding.

"Just keep 'em coming," Jonas screamed
at her. "You're doing bloody great."

And that was all she wanted to hear.
From that moment on, her nervousness
vanished and she gave every instruction
at exactly the right time, even remembering to shorten the yardage on the corner
that Bert had pointed out. Jonas realized
what she had done when they rounded

the hundred-degree turn, letting out a yelp of triumph as the car ran inches from the ditch on the left-hand side.

At the bottom of the road, they swung out onto the stretch that Jonas had been practicing on for the past eight months.

"Relax, I'll take it from here," Jonas called out.

"No, just keep listening," Claire yelled back, now feeling in total control of the run. "I'll beat your time."

She gave every direction as she had them written down and it wasn't until the last corner that she knew she had really cracked it. The car took it at speed, its back end never wavering from control, and then she saw Bert at the end of the straight, jumping up and down on the high bank.

The car flashed past the finishing mark and Jonas applied the brake, slowing the car down before he swung it round in the turning circle. He had unbuckled his safety harness and was out of the door before Claire had time to catch her breath. She watched Bert clamber down the bank and run towards Jonas, the stopwatch held in his outstretched hand. Jonas grabbed it from him and stood for a moment just staring at it before he started pacing fast back and forth up the road, punching the air every time he consulted the stop-watch.

Unbuckling her harness, Claire got out of the car and took off her helmet. "How did we do?" she asked as she walked to-wards Bert.

"Unbelievable, lassie," Bert said as he approached her. "That was unbelievable. I had a time in mind of just under three min-utes and you two have just done it in two twenty." He put his arm around her shoul-ders and gave her a tight squeeze.

They walked together back to where Jo-nas was still pacing and yelling out in tri-umph.

"Well, what did I tell you?" Bert said, smiling proudly at Claire. "I told you she was good."

Jonas approached her, a wide grin on his face, and Claire was convinced that this was the moment she had been waiting for. The barrier was about to be shattered.

"Rock-solid, Claire, rock-solid," he said, his hand coming out towards her, but it was a punch to her arm that it delivered, the adrenalin pumping in his body making it much harder than perhaps he had meant. He glanced once more at the stopwatch and with a loud triumphant "Yesss!" he headed past her up the road towards his car.

In that moment, Bert saw the look of complete dejection on Claire's face as she turned to watch Jonas's retreating figure. He smiled and nodded slowly, suddenly understanding everything. "Not quite the congratulations you were hoping for, was it, lass?" he said quietly.

Claire did not reply but looked up into his kind weather-beaten face. She let out a laugh that verged dangerously close to the brink of misery.

"Ah, well, give it time," he said, putting his arm around her again, "give it time." He planted a kiss on the side of her head. "And for now, you'll just have to make do with that one from his daffy old father."

Over the next year, Claire continued to navigate for Jonas on the forestry road, but they only once managed to beat the time of their first run. Jonas never held her at fault, but she knew that her true motivation for doing it had been lost on that first day. But she was willing to "give it time," as Bert had said, and she knew that if even the slightest opportunity arose to break the barrier, then she would take it.

The bond, however, grew stronger between her and Jonas, mainly because she was so much part of his dream to succeed. Claire spent every spare moment of her time at the farm, chatting away with Jonas in the workshop as he carried out yet another modification to his car's engine, and rarely returning home until well after dark. This close contact gave her even greater hope that their relationship might eventually come to fruition after all, but then after that one evening during the Christmas holidays, when they had been together in the workshop until well after midnight, everything changed. It was as if an impenetrable wall had suddenly been dropped in front of her, cutting off all means of communication with Jonas. Thereafter, there was no contact between them, and it broke Claire's heart.

It had always been her plan to go straight to university from school, but now she wanted nothing more than to get as far away from Jonas as she possibly could. She organized her gap year to travel round the world, knowing that it would not only broaden her horizons but also give her a chance to put Jonas out of her mind. She did not realize when she drove away from the Dragon Plant House on that warm July morning that she was leaving the remnants of her youth there like Peter Pan's unruly shadow, and that it would be a very different person who would eventually return.

A young woman, married and fulfilled.

21

Alloa—September 2004

During the week following the funeral, Claire busied herself with the heart-rending task of clearing the wardrobes and cupboards of Daphne's belongings. She tried to switch her mind off as she stuffed all-too-familiar clothes into black bin bags, destined for the charity shop, but every now and again Daphne's scent wafted up from a shirt or a jersey, invading her senses with nostalgia and breaking her resolve. She would sit on the edge of the bed, which now seemed depressingly large for Leo alone, and press the garment to her nose while tears rolled down her cheeks.

Consequently, a job that should have con-
stituted a morning's work took more than
two days.

Art never knew about these moments of
private mourning, and Claire was glad of it.
He had thrown his energies into research-
ing the idea of turning Croich Into a conference centre, having chosen his time
well to speak to Leo about it all. It transpired that Marcus had spoken with his father on the telephone the day after Daphne
died, saying that Leo should give careful
thought now to what should happen to the
property, and that both Charity and he had
made their homes in London and therefore had no wish to live in Croich at any
time in the future. With the housing market
being so buoyant, he felt that there would
never be a better time to put the property
on the market and that it was an ideal opportunity for Leo to downsize to a smaller
house.

It was only when Art explained his pro-
posal to Leo, telling him that the main crite-
ria behind the idea was to keep the house
in the family, and subsequently learning
that Marcus's ideas were to the contrary,
that he realized how much this had been

adding to the old man's misery. The furrowed eyebrows lifted the moment Art began carefully to outline his plan, and even a glint of brightness returned to Leo's eyes as he sat forward in his armchair, listening intently. His acceptance of the idea became apparent when, half-way through Art's explanation, Leo slapped his hands decisively on his knees, got to his feet and walked purposefully over to the door of the sitting room. He threw it open and from the hallway called out to Art, who was left dumbstruck by this sudden metamorphosis, "Better get on with it, then. No time like the present. I'll be in my office if you want me."

The news not only gave Claire a much-needed boost, but she was also amazed by the effect it had on Leo. At supper that evening, the usual stilted silence that surrounded their meals was blown away by Leo's enthusiastic suggestions of how best the house could be set up as a conference centre and his agreeing with Art that the conversion of one of the greenhouses into a "bachelor pad" would suit him perfectly in the future. At the end of the meal, he got to his feet and started to leave the kitchen, but then turned to announce that he wanted Art and Claire to return to New York at the end of the week, that he had imposed on their time too long. He had given it thought that afternoon in his office and felt that now he had to make the best of things and get on with his life, and he was sure he was going to be absolutely fine rattling around the old house with Agnes giving him a hand. He then cut across Claire's concerned response to this by telling them that he had arranged a meeting with John Venables, his solicitor, in two days' time for the reading of Daphne's will, so they must take that into consideration when fixing their time of departure. He then left the room, leaving Art and Claire staring at each other in surprise and little to say except "Well, that's a bit of a turnaround, isn't it?"

The following afternoon, much to his delight, Art was asked to play golf with the managing director of a local timber company with whom he had made contact to sound out his ideas on the house. However, when he returned home that evening and sought out Claire in their bedroom, he was in a surprisingly sombre mood.

"The borrowed clubs let you down, did they?" Claire asked teasingly as he stared morosely out of the window.

He shook his head. "No, actually they were fine. I played pretty well."

"So why the glum face?"

Art turned and scratched at the back of his head, for a moment delaying his response. "Ben Cohen rang me just after I got back to the clubhouse."

"Ben Cohen? You mean the lawyer in New York?"

"Yeah."

"What did he want?" Claire asked, her voice now edged with concern.

Art let out a long sigh. "You know the art gallery next to the restaurant?"

"Yes."

"It's closing down and the place is up for lease."

Claire gasped. "Wow, that was unexpected. I thought they were doing really well."

"Ben reckons a marriage split was the cause. Anyway, he's been on to the realty that's handling the re-leasing, and there's already been a hell of an interest in the place." He looked at her, a pained expression on his face. "I have to take it, Claire. I can't lose out on this opportunity."

"Ah," Claire said solemnly, suddenly realizing the implications this had on Art's plans for the house. She sat down heavily on the bed and stayed silent for a moment, her hand covering her mouth. She shook her head. "You've got to go for it."

"I know. I just wished I'd never mentioned—"

"It's not your fault. It's just bad timing." She pushed herself to her feet. "But I'm not sure what we're going to say to Leo."

Art stuck his hands in the pockets of his chinos and leaned a shoulder against the window recess. "What about we don't say anything for now? I reckon it's still a good plan, just we have to put it on hold for the time being. I was going through some figures in my head on the way back from golf, and I'd say a year, maybe two, would see us through payback on all the conversion costs to the new premises in New York, and then we'd be in the position to give the project over here more thought."

"Will Leo not question why it's taking so long?"

"I don't think so. I told him nothing would

happen immediately, and anyway we've given him peace of mind about his place. As soon as we're gone, he'll just lose himself in his plants again and put the whole idea out of his head until we're ready to roll with it." He pushed himself away from the wall. "One good thing is that Leo is not going to say anything to Marcus or Charity until I've had the chance to work out if it's feasible."

"But won't Marcus keep on top of Leo about selling the house?"

"I don't think so. Marcus has this big project on in London right now and it's my guess that'll occupy his mind completely for the time being. Same thing with Charity. She'll get involved with her kids and her high-flying social life and not give it another thought."

"Are you saying that Charity knew about Marcus's idea to put the house on the market?"

"I think that's what really got to Leo. He reckons they've both been working in cahoots over the whole thing."

Claire sighed. "Poor Leo, he really doesn't need this kind of thing happening at his stage of life."

Art walked over to her and planted a re-assuring kiss on the cheek. "Don't worry, he's on the mend and we'll make sure we keep in close contact with him when we're back in the States." He pulled his sweater off over his head. "Hey, guess what, I got two birdies during the round of golf today. Pretty good, huh?"

22

Claire opened the door of the sitting room and showed in the solicitor. John Venables had the deportment of an elderly stork, tall but stoop-shouldered, making the jacket of his dark suit look as if it were a couple of sizes too large for him. His demeanour was so serious that when Claire answered his ring at the front door, she had first thought him to be a representative of the undertaking firm that had handled Daphne's funeral.

"We could have our meeting over there," she said, pointing to the round table by the window. "Is that all right?"

"Perfect," the solicitor replied, putting

down his laden leather briefcase by one of the chairs.

"Would you like tea or coffee?"

"Coffee would be just the ticket."

"Right, I'll just go and find Leo and my husband, Art."

Claire left the room and walked out into the hall, where she found Leo sitting on a chair pulling on his Wellington boots. He was dressed in an old pair of cavalry twill trousers and a threadbare tweed jacket.

"Leo, what are you doing?"

He looked up at her and smiled. "It's damned wet after last night's rain. Don't want to get my feet wet."

She frowned at him, first baffled by the reply and then worried by his apparent confusion. "But John Venables is here in the sitting room. We're meant to be having a meeting. Had you forgotten?"

Pushing himself to his feet, Leo picked up a pair of battered leather gloves from the pine table. "No, I hadn't, but there's no need for me to be there. I had a long meeting with John yesterday morning when you and Art were out shopping. I've asked him to fill you in on all that we discussed before the reading of your mother's will."

"But you'll probably be involved in that, Leo. Don't you want to hear it?"

His smile was forced. "No, better not. I'll learn anything that concerns me from John at a later stage. All a bit recent, you know." He took a tweed hat from the coat stand by the stairs and pushed it onto his head. "If you do want me for anything, though, I'll be in the greenhouse." He walked over to the front door and pulled it open. "Probably have to beat my way in with a machete," he said with a laugh. "Haven't been near the place for ages."

After introductions and a brief informal chat, Mr. Venables laid his coffee cup down on its saucer with a sinewy hand. "Well, shall we make a start to proceedings?" he said, flicking off the elastic bands from the file that sat on the desk in front of him. "If you don't mind, Claire, Leo has asked that we go through some changes he has made to his own will before we start on your mother's."

"Of course," Claire replied, glancing across the table at Art. "He did say as much before going out to the garden."

"Good," the solicitor said, putting on his reading spectacles. He opened the file and took out two typed documents and slid them across the table to Claire and Art. "Now, Leo's previous will had taken into consideration the fact that he would most likely predecease your mother, Claire." He smiled sympathetically at her. "Unfortunately, that was not to be." He glanced down at his own document. "Nothing really has changed with the basics, in that most of the household furnishings that were here before your mother married Leo are to be divided between his own children, Marcus and Charity—"

"Mr. Venables," Claire cut in.

"Oh, John, please," the solicitor replied.

"All right . . . John," she continued, "if we're to be going through Leo's will in detail, does it not matter that the main beneficiaries aren't here?"

John smiled awkwardly. "That is a good point, but I shall in fact be sticking to those few salient points that have some bearing on the plans Art has for this property."

Claire glanced concernedly at Art, but he dismissed it with a brief shake of his head.

"Are you quite happy to continue?" John asked.

"All right," replied Claire.

"Very well, then," John replied, smiling reassuringly at her. "When Leo first bought Croich, a fair proportion of the considerable capital generated from the sale of his brewery thirty years ago went into the property and its subsequent upkeep. Nevertheless, he still has a fairly healthy investment portfolio with a present-day value of two hundred and seventy thousand pounds, and accordingly, in case of his own infirmity in future years, he has granted joint power of attorney to both Marcus and Charity to administer to this. However, during our meeting yesterday, Leo briefed me fully on your plans for this house, Art, and understanding this won't happen immediately, he has decided that, in the event of his demise meantime, to name two unrelated executors for the eventual distribution of his estate. They are to be myself and Jonas Fairweather."

"Jonas Fairweather!" Claire exclaimed, immediately sensing a bubble of resentment seep out from that hidden vault deep within her and burst in her head.

"That's right," John replied tentatively, reading Claire's tone as disappointment that she herself had not been asked. "I did suggest that you should also be made an executor, but Leo felt there might well be a conflict of interests if that were to happen and he thought it best not to give reason for 'the boat to be rocked,' so to speak."

"Who is this guy Jonas?" Art asked, still noticing the dismay on Claire's face.

"His family were tenants of the neighbouring farm for many years," John continued. "He's been away for quite some time, working in the south and abroad, but he returned last year and subsequently bought the farm from Leo. Despite being a very successful businessman and having gathered for himself some considerable wealth, he has been nothing but supportive of Leo over the past year. You will know, Claire, that it was Jonas who organized your mother's funeral."

"Yes, I'm aware of that," Claire replied tersely.

"Really?" Art said with surprise. "I thought you said Leo had organized the funeral himself."

Claire felt colour rise to her face. "I never did."

"Well, you certainly gave me that impression."

Claire shrugged. "I have no idea why," she replied, deciding that now was a good time to deliver a counterpunch to allay Art's curiosity. She turned to John. "Don't you think that having Jonas as an executor might not cause an even greater conflict of interests?"

"In what way?" John asked.

"Well, on one hand, being the executor, he'll no doubt be made aware of Art's plans for the house, and then on the other, being the owner of the neighbouring property, he might want to stop the whole thing. No one is in a better position to do that."

"I see no reason myself why there should be any mention of this for the time being," John said, "and I'm quite sure Leo has considered every eventuality. He knows that Jonas has the best interests of this family at heart." He took off his spectacles and sat back in his chair, fiddling with one of the thin gold legs. "You know, Claire, I have been acquainted with your stepfather for over thirty years now, and in that time he has become a very close friend. As such, we have shared many confidences, some of which have had a marked bearing on the changes he has made to his will." He paused, tapping a finger on the table, as if giving himself time to choose his words carefully. "Leo is perhaps one of the most trusting and trustworthy people I know, and I think he finds it very . . . saddening when this important quality is not reciprocated in the nature of others." He smiled reassuringly at Art and Claire. "Now, I am certainly not casting aspersions here, but I want you to be aware that Leo has given a great deal of thought to the various decisions he has made." He leaned forward again, shifting Leo's will aside, and in doing so, finalizing its discussion. "So let's move on to your mother's will, shall we?" He slid a copy across to both Claire and Art. "I have listed all her belongings, Claire, the majority of which will go to you, excepting some special bequests she has made to Leo, Art and your daughter, Violet. You will no doubt be aware that your mother had little financial capital herself. Her main source of income came from a legacy left to you by your father, the late David Barclay, from which your mother drew interest and which would then pass to you on her demise.

Now, since your mother married Leo, he has been looking after this for you, managing it alongside his own portfolio of investments. Its present-day value is just over three hundred and fifty thousand pounds."

Claire gasped in amazement. "I don't believe it! I mean . . . I had no idea!"

John smiled broadly at her. "Well, it has been carefully managed. Leo has done an excellent job in building up its worth." He leaned his elbows on the table, putting his long hands together. "Now, depending on your own present financial position, you can either take over the portfolio as it stands, or I can arrange for it to be converted to cash. It's entirely up to you."

Claire glanced at Art, who was rubbing a finger thoughtfully against his mouth. "What do you think?" she asked him.

He paused for a moment, leaning back in his chair. "Well, I do have an idea," he said, looking towards the solicitor. "You've talked a lot about confidentiality, John, and I'm going to ask you to do the same here and keep this very much to yourself. It wouldn't do any good for it to become common knowledge."

John nodded. "Of course."

"You said that Leo has informed you of the plans we have for this house."

"In detail."

"Well, I'm afraid we're going to have to put them on hold. A property has come up for lease next door to our restaurant in New York. It's ideal for expanding the enterprise and I have to strike while the iron's hot, consequently the capital I had earmarked for this venture will now have to be directed towards that." He paused. "Now, I do realize the idea of this project has been instrumental in giving Leo's spirits a real boost, so I don't want him getting wind of this, as it's simply our intention to delay matters for the time being until we have recapitalized." He tapped a finger on the document in front of him. "Now this, of course, throws a completely different light on the whole issue and would allow us to reduce that timescale quite considerably." He looked at Claire. "How would you feel about putting your investment towards the purchase of this house?"

Claire answered immediately, a broad grin on her face. "I think it's a wonderful idea. The house would then become not only part of Leo and Daphne, but my father as well."

Art smiled at his wife. "My thoughts exactly." He looked back at the solicitor. "So my suggestion is that we maintain the status quo. We're going to have our hands full over the next couple of years with the expansion of the New York operation, so how about we just leave the portfolio in Leo's control? It'll be like our down payment on the place."

John Venables nodded slowly. "That would seem to me a very sound idea. Leo is more than capable of continuing to oversee your investments, and I'm sure that when I ask him, he will be delighted to do so." He turned back to the first page of the document in front of him. "So, why don't we now read through the will in its entirety and you can make comments when you wish?"

An hour later, having seen John Venables to the front door, Claire returned to the sitting room to find Art standing at the window facing out onto the side lawn and the greenhouses beyond. She came up behind him and put her arms around his waist. "Thank you, my dear man. That was not only a wonderful idea, it was thought-ful as well."

Art continued to stare out of the win-dow. "Yeah, well, in the long run, it'll help us both."

Claire relinquished her hold and peered round at his face. "You okay?"

Art nodded. "Sure."

"What are you thinking about?"

He turned, a light smile on his face. "Tell me about Jonas Fairweather."

Claire sighed. "What do you want to know about him?"

"For a start, what age is he?"

Claire turned away from him, feeling co-lour rise to her face once more. Hoping to give it a chance to settle, she walked over to the table and sat down on the chair she had occupied during the meeting. "He's about a year older than me."

"So you knew him quite well."

"Yes."

"And you knew he'd given Leo a hand with the funeral."

She paused, her eyes closed as she rubbed a hand against her forehead. "Yes, I did."

"So, what gives with all this subterfuge?"

She shook her head. "There's no 'subterfuge,' Art. I just didn't think it was that . . . important."

Art nodded. "Right." He came over and sat down on the chair opposite her. "So, did you two date?"

"No . . . no, we never did."

"But you were close."

"Yes, he was my best friend. We went right through school together and spent most of our free time in each other's company. He made my life bearable when Marcus and Charity were at home."

"So, what happened? You obviously don't have much time for him now."

Claire paused, turning her head and fixing her gaze out of the window on the swaying tops of the fir trees at the far end of the lawn. "Well, we had this falling-out."

"Over what?"

Claire turned to glare at him. "I don't know what. He just . . . stopped communicating with me. And to this day, I never found out why."

"Did you . . . love him?" Art asked quietly.

She smiled distantly. "I suppose it was more of a teenage crush."

"Wow, those can be pretty heavy," Art said with a quiet laugh. "I'm surprised you never told me about him. Was it all over and done with when you went off to Australia?"

"In practical terms, yes, but not in my head . . . nor my heart, for that matter."

"What about when you met me? What were your feelings about him then?"

She paused, looking directly at him. "My feelings weren't directed just at him, but at every member of the male sex under the age of twenty-five."

"And they were?"

"That I really didn't need men in my life because they couldn't be trusted not to leave you sinking slowly into a great swamp of emotional quicksand."

He laughed quietly. "Hopefully, that's changed."

She got up from her chair and went round the table and sat down on his lap. She put her arms around his neck and gave him a kiss on the mouth. "Oh, yes, that changed almost the moment I met you."

He grinned. "Well, I'm truly glad to hear it!"

23

New York—June 2006

Two hundred and four covers for the evening. That was an all-time record. Not only was every table taken both inside and outside on the cordoned-off part of the sidewalk, but seven had been early pre-theatre bookings so were now occupied by later reservations. Though in his renovation plans Art had made the passage between the extended kitchen and the restaurant area much wider, it was as chaotic as the Pamplona bull run, the four table servers having to dodge past each other with laden plates held on high. Even Claire and Art had been pressed to join in the fray, forsaking their usual ambulatory roles as front-of-house hosts to don the white-aproned uniforms of Barrington's. As they came face to face with each other in the passage, they stepped the same way, and then the other, and then both stopped, laughing and shaking their heads.

Art breathed out exhaustedly. "I sometimes wonder."

"What?" asked Claire.

"Whether we shouldn't have just kept the place to its original size." He slumped against the wall. "This is nuts. We shouldn't even be here today. This is our daughter's ninth birthday and we've managed to spend all of two hours with her."

Claire smiled sadly at him. It was not just that it was Violet's birthday. The neverending work in the restaurant had relegated their daughter's existence to no more than a walk-on part in their lives and the feelings of guilt and frustration over this were never far from Claire's mind.

"In that case, let's do something about it," she said.

"What do you suggest?"

"I think it's high time we took on a manager," she replied.

Art smiled. It was not the first time she had suggested this. He stood for a moment surveying the mayhem in the corridor before nodding decisively. "Okay, let's do it," he replied, pressing his back against the wall to allow a rushing waitress past. "We'll get on to it tomorrow."

Claire felt like giving out a loud cry of jubilation as she hurried on her way to the kitchen. At last, she thought to herself.

There had not been a holiday, hardly a weekend break, since they had extended the restaurant into the next-door premises. From the outset it had been a much bigger operation than they had at first envisaged. The initial thought was that it would just be a case of busting a hole through the wall to connect the two properties, and then a bit of wallpapering and parquet-floor matching before scattering around a few extra tables and chairs. But then further practicalities and health and safety regulations caused havoc for a while. The kitchen was not big enough, nor met with the correct specifications to cope with the increased seating, so the small administration office had to be sacrificed to allow for its extension. Art thought they could survive without the office, but four weeks into the refurbishment the filing cabinets and desk, now mono-coloured with red brick dust, were seriously hampering work progress. So Art was forced to prioritize, stopping the construction work until an area had been partitioned off at the back of the new premises and the office equipment had been cleared out of the way.

Even though Art pushed the contractor to have the work finished as fast as possible, the restaurant was still closed for a total of three months. With every day that passed, his agitation grew, thinking that his established clientele would take their allegiance elsewhere and never return. He needn't have worried. Claire sent out ninety invitations to both corporate clients and everyday customers for the opening night and there had only been three refusals. The restaurant was mobbed on that night and had been ever since.

Consequently, their plans for a Scottish conference centre were not so much put on the back burner as being forgotten completely, and despite their assurance to Leo that they would be in constant contact, it usually all came down to a brief telephone call on a Sunday night. It was a time when Claire was never at her best, trying to play catch-up with her energy levels while having a bit of quality time with Violet, whom she felt had been quite abandoned since they started the expansion of the business. Claire always felt guilty after these calls, not because of their irregularity, but because she found herself more often than not telling Leo how hard their lives were, and what little time they had to enjoy themselves, rather than vice versa. In fact, it was always Leo who was much more upbeat and talkative, especially after his own existence had been given greater interest by the arrival of a young Czech couple who were helping both him and Agnes in the garden and the house, respectively. Claire's reaction to the news, however, was mixed when she learned that it was Jonas who had arranged it. Despite the assurances of Leo's solicitor at their meeting, she had nevertheless been left with an uneasy, yet unquantifiable feeling over Jonas's close relationship with her stepfather. But then by the following morning, when another frenzied week had begun, she had no time to give it any further thought.

Five people answered their classified for the new managerial position at Barrington's and interviews were held over two days, but, with the first, both Art and Claire knew immediately that they had found the person they wanted. Luisa Gambini was twenty-seven years old, a small dark-haired bundle of Italian exuberance with a constant smile on her wide lipsticked mouth. Ever since leaving school, she had worked in her family's restaurant in SoHo, first as a waitress before taking on front-of-house. Her sister had now joined the staff at the restaurant, and Luisa, with the blessing of her parents, was looking for a new challenge in life. From the moment Art and Claire showed her round the restaurant and introduced her to the other members of staff, they could tell that her communication and organizational skills were both instinctive and professional.

The other interviews were mere formalities. Luisa started on a two-month trial period almost the moment the final interviewee left the premises.

Art was comfortable with the new arrangement from the start, even taking two days off during Luisa's second week to go and play golf. It was his first game for over a year. Claire, however, found it more difficult to let go of the reins. Luisa now commanded the running of the restaurant, from taking bookings down to ordering the wine and food, and Claire could see that she was not only given complete respect by the other members of staff, but her open and friendly manner charmed even those customers whom Claire had found difficult to handle in the past. Claire was beginning to find her own role superfluous, and the occasions became more frequent when she and Luisa would bump into each other as they went to carry out the same task. But then Luisa would just smile sweetly at her and say, "Oops, sorry, I'll go find something else to do."

And then small changes started to happen, almost without Claire noticing them. Violet rang one afternoon from school to say she was feeling unwell and that she hadn't been able to get hold of Pilar, so Claire said, without hesitation, that she'd come to get her. As it turned out, Violet was indeed running a high temperature, so Claire put her to bed and stayed with her for the rest of the day. And then Pilar caught the same bug and Claire found herself having the time to take Violet to school before going on to spend a leisurely hour shopping at the food store. A few days after that, a friend came into the restaurant to have an early supper before attending the opening of a new art exhibition in Broome Street. When she left, Art and Claire went with her, and having spent an hour drinking wine and viewing some quite unintelligible paintings, they took their leave of the friend and went to eat in a small Thai restaurant just off Canal Street. And it was as they sat there, with Claire using the rare moment of privacy to air her concerns about Luisa, that Art leaned back in his chair, folded his arms and grinned at her. She stopped talking in mid-sentence and frowned quizzically at him.

"What's the matter?"

"I just wondered if you realize what we were doing."

Claire shrugged. "I thought we were talking about the restaurant."

"No, I mean right here, together." He leaned forward on the table. "I can't remember the last time you and I did this." He twisted up the side of his mouth as he gave it thought. "I think it could have been our fifth wedding anniversary."

She stared at him for a moment and then smiled. "My word," she replied quietly.

"Exactly, and this is going to be the way of things in the future. It's all change, Claire. The restaurant is running as well, if not better, as when we were slaving our guts out at the job. We've done our bit in building up the business, and now we can just hand over the running to Luisa. She's doing good work, you know. The reason why you two keep stepping on each other's toes is that she's been intuitive enough to come up with a routine that matches your own. You might not have noticed, but she watched you intently during that first week she was with us. You were her teacher"—he laughed—"and the chief orchestrator of your own downfall."

Claire sat open-mouthed as his words began to register, and then it dawned on her that Luisa's presence in the restaurant had been allowing her to act spontaneously. Never before had she simply walked out of the place at a moment's notice without feeling guilty for having done so or

without having to organize some complicated back-up plan beforehand. She shook
her head as if waking herself up in this new
world of freedom. "You're right," she said,
glancing around the small dimly lit confines
of the Thai restaurant. "What on earth are
we doing here?"

Art smiled. "Do you want to go back to
work?"

She gave it a moment's exaggerated
thought. "No," she replied lightly.

"Good." Art picked up his wine glass and
held it out to her. "So how about we drink
to this occasion as being the first of many
more?"

24

And from that moment their lives did change. The strict daily routine that had been their norm for the past sixteen years was thrown to the wind as leisurely breakfasts, impromptu shopping trips, theatre visits and weekends with friends took over. In the first month of his new-found freedom, Art played golf more than he had in the preceding four years and managed to cut his handicap by two shots into the bargain.

It did, however, take time for both Pilar and Violet to get used to the new arrangement. For Pilar, the easy pottering around the empty flat in Gramercy Park was now disrupted by the presence of others. It had always been her domain during the day, and now her well-ordered schedule was completely thrown. No longer could she arrive in the morning and set about clearing the breakfast table, because Art was invariably still there, drinking coffee and reading the newspaper. She would walk past him, a scowl on her small dark features, and take herself off to start elsewhere with her broom and bucketful of cleaning fluids. Loud sighs and muted expletives in Spanish would then ensue when she found the beds already made or the washing machine in the corridor recess whirring to a finish on its spin cycle. It took Claire little time to realize that this intrusion was as difficult for Pilar to come to terms with as it had been for her to accept Luisa's involvement in the restaurant. And so she ceased forthwith all forms of this new-found domesticity, leaving the beds unmade and the dirty washing piled in the laundry basket, and it was not long before Pilar's happy disposition returned.

However, it took Claire longer to realize that Violet was exactly as she herself had been when she was nine years old. She was aware of there being a striking resemblance between them at that age, Violet having the same short dark hair, brown eyes and small mouth that could change in a flash from pouting disapproval to a gleeful smile. But Violet too had developed a similar fierce sense of independence and love of her own space that came from having a mother who worked all hours, as Daphne had done in her gardens in West Sussex. Violet was quite happy to be alone in the flat with Pilar because she knew the Spanish maid would make no demands on her, there being only gentle reminders to do her homework or to turn off the television when it was time for supper. During the holiday break, as it was now, it meant she didn't have to get up until Pilar came quietly into her room and sat her squat frame down on the edge of her bed. She would push a wisp of hair away from Violet's sleeping face and whisper, "Hey, cariña, it's time to meet the morning. I'll come back in five minutes, right?"

Now every morning was a rude awakening, and every moment in front of the television was threatened with invasion, with the consequence that Violet found more reasons than ever before to set her mouth in a near permanent pout. But then, in time, it was Claire who came to understand that this change to Violet's ordered life was as drastic as when she herself had made the move to Scotland with Daphne all those years ago. So Claire compromised, but only in her own mind, allowing Violet to enjoy her solitary moments and waiting for the time when her daughter happened to decide for herself that having her parents around on a regular basis was actually quite a welcome development in her young life. With the new shopping trips uptown, games of tennis in East River Park and the now-frequent visits to the multiplex in Union Square, it was not long before Violet, of her own accord, would vacate her bed by half past eight every morning and the television remained darkly dormant in the corner of the living room.

Claire heard the telephone ringing in the flat the moment she stepped out of the elevator, laughing at Violet's near-perfect recollection of every moment of action in the film *Charlotte's Web,* from which they had just returned. Hurrying across to the door, she quickly let herself in and went into the kitchen, grabbing the telephone off the wall.

"Hullo?"

"Oh, hullo. Excuse me, but I wish to speak with—er—Mrs. Barrington." It was a young man's voice, heavily accented.

"Speaking."

"Ah, Mrs. Barrington. I sorry, but my English is not so good. My name is Pavel, and I am living in the house in Scotland with Mr. Harrison."

Claire hushed Violet, who had taken her mother's momentary silence as a cue to continue her account of spidery adventures. "Yes, of course, Pavel, Leo told me about you. How is everything going?"

"All is going very well until this morning, I am sorry to say this."

"What's happened?" Claire asked, feeling her cheeks flush with sudden anxiety.

"I was in the garden when Gabriela—that is the name of my girlfriend who lives in the house with me . . ."

His explanation was too painstakingly slow for Claire. "Yes, Pavel, but is Leo all right?"

"Gabriela comes to tell me that Leo has fallen down the stairs, and I have to . . ."

Claire closed her eyes tight. "Oh, no," she said quietly.

"He is good, though!" Pavel replied quickly. Claire heard him say something unintelligible down the line. "Is difficult to say in English." Claire now heard another voice speaking, farther away. "Wait, I hand you to—"

"Hullo, who is this?" The voice was still male, but this time the accent was Scottish.

"It's Claire Barrington."

There was a moment's silence. "Ah, Claire, this is Jonas Fairweather."

She had not heard his voice for over eighteen years, more than half her lifetime, but she recognized immediately its flat, slightly hesitant tone. In the few wordless seconds that followed, her mind went into overdrive as she went through the emotions of shock, anger, even for some ridiculous reason embarrassment, before complete confusion set in. She made to put down the receiver to end the call, but then stopped herself, knowing that she had to continue the call for Leo's sake.

She swallowed hard. "Yes, hullo."

"I'm sorry about Pavel. You'd noticed his English is not the best."

Claire was not remotely interested in this observation. "Could you please just tell me what's happened to Leo?"

"Right, well, I'm afraid he did have a pretty bad fall coming down the stairs this morning, and he's gone and broken his hip. He was taken into Stirling Infirmary and they decided to operate on him straight-away."

"Do you know how it went?" she asked.

"All good, I think. He had to have a new hip joint put in, so it was a lengthy opera-tion, but he's come out of the anaesthetic all right. He's looking pretty washed out, though."

Claire frowned. "Have you seen him?"

"I've been at the hospital all day. I wanted to make sure that everything went well. I've just this moment got back."

Claire noticed now that his tone was a little deeper with age, and the lengthy time he had spent away from Scotland had stripped the strong, guttural intonation from his accent. It all seemed quite surreal to her that she should be standing there talk-ing to Jonas about Leo. He was the com-mon denominator, the person with whom they had spent so much time together in their youth, and she almost felt that the most natural thing she could do was to ask him to explain, there and then, what had happened all those years ago to cause such a seismic change in their relationship. But, of course, it was absurd to think such a thing, especially at this stage and under these circumstances. Anyway, did it really matter anymore?

"Listen, Claire," Jonas continued, "I was meaning to call you."

"Yes, well, I think it's probably a bit late for all that."

"I'm sorry?"

Hearing the puzzlement in Jonas's voice, Claire screwed up her eyes, realizing that her misunderstanding of what he had just said had allowed her thoughts to spill out.

She quickly said, "No, nothing. You said you were going to call me."

"Yes, it's just that I've not been in contact with anyone else in the family about Leo."

"You mean Marcus or Charity."

There was a pause. "Exactly. I tried to call you a number of times earlier in the day, but there was no reply. I left a couple of messages for you."

Claire glanced over to the sideboard and saw the red light blinking on the answering machine. "I'm sorry, I've been out all afternoon."

"Well, I told Pavel to keep trying you. I wanted you to know—as soon as possible."

Claire sighed edgily. "Look, I'll phone Marcus and Charity."

"That would be the best."

"All right—and thank you for letting me know about Leo. I'll have to think what we can do about all this."

"I'm sure."

"Well, goodbye . . ."

"How much do you know, Claire?"

She had already anticipated the end of the call and had turned to hang up the receiver when his question took her by surprise. "What about?"

"Leo."

"What do you mean?"

"Well, over the past year, he's been getting more . . . confused."

She shook her head. "I think that's probably his age, Jonas. He is seventy-eight, after all."

"No, it's dementia."

"Why on earth would you say that?"

"Because I took him to the doctor. I was there when he was diagnosed."

Claire did not speak for a moment, but stood twisting the cord of the receiver around her fingers. "Well, if he does have it, then it must be at a very early stage. I talk to him every Sunday night and he never seems confused to me."

"He always calls you, doesn't he?"

"So?"

"He didn't want you to know. He has lists."

"What do you mean, lists?"

"When he calls you, he always has everything written down in front of him. Hang on a moment . . ."

Claire could hear him talk to the young Czech. She waited a further thirty seconds before Jonas resumed speaking. "Right, Pavel's just got one for me. Reading from the top, it says Claire and Art, then Violet, aged nine, then it says Barrington's Restaurant and in brackets, ask about renovations. Then it has Agnes, housekeeper, and Pavel and Gabriela from Czechoslovakia . . ."

"Is he really that bad?" Claire asked

quietly, not really believing what she was being told.

"I'm afraid so. There are times that he's fine, but then a couple of months ago, he went wandering off in the middle of the night and was picked up by the police in the centre of Alloa. He told them he was going to meet your mother at the bus station. Luckily, the desk sergeant happened to be a friend of mine and called me and I went in to fetch him back. It was after that happened that I arranged for Pavel and Gabriela to come to live with him."

"But why . . . I mean, do Marcus and Charity know anything about this?"

"Not about my involvement, but they do know about the dementia. Charity was up staying a couple of months ago and put two and two together." He paused. "I'll let you get on and call her, then."

It was abrupt. He'd said all he wanted and obviously didn't want to engage in small talk with her.

"Right. Well, thanks for letting me know. Bye."

Claire hung up the receiver and leaned her shoulder against the wall, rubbing a hand against her forehead. Everything had been going so well for them up until that moment, and now the last thing she wanted to do was speak to Charity.

"Can I have a glass of milk, Mom?" Violet asked without looking up from the screen of Claire's laptop on the kitchen table.

"Of course you can, darling," Claire replied, laying a hand on her daughter's shoulder in passing as she walked over to the fridge.

"Oh, why is this not working?" Violet exclaimed, slewing the mouse across the table.

Claire put a glass of milk on the table and leaned over her daughter's shoulder. "What are you trying to do?"

"I want to find the *Charlotte's Web* page on the Internet."

Claire clicked the mouse, typed in a few words on the keyboard and clicked the mouse again. "There it is."

"Thanks, Mom," Violet said, taking a sip of the milk. "Do you want to have a look at it with me?"

"I will do in a moment," Claire replied, picking up her handbag from where she had discarded it on the floor when she entered the flat. "I've just got one quick telephone call to make."

Taking out a large moleskine notebook from the bag, she flicked through the pages and then took the receiver off the wall and stuck it under her chin as she dialled the number. She lobbed the notebook onto the table and let out a long sigh of trepidation as she heard the double burr of the British ring tone.

"Hullo?" Charity's voice had a perfect English drawl, her greeting sounding more as if she had said "Hell-air."

"Charity, it's Claire."

"Oh, darling, I was just going to call you. Tarkie's come back from school with a ghastly temperature, so I'm going to keep him at home tomorrow. You don't mind doing the run, do you? It's just that . . ."

Claire gritted her teeth. "No, Charity, it's—it's Claire Barrington."

"Ah." There was a moment's pause. "Sorry, I thought you were someone else."

"Yes, I gathered that. So . . . how are you?"

"Run off my feet, actually. I have one child lying prostrate in bed and I'm meant to be going down to Berkshire tomorrow for James's Speech Day." Claire heard her sigh. "Oh well, I suppose I'll cope."

"I'm sorry."

"These things happen."

Charity went silent, offering no reciprocal conversation. Claire felt there was little point in prolonging the call any longer than was necessary.

"The news I'm going to give you, then, is not going to help."

"Oh? What's that?"

"I'm afraid Leo has had a bad fall. He's broken his hip and has had to undergo a pretty major operation today."

"Who told you this?" Charity asked, almost spitting out the question.

Claire thought it best not to mention Jonas. "The young Czech boy who lives with Leo. He called me just a moment ago."

"For heaven's sakes, why was I not told about this? What's the point in telling you when you live in another country?"

It was a fair observation. "I didn't ask that question, Charity."

"It's quite ridiculous." Claire heard her sigh again. "He shouldn't be living in that house by himself, you know."

"Well, he's hardly alone. He has Agnes and the two Czechs—"

"And a fat lot of good they are. They let him fall down the stairs, for goodness' sakes!"

"It was an accident, Charity. I don't think you can blame anyone for that happening."

"That's as may be, but he needs proper professional care, especially now that he's losing his marbles."

"Yes, well, I didn't know about that."

"Marcus and I have been trying to get him to move into a home for the past year," Charity continued, ignoring Claire's pointed remark, "but he's such a stubborn old devil. He can't seem to understand that he's far too old to be living on his own."

Claire pressed her fingers hard to her forehead. She had had no idea about this. Leo had never mentioned it. But then he had gone to painstaking lengths not to reveal his condition to her. "He does love that house, Charity, and the gardens, and all his memories."

"Oh, for God's sakes, Claire, you have no idea, do you? He's got no memories. He hardly knows what time of day it is. And tell me, what's going to happen to him now? He's going to be totally incapacitated, both physically and mentally."

Claire shook her head slowly. Charity had summed up her case perfectly. Leo's falling down the stairs had all but precipitated him into a home. A thought suddenly occurred to her. If that happened, what was to become of the house? She was trying to think of a way to stall the inevitable when Charity herself came to the rescue.

"Oh, the timing on this is just so impossible. We're off to the south of France in three days' time for two weeks and Marcus is already in Tuscany with his family. I suppose we'll just have to hope that those young Czechs can cope for the time being, because I can't see us being able to do anything until after the summer holidays."

Claire was so relieved that she started to speak without giving it any thought. "Well, I suppose we could—" She stopped, suddenly realizing the complete idiocy of what she was about to suggest.

"You could what?"

"I'd have to speak to Art, but I suppose we could go over to Scotland for a bit to look after Leo."

"Really? But what about your tea room?"

Claire grimaced at Charity's derogatory remark. She wasn't even going to bother to explain that Barrington's was listed as one of the top restaurants in downtown Manhattan. Charity knew this only too well. "I'm sure we can find someone else to make the tea," she replied acidly.

"Well, if you're sure, that would be most helpful."

Most helpful? Claire thought to herself. Who on earth does Charity think she is? She sounds positively regal. "As I said, it depends if Art thinks we can."

"Of course." There was another of Charity's inevitable sighs. "Well, I suppose I'd better try to call the hospital to find out how he is. You wouldn't happen to know which one it is?"

"Stirling."

"Oh God, these provincial places. I hope he doesn't pick up one of those ghastly hospital bugs. That would just be the crowning glory, wouldn't it? Could you give me the telephone number?"

Claire gritted her teeth. "No, I haven't got it, but I'm sure you'll get it through directory enquiries."

Yet another sigh and Claire felt like coming out with the old adage about one more drop of blood. "Just another thing to do. I'll say goodbye, then."

"Have a good holiday," Claire trilled merrily before replacing the receiver. "And good riddance to you too." With a sigh of relief, she walked over to Violet and planted a kiss on the top of her head. "So, what have we found out about Charlotte the spider, then?"

Art poured out two glasses of red wine and handed one to Claire. "Wow," he said, sitting down heavily on a kitchen chair and putting his hands on his head. He looked tired and red-eyed, the consequence of having been holed up in the office at the restaurant with the accountant all day, staring at the computer screen. "That was a bit impulsive of you."

Claire took a sip of wine and sat down next to him. "I know, it was just that Charity seemed so unconcerned about Leo, and what with her and Marcus trying to move him into a home, I felt Leo needed a bit of loving care and support from, well, a member of the family." She paused, leaning her elbows on the table and running a finger round the rim of her wine glass. "I suppose guilt played its part as well. I haven't seen him since my mother died and that was nearly two years ago."

Art leaned back in his chair, stretching out his long legs. "So how long do the English summer holidays go on for?"

"All their children are at private schools, so it'll be early September."

He nodded slowly. "And if they move Leo into a residence at that point, they'll no doubt put the house straight on the market."

Claire shrugged. "I'd say that's a fair assumption. I'm sure neither of them will have changed their minds about living in the south." She leaned across the table and put her hand on his. "I'm sorry, I shouldn't have opened my big mouth. It's just that . . ."

"No, I'd have said the same thing under the circumstances." He clenched her hand reassuringly. "Funny thing is the accountant was saying today that he thought we should be considering further expansion, not where we are right now but further uptown."

Claire was astonished. "Is it really going that well?"

Art smiled. "Looks to be." He let go of Claire's hand and folded his arms. "So maybe this would be an opportune time to get moving with this conference-centre idea."

Claire's eyes brightened. "Are you saying we should go to Scotland?"

He nodded decisively. "Yeah, let's do it. Luisa's more than capable of running Barrington's without us, and dammit, we haven't had a family holiday for God knows how long."

Jumping to her feet, Claire went and put her arms around his neck and gave him a smacking kiss on his forehead. "Thank you, I really do appreciate this."

He laughed. "Hey, this is for myself as well, you know," he said, "because I'm sure as hell taking my golf clubs with me this time!"

25

Alloa—July 2006

Liv Fairweather glanced at the clock as she entered the kitchen. It was just coming up to 9:00 A.M. She walked over to the wide window and leaned on the sink as she looked out at the steady stream of young Eastern European students walking across the courtyard on their way to the polytunnels out in the fields. The strawberry picking being at its peak, Jonas had them working on three separate shifts, and he had already been out of the house for the past three hours to oversee a changeover.

One of the boys caught Liv's eye and smiled, nudging the elbow of his friend, who spun his head round and grinned at her. That happened to Liv quite often, not only here on the farm, but everywhere she went. Even though it had been ten years since she had worked as a fashion model, she had not lost her front-page looks, and the sight of her tall slender figure striding along a street with her long blonde hair flowing still caused men to turn their heads.

Giving the two boys a friendly wave, she turned away from the window and prised a mobile phone from the back pocket of her skin-tight jeans. She keyed in a number and held it to her ear. "Hey, Rory, not so much sugar," she said in a gentle lilting voice to the young boy who was seated at the table. He quickly emptied the spoon onto his cornflakes and smiled wickedly at her, his blue eyes twinkling beneath his straight blonde fringe.

Liv admonished him with a shake of her head just as her call was answered. "Hi, where are you?"

She laughed and turned to find her husband waving at her through the kitchen window, his mobile held to his ear. "Well, in that case, I'll say goodbye then," she said, blowing him a kiss.

She poured out a cup of black coffee from the pot that was sitting on the Aga and walked over to the back door, timing it perfectly as Jonas entered. She handed it to him and gave him a kiss on the cheek. "Is everything going well?"

"Fine," Jonas replied, ruffling his son's hair as he walked round the table and sat down at the head. The weather had been warm for the past week, both day and night, so he wore nothing other than a T-shirt and a pair of jeans. "Ivan didn't turn up for work, so I had to load the lorry. That's why I'm a bit late."

"Is he all right?"

"A dose of the flu, according to Paul. Hopefully a day in bed will see him better."

Every year, more than a hundred and fifty students made their way across Europe by train, bus or battered motorcar to endure the long working shifts on the farm, eager to bolster their finances before starting back at university after the summer break. Ninety per cent of them turned out to be new faces, and it always amazed Liv that Jonas seemed to know each by name almost within the first week.

"Are you going to be around today, then?" Liv asked.

"I'm not going to the dealership, if that's what you mean. Why do you ask?"

"I thought I might take Asrun to Edinburgh. There's an exhibition of antique dolls on at one of the galleries."

"Where is she?" Jonas asked.

"Still lying in bed," Rory replied through a mouthful of cornflakes.

"Well, then, she'd better get her skates on, hadn't she?" Jonas said, peering at his son.

"So, would you be able to look after Rory?" Liv asked.

"What? You don't want to go to see the dollies?" Jonas asked his ten-year-old son, a teasing smile on his face.

"No way!" Rory replied forcefully.

Jonas nodded his agreement. "All right, you're with me for the day, then. I'm heading over to the Dragon Plant, so you can go and give Pavel a hand in the garden. He'll be wanting to get it looking good for Leo coming back."

"Is it today he's coming out of hospital?" Liv asked.

"Yes, should be home by lunchtime. I want to be around when the ambulance arrives, just in case I'm needed to lend a hand."

"I hope Pavel and Gabriela will be able to cope with him."

"They'll do fine. Anyway, Leo's step-daughter and her family will be arriving the day after tomorrow, so there'll be enough hands on deck after that."

Liv smiled knowingly at her husband. "Ah yes, that would be your old girlfriend, would it not?" She laughed. "Maybe you'll be going over to the house quite a lot during the next few weeks."

Jonas did not rise to his wife's light-hearted taunt, his face remaining serious. "I don't think so. I'll get Leo's correspondence cleared today so I won't need to bother them while they're there."

Liv shook her head. "It all happened so long ago. Why not take this as an opportunity to sort it all out?"

Jonas drained his cup of coffee and got to his feet. "Oh, I'll do just that one of these days, but only when I feel the time is right."

He gave his wife a kiss before putting his hands lightly round his son's neck, pretending to throttle him. "Are you ready for a bit of physical labour then, my lad?"

"If you could bring him in here, that'd be grand," Jonas said as he walked into the sitting room in front of the paramedic who was pushing Leo in the wheelchair. The room was like a furnace, Agnes having taken it upon herself to put light to a roaring fire, despite the sultry heat of the day. Jonas pushed the wide stool that stood in front of the fire over to Leo's chair and then helped the paramedic to transfer him over.

"Look after yourself, then," the man bellowed loudly into his patient's ear as he left with the wheelchair. Leo winced sharply in reaction to it.

"Thank you for your help," Jonas said before turning to the young Czech girl who was standing by the door. "Could you see him out, Gabriela?"

As soon as they had left, Leo looked up at Jonas with tired eyes and shook his head slowly. "Thank goodness I'm back. I thought I'd go mad in that hospital. Everyone treated me like a bloody imbecile."

"So how're you feeling?" Jonas asked, sitting down on the sofa next to him.

"A bit groggy, a bit sore—and a bit old, to be quite honest."

"You've gone through the mill."

Leo grimaced as he took hold of the leg that was resting on the stool and moved it a fraction. "Stupid thing to do. I don't know what I was thinking about."

"Best to forget that and concentrate on getting better."

Leo nodded. "You're probably right." He smiled at Jonas. "So, did you give the Humber a run while I was away like I asked you?"

"Of course I did," Jonas replied without a moment's hesitation. It saddened him to see Leo as he was now, grey-faced and wizened, a shadow of the man he had come to admire so much in his youth. But what ate away at him was the steady mental decline the old man was being made to suffer. Jonas himself had taken the Humber on its final journey to the car breakers' over fifteen years ago, but what was the point in telling him that? Going along with what he said was so much easier—and kinder. "She's going like a dream," he continued. "There's a lot of life left yet in that old girl."

"Of course there is." He glanced wearily around the room, as if searching out some-one or something.

Jonas followed his eyes. "What are you looking for?" he asked.

"Where's Claire?"

This time Jonas paused. It was that association of bygone memories again. Himself, the Humber, and now Claire. The old boy was way back in Dragon Plant House days. Maybe that was the upside of dementia, being able to live in one's own private world of happier times.

Even now, Jonas still often thought of Claire. From the outset, their friendship would seem to be mismatched, the farm boy and the London girl, yet it had been totally natural and sustained over the years through a mixture of strong character and pure innocence. At school, they were as open about their fondness for each other as they were at home, yet they were never subjected to stigmatic accusations about "walking out together." Everyone just knew them as being inseparable friends. And he still missed her, not as a deep, near-forgotten

memory, but one that was too easily ac-
cessed in the forefront of his mind. Of course
he had told Liv all about Claire, but he certainly wouldn't tell her about that, nor the
true reason why their friendship had come
to such an abrupt end.

"Claire's not here just now, Leo," he said
gently to the old man. "She's living in
America."

"Oh, I know that, but she's coming to
see me."

Jonas smiled and shook his head. Confusion was then followed by that moment
of perfect clarity, completely unscheduled
and unforeseen. "Yes, you're right, she's
arriving in two days."

Leo pointed a shaky finger in the general direction of the dark-wooded bureau
in the corner of the room. "There's a list
over there somewhere."

Jonas got to his feet and walked over towards the desk. "Do you know where it is?"
He turned when there was no answer. Leo
had dropped his hand limply onto his lap
and was staring fixedly at the fire. "Leo?"

The old man turned round slowly. "Sorry,
what?"

"Do you know where the list is?"

Leo closed his eyes tight and rubbed a shaky hand against his wrinkled forehead. "List?" he said quietly.

"Don't worry," Jonas replied and began opening the drawers of the bureau.

Five minutes later, concealed amongst a pile of horticultural press cuttings in one of the cubbyholes, he found an envelope with his own name written on it in Leo's spidery handwriting. He took it back to him. "Here you . . ."

The old man had fallen fast asleep in his chair, snoring quietly with his mouth open. Jonas tapped the edge of the envelope on the palm of his hand before slipping it into the back pocket of his jeans and leaving the room. He walked across the hall to the kitchen door and put his head round the side. Gabriela was standing pummeling bread dough on the table, her arms white with flour right up to her elbows.

"Is Agnes not about?"

"No, she will be back soon. Went to get some tomatoes from Pavel."

"Right. In that case, can you leave what you're doing and go and sit with Leo?"

"It's no problem," the girl replied,

hastily wiping her floury arms with a dish towel.

"And he shouldn't be left alone at any time, right? Either Agnes, you or Pavel have to be with him."

"It's no problem," Gabriela said again as she walked past him towards the door of the sitting room.

Having been in the toasting confines of the sitting room for the past quarter of an hour, Jonas found his bare arms rising in goosebumps from the cold even before he reached the bottom of the spiral stone steps that descended at the rear of the house. He walked along the basement corridor, its subterranean length lit only by weak shafts of light coming through two small grimy windows that faced out onto the cobbled courtyard. It was where he always parked his car when he came to see Leo. He had a key for the lower back door, so it meant he could let himself in and see to Leo's affairs in the office without disturbing anyone in the house.

He had been doing this for Leo for over a year now, from the time when he first started showing signs of dementia. It had all come about when Leo had asked him if he could recommend a good accountant because his books were in need of "a good seeing to." He had shown Jonas to the office in the basement, but he did not enter himself, and the way he scuttled back along the corridor and up the stairs made Jonas wonder if the room didn't contain some dark secret of which Leo was terrified. He had to open the door by force, it being held fast by some form of resistance, and on entering the room he realized immediately that it was not an accountant Leo required, but more a waste-paper lorry. It would have taken the felling of a small forest to supply the amount of paper that filled the place. It was impossible to see the surface of the desk for old newspapers, magazines and junk mail, these being liberally interspersed with unopened envelopes that turned out to contain long-overdue bills, unread bank statements and stock reports. The tops of the two filing cabinets were heaped almost up to the damp paint-stripped ceiling with yellowing A4 sheets that curled at the edges, and the two drawers that were open had been left so because Leo's haphazard filing system had deemed them impossible to shut.

It took Jonas the best part of two weeks to get the place sorted out, and the massive bonfire that had kept alight for days at the far side of the courtyard was still glowing hot when he slid shut the cabinet drawer for the final time and clamped the last piece of paper into its designated Arcadia file before placing it on the shelf alongside twenty others. Jonas knew there was no point in asking Leo if he should continue doing this for him. There was just no alternative.

Jonas entered the office and saw that the pile of envelopes Pavel had stacked neatly on the desk was not big. He flicked on the switch of the small electric heater and then began discarding the obvious flyers straight into the waste-paper basket. Sitting at the desk, he took his mobile from his pocket and sent a text message to his farm foreman saying that he would be back within the hour. That was ample time to clear Leo's desk and collect Rory from wherever he was working in the garden with Pavel. Reaching across the desk, he took Leo's silver letter knife from the pen stand, picked up the first envelope and slit it open. It was a bill from the newsagent. He put it into the red wire tray and opened the next. This one was a bank statement. He put it to the right-hand side of the desk, ready for filing away later, and picked up the next envelope. He stopped, put down the envelope and reached across for the bank statement again and studied it, frowning as he did so. He got up from the desk and walked over to the shelf and took down one of the Arcadia files. He laid it on the desk and undid the spring holder and began leafing through the past statements.

"What the hell . . . ?" he muttered under his breath.

Returning to the desk, he began going through the envelopes, picking out four that were of the size he was looking for. He opened each and glanced through them, and then again went back to the shelf and took down the four corresponding files. He thumbed through the pages in turn, comparing them with those he held in his hand. He dropped them on the desk, almost as if they were burning coals, and stood back, pulling a hand across his head, his eyes darting from the sheets of paper to the files.

He blew out a long breath. "Well, well, what do we have here?" he said out loud.

He walked round the desk and flumped down into the chair and sat staring straight ahead at the bare wall, every now and again twitching his eyes as if comprehension of what he had just seen was way beyond his reach. And then a moment of lucidity, an association of a name, and he leaned to the side and took from his back pocket the letter that Leo had told him to fetch from the bureau. Without bothering to use the knife, he ripped open the envelope, took out the letter and began to read. It was no more than a list, written haphazardly and quite lacking in any sense or form, but Jonas understood everything that Leo was trying to convey. As he went through it for a second time, he pulled a pad of paper towards him, took a ballpoint pen from the stand and began to write, his thoughts coming from what he had just seen and what he had just read.

When he did eventually arrive back at the farm with Rory, it was two hours later than his estimated time.

26

Leo woke in his chair with a start, feeling the gentle pressure of a hand on his. For a moment, he stared bleary-eyed and disorientated towards the unlit fire before turning his head to see the dark-haired woman sitting next to him on the adjacent sofa, silhouetted against the glare of the late-morning sun coming through the window. "Gabriela," he said, smiling at her, "how are you, my dear?"

"It's not Gabriela, Leo," the woman replied. "It's me, Claire."

Leo screwed up his eyes. "Claire. You live in America."

"You're right, I do, but I've come over to see you, to look after you."

Leo put his other hand on top of Claire's and gave it a pat. "How nice."

"And Art and Violet are here as well. We're going to spend our summer holiday with you."

"Oh, that's nice," he replied distantly. "I do hope the weather turns for the better, then. We've had a lot of rain lately."

Claire smiled sadly at him. The sun was not only shining brightly in a cloudless sky but on their arrival ten minutes before, she had noticed that the lawn at the front of the house had begun to turn yellow through lack of water.

"I'm sure it'll be fine." She gave his hand a loving squeeze. "So, how are you feeling?"

"Oh, not so bad," he said, grabbing at the trouser leg that was stretched out on the stool, "except I did a stupid thing and fell down the stairs."

"I know all about that."

"Broke my hip, you know. Had to have an operation."

"Yes, I know."

He turned and frowned questioningly at

her. "Have you been out to the greenhouse today?"

"Not yet. We've only just arrived."

"Ah well, you should. The plants are looking wonderful. That Jonas lad is doing a very good job."

Claire bit at her bottom lip. "Is he?"

"He knows a lot about gardening, you know. Used to work in the parks in Prague."

"Ah, you must be talking about Pavel."

Leo nodded. "Yes, that's the boy. Very good indeed."

The door of the sitting room opened and Art walked in. Claire smiled up at him. "Here's Art come to see you."

Art placed his hand on Leo's shoulder as he came round his chair to stand in front of him. "Hi there, Leo, sorry to hear you've been in the wars."

The old man looked up at him with little recognition in his eyes. "Not so bad, not so bad."

"Is Violet all right?" Claire asked her husband.

"She's fine. Gabriela took her out to the garden to meet Pavel." He turned his attention back to the old man. "So, here we all are, Leo, over from the States to find out how you're doing and see if we can't do something about this house."

Leo dropped his eyes to his lap and began fiddling with his thumbs. "I'm not going into a home. I'm staying here."

Art sat down on the edge of the stool on which Leo rested his leg. "Of course you're staying here," he said, reaching forward to give Leo's clenched hands a reassuring pat. "That was always our plan, don't you remember?"

"My children want me to move into a home," Leo grumbled moodily into his chest. "They're going to sell the house because none of them want to live here."

"You don't need to worry about that, my friend," Art said. "This is your place and Claire and I are going to make sure you stay here as long as you want."

Although there seemed to be little understanding on Leo's part of what was being said to him, Art continued to talk in a quiet, gentle manner, telling him about their trip over from the States and how Violet had stayed awake most of the journey, reckoning that she must have watched three full-length feature films on the way. Claire moved over to the unlit fireplace and

leaned her shoulder against the mantelpiece. She smiled as she watched Art,
with his long legs bent up as awkward as
a giraffe, coaxing a brief spark of remembrance from Leo, resulting in a momentary
brightness in his eyes. In that instance,
she felt a sudden burst of love for her husband that coursed through her body like
liquid gold. Not for the first time she re-
flected on the fact that she truly had been
blessed to have walked into Barrington's
Restaurant on that cold February night
sixteen years ago. She had never told him
about her past, and he had never ques-
tioned her about it, so it was simply his
kindness, his humour and his complete
adoration of her that had healed over those
raw wounds of devastation and male distrust that had lain festering deep within her
at that time. She hadn't fallen in love with
him immediately. There had never been
the sparks and the stars and the rainbows
floating around her head, making her
dizzy with infatuation. That had happened
once before and it had led to nothing. But
eventually, there had come about the realization that Art was her best friend, her
confidant, her world, and that she was

deeply in love with him. And that feeling had remained to this day.

She turned and looked out of the window at the far end of the sitting room, seeing the long side lawn and the trees beyond it that hid from view the track that led down to the farm. She had always loved coming back to the Dragon Plant House with Art and Violet, but a two-week holiday had always been long enough. Here she had never felt that she owned her own life. She had left the place forever at a deeply unhappy time, and the association of just being there formed too strong a bridge with the past. And this time, not only were they to be spending longer, but Jonas was back, just along that hidden track.

Art pushed himself to his feet and walked over to her. "Listen, do you mind if I head off? I have a meeting with John Venables in half an hour."

"Already?" Claire said in amazement. "We've only just arrived."

He leaned forward and planted a kiss on her cheek. "I know, but he's going to be away all tomorrow, and I need to find out if anything has changed with the plans for

the house"—he lowered his voice—
"considering Leo's state of health."

"Are you going off?"

Both Art and Claire turned with surprise
to Leo, who had put the question.

"Yes, I am, Leo," Art replied. "I have to
go see someone, but I'll be back real
soon."

"Before you go then," Leo said, pointing
at the bureau desk that stood at the far
side of the mantelpiece, "have a look in
there. I've left a list for you."

Art glanced round at the bureau and
then at Claire, raising his eyebrows hopefully at Leo's sudden recollection. He
walked over to the bureau and pulled the
lid open. Nothing immediately came to
hand, so he began to sift through the papers that were pushed into the cubbyholes. After a couple of minutes of
searching, he closed the desk and walked
back to Claire.

"Nothing there," he said quietly, giving
her arm a squeeze. "I'd better head off."

"Did you find it?" Leo asked as Art
walked round behind his chair.

Art patted him on the shoulder. "No,
Leo, I'm afraid not."

"Oh, that's strange," Leo said, scratching at his forehead. "It was there. Maybe Pavel took it."

"Okay, I'll ask him," Art replied as he opened the door.

"Or it could have been Jonas."

Art stopped in the doorway and glanced back at Claire. She made a circular motion with her two forefingers to signify that Leo was mixing up the two names. Art ackowledged this with a nod and left the room.

"Yes, I think it was probably Jonas," Leo said as Claire sat down on the sofa next to him.

"Or Gabriela?" she asked.

Leo smiled at her. "She's a very good cook, you know. Makes the most wonderful bread." He licked his lips and turned to pick up the glass of water on the table beside him and put it to his mouth. Claire could see that there was nothing in it.

"Do you want me to fill that for you, darling?" she asked.

Leo held out the glass in front of him and studied it before handing it to her. "Could you? That would be very kind. It's only water."

"All right," she said, getting to her feet. "I'll be back in a moment."

When Claire entered the kitchen, Gabriela was standing at the table peeling potatoes and chatting to the small white-haired woman who sat opposite her laboriously cutting the ends off a basketful of French beans. It was the first time Claire had seen Agnes since she arrived. She caught Gabriela's eye and held a finger to her lips, and creeping up behind the old housekeeper, she covered Agnes's eyes with her hand.

"Oh, michty me!" Agnes cried out in surprise.

"Guess who?"

Claire took her hand away and Agnes slowly turned her head to look at her. "Oh, my word, it's the wee girl herself." She got slowly to her feet and put her arms out to Claire, tears already welling up in her pale blue eyes. "Come on, let's be havin' you, then."

Claire bent forward, feeling the feeble grasp on her arms and the bristly mouth land a loud kiss on her cheek. Agnes took a step back and looked her up and down.

"Oh, you're lookin' fine, so you are, and puttin' on a bit of weight too."

Claire gasped and glanced across at Gabriela, who had covered her mouth to stifle a giggle.

"That's not a very good thing to say, Agnes," Gabriela said.

"Oh, you just hush yerself, young 'un," Agnes replied in admonishment. "I've known this lass since she was knee-high. I can say what I like to her." She reached up and lightly pinched Claire's cheek. "Isn't that so, my dear?"

"It appears so," Claire said with a laugh.

"So how's life been treatin' you in America?" Agnes asked, sitting down at the table and resuming her work.

"It's good."

"And that restaurant of yours?"

"That's going well too."

"Aye, but you're workin' way too hard, I can tell that. Just like your mother."

"What makes you say that?"

"You only had time to produce one bairn, both of you. That's a good-enough sign for me."

Claire smiled. "You could be right, Agnes."

"Aye, but she's a fair cracker, that wee daughter of yours, the spittin' image of yourself at that age." She threw a bean into the pot and turned to look at Claire, a sad expression on her face. "So how did you find your stepfather?"

Claire toyed with the empty glass in her hand. "He's . . . changed a lot."

"Aye, you'll be seeing the difference. It's never a good thing, losing your mind, and that operation has fair taken the sense out of him, but you wait and see, there'll be times when he's his old self, remembering things and all." She smiled at Gabriela. "That's when he writes his lists for us, isn't it, dear?"

Gabriela wiped her hands on her apron and came round the table. "Would you like me to fill that for you?" she asked, putting out a hand for the glass.

Claire handed it to her. "Thank you," she said, following the girl over to the sink. "Gabriela, Leo has just mentioned one of those lists. He said he'd put it in the desk in the sitting room for Art and me. Do you know anything about it?"

Gabriela shook her head. "Maybe Pavel will know. He puts all papers in Leo's office down the stairs." She gave Claire the full glass of water. "Maybe Jonas has seen it too."

Claire stared at her. "Jonas? Why would he have seen it?"

"Because he does much work for Leo in the office."

"When was he last here?"

"This morning, before you arrived. He comes every day since Leo has returned from hospital."

"Would he have been into the sitting room?"

"Of course he would," Agnes piped up. "He spends as much time as he can with Leo, chatting away with him. Jonas is awful patient that way." She stopped her cutting and sat back in her chair, fixing her eyes on a point above the kitchen cupboards. "Aye, I remember the two of you were almost inseparable back in the old days, always in and out of that greenhouse or playing on the lawn out there. And then when you were a bit older, you'd be over at his dad's farm, mucking about with those old cars of his." She looked round at Claire, a twinkle in her rheumy eyes. "I always had the notion the two of you might take it a bit further, but that wasn't to be, was it?"

Claire darted a look between Agnes and Gabriela. She had been no more than one hour in the house and already that bridge with the past had been reopened. She forced a smile onto her face. "I think I'd better take this back to Leo," she said, holding up the glass.

"You do that, dear. He'll be needing his water. It's all those tablets he's having to get down him. Makes his mouth awful dry."

Agnes followed Claire with her eyes as she left the kitchen and then turned with a sigh and continued to cut the beans. Gabriela pulled out the chair opposite Agnes and sat down. She pushed a strand of dark hair away from her eyes before leaning on the table and cupping her face in her hand. There was intrigue in her eyes as she stared fixedly at the housekeeper.

"What are you lookin' at, young 'un?" Agnes asked.

"I want you to tell me about Jonas and Claire. Were they going out together?"

"Never you mind," Agnes replied, concentrating on her task.

"Oh, please, Agnes, I would really like to know."

Agnes dropped her knife on the table and heaved out a resigned breath. "I don't suppose you'll be getting on with your work until I've told you."

Gabriela smiled and shook her head.

"I thought not." The housekeeper paused for a moment, rubbing her hands on a dish towel. "Och well, I don't suppose it can do any harm."

27

Violet was beginning to feel really bored and showed it by digging carelessly at one of the small plants that Pavel had asked her to transplant into flowerpots. She thought there would have been a bit of excitement in the house after their long overnight journey from New York, but everyone had greeted them with sombre faces and hushed voices and she felt it had been rather like walking into a church. And then, almost as soon as they had got their suitcases in the door, her father had suggested that she go with Pavel to the greenhouse because he had some business to attend to and her mother had to have a bit of peace and quiet with Leo. She hadn't been in the house since she was about four years old and she would much rather have been allowed to run around and find where everything was again, but instead she had to go out to the greenhouse with this funny-looking man with long hair and little round spectacles she had never met before. And now she was wondering if every day of their holidays was going to be like this, with her father having to work and her mother going off to have peace and quiet with Leo. That would mean she would have to entertain herself, just as it always was when her parents had to work all the time at the restaurant.

"You be more gentle with it, yes?"

She turned to find Pavel standing beside her. He put down his watering can on the ground and took the trowel from her hand.

"You need to start far from the roots, like this." He pushed the trowel in around the plant and levered it out of the soft dark earth. "There, it comes out easy that way, no?"

Violet rubbed her hands together to get

rid of the loose dirt. "Did you know a lot about gardening before you came here?"

"Of course," Pavel replied, placing the plant into one of the plastic pots lined up on the raised flower bed. "It is my job when I leave school."

"Did you work in a garden like this one?"

"No, not a private one, but very special. It is the oldest garden in Prague."

"What's it called?"

"Vojanovy Sady."

Violet screwed up her face. "That sounds like you're talking nonsense."

"That is because you do not understand the Czech language"—he laughed—"like sometimes I do not understand your language."

Violet shrugged. "You speak it okay. Maybe not as good as Gabriela."

"Ah, but that is because she study English at university. She is more clever than me."

"I bet she doesn't know as much about plants as you do."

Pavel looked up from his work and smiled at her. "Thank you, that is a kind thing to say."

Violet watched as he began digging

around the next plant. "Are you and Gabriela dating?"

Pavel frowned. "Okay, so what is the word, dating?"

"It means you're going out together, that she's your girlfriend."

"Ah, in that case, I answer yes. We are dating for two years now."

"And are you going to live in Scotland forever?"

"No, in the middle of September, we go home. Gabriela returns to her university." Finishing off the last pot, he dug the trowel into the earth and leaned against the edge of the raised flower bed, crossing his arms. "And you, how long here?"

Violet turned down the corners of her mouth and shrugged. "Not sure. Probably until September as well."

Pavel smiled. "You are not very happy about this. You are not liking Scotland?"

"It's okay."

"You have many friends here?"

Violet shook her head.

Pavel winked at her. "Okay, so Gabriela and I make sure you have fine time." He picked up the watering can and began filling it up at the tap. "We go to the garden centre after we have lunch. You like to come too?"

"Okay," she replied with little enthusiasm.

There was a thumping noise at the far end of the greenhouse and both Violet and Pavel turned to see the warped door fly open. A young boy with blonde hair entered and pushed the door closed, and then stood on the central path watching them. He was dressed in a T-shirt and shorts, his hands thrust into his pockets, and Violet's first thought was that he must spend a lot of time outside because his face, arms and legs were very brown.

Pavel waved a hand at the boy. "Hey, Rory, how are you?"

"Good," he replied, nonchalantly brushing a hand against the leaves of the plants as he approached them.

"Your father is here?" Pavel asked as he liberally watered the four growbags of tomato plants.

"Yes, in the office," Rory replied quietly.

Pavel put down the watering can. "So, Rory, this is Violet. She arrives today and is here to September."

Rory nodded a shy greeting at Violet.

"She is the granddaughter of Leo," Pavel continued, smiling to himself at their obvious awkwardness.

"Actually, I am his stepgranddaughter."

"Oh?" Pavel said with a frown. "What is this?"

Violet wished she hadn't been so clever in saying that. She bit at a fingernail as she thought how to explain.

"It means that her grandmother must have married Leo and she'd had a child before that," Rory said confidently.

Pavel nodded. "I understand. And your mother is that child."

Violet nodded and beamed a smile at Rory for helping her out.

"So your mother, who is Claire, is the . . . stepdaughter of Leo, right?"

"Yes," Violet replied.

Pavel looked pleased with himself. "That is great, then," he said. "Another few English words for me." He picked up the tray of plants that he and Violet had just finished potting. "How long is your father in the office, Rory?"

"Only about half an hour," the boy replied. "We have to be home for lunch."

"You have time to plant this in the border by the wood?"

"Sure," Rory said, taking the tray.

"Good, I can do more things, then," Pavel replied, pulling the trowel out of the flower bed and handing it to Violet. "And maybe she goes with you? It is quicker when you are helped."

There was no verbal agreement to this, the two just turning and walking back down the path towards the door.

"And do not plant too close together, okay?" Pavel called after them, a contented smile on his face.

Rory put the tray down on the grass at the edge of the border and took the trowel from Violet's grasp. "I'll do the digging and you can plant." He knelt down and thrust the trowel into the earth.

"Do you live around here?" Violet asked as she watched him work.

"At the farm."

"Where is that?"

Rory pointed the trowel towards the high wall that ran the length of one side of the garden. "Over there." He continued digging. "You're from America, aren't you?"

"Yeah, New York."

"I thought so from your accent."

He started on another hole and Violet took this as her cue to start planting. She took one of the pots out of the tray, carefully extracted the plant and put it in the hole, pressing the earth in around it. "How old are you?" she asked.

"Ten," Rory replied, removing a large stone from the new hole and throwing it with force deep into the wood beyond the border. "You?"

"Nine." She didn't say that her birthday had only been the previous month in the hope that Rory might think they were much closer in age. She knelt down beside him so that she could plant as soon as he had finished digging. "Do you have brothers and sisters?"

"A six-year-old sister. What about you?"

"No, it's just me. What is your sister called?"

"Asrun."

Violet thought he said it in rather a funny way. "That sounds foreign."

"It's Swedish. My mother's from Sweden."

"Can you speak Swedish?"

"A bit, but not very well." He watched Violet press in one of the plants. "That's too deep. You're covering the bottom leaves." He dug it up and pushed earth into the hole with the back of the trowel before replanting it. "My dad knows your mother," he said, fixing her with his pale blue eyes.

"Who's your dad?"

"Jonas Fairweather."

Violet shook her head. "I don't think I know him."

Rory laughed. "Why should you? You live in New York."

"I've been here before, though," Violet replied indignantly. "I could have met him then."

"Yeah, maybe," Rory said, shuffling farther across the flower bed on his knees. "Do you know what my dad and your mum used to call this place?"

"No."

"The Dragon Plant House."

"Why?"

"Because Leo grew hundreds of dragon plants in his greenhouse. When they were young, they both used to go and help him there."

"Who told you this?"

"Leo did. Me and my sister helped him too until he got ill. We always call it the Dragon Plant House as well."

Violet looked perplexed. "Did your dad and my mom know each other very well, then?"

"Seems so. My mum calls her his old girlfriend, but I don't think they get on well now."

"Why do you think that?"

"Because I heard Dad say he was not going to see your mum when she was here, and my mum said that it all happened a long time ago and he should sort it out now."

Violet held the last plant in her hand, pulling at the earth on its roots. "Have you asked your father about it?"

"No."

"Should I ask my mother?"

"If you want." Noticing that the roots of the plant Violet was holding were almost bare of earth, he took it from her and placed it in the hole and covered it over. "That's it done, then."

They both got to their feet and Rory brushed the dirt off his bare knees with his hands. They surveyed their work in silence, standing awkwardly apart, Rory swinging the trowel in his fingers like a pendulum. He glanced across at Violet. "Dad put up a cool rope swing for us in the wood. If you want, Asrun and I could meet you there after lunch and you could try it out."

Violet thought that it sounded exactly what she wanted to do. "I can't," she replied dejectedly, "I'm going with Pavel and Gabriela to a garden centre."

"That's not very far away, so you won't be the whole afternoon. We could meet you at the swing later."

"Where is it?"

Rory pointed towards the drive. "There's a track just over there that leads through the wood, and at the end of it, there's a gate. The swing's just beside that. We could meet you by the gate at four o'clock."

"All right. I don't have a watch, though."

"Well, ask Pavel the time or look at the clock in the kitchen. It's above the cooker."

Violet now wished she hadn't said she didn't have a watch. She did have one but it got broken and now it was as if she was really stupid and childish and couldn't tell the time. And she knew that there was a clock in the kitchen. She had seen it there that morning.

A shrill whistle sounded out from the far side of the lawn and they both turned simultaneously to see a tall dark-haired man standing at the corner of the house. He waved a hand at them.

"That's Dad," Rory said. "I'd better get going." He handed Violet the trowel. "Can you put that and the tray back in the greenhouse?"

"Sure."

"See you at four, then," he said before running across the lawn.

As Violet began ambling slowly back to the house, she glanced up at the kitchen window and saw Agnes's little white head looking out at her. When the housekeeper waved, Violet broke into a run, taking this as a sign that lunch was ready.

Inside the kitchen, Agnes turned away from the window. "Oh my word, now that could put the cat amongst the pigeons," she said quietly to herself.

"What did you say?" Gabriela asked, holding a wooden spoon poised over a bubbling pot on the cooker.

Agnes shook her head and smiled. "Nothing, lass."

Shadows cast out by one of the tall beech trees on the lawn were shading the late-evening sun from the front of the house as Claire opened wide the window in Violet's bedroom and pulled the heavy curtains together. She turned and moved in the half-light over to the bed where her daughter lay, looking up at the ceiling with thoughtful eyes. Claire sat on the edge of the bed and reached out to push the short dark hair away from Violet's forehead.

"You must be tired. You didn't get much sleep last night on the plane."

"I did a bit after I'd watched the movie."

"Well, you can have a good lie-in tomorrow. There's nothing to get up for."

Violet turned her head on the pillow to look at her mother, a faint smile on her face. Claire thought she understood its meaning.

"I'm sorry, darling, I rather deserted you today, didn't I?"

"That's okay."

"I just had to spend some time with Leo."

"I know."

"Maybe we could do something tomor-row afternoon."

Violet thought about this. She had al-ready made a plan for that time with Rory and Asrun. "Or in the morning?"

Claire sighed. "That's a bit difficult, dar-ling. Pavel and Gabriela are going to the supermarket and I said I'd stay here to keep an eye on Leo."

Violet nodded. "Maybe I'll do something with Daddy then."

"We'll see. It depends if he's working or not."

"I thought he was coming here for a holiday. Why is he working?"

"He's having to meet lots of people, be-cause he's trying to see if it's possible to turn this place into a conference centre."

"What? The Dragon Plant House?"

Claire stared open-mouthed at her daughter. "Where did you hear that from?"

Violet smiled and sat up, her eyes los-ing all signs of tiredness. "Mom, do you know a man called Jonas something-or-other?"

This felt like a double punch to Claire. "Yes, I do," she replied quietly.

"He was your friend when you were little, wasn't he?"

"He was."

"But something happened and you don't speak to him anymore."

Claire smoothed a hand across Violet's sheet. "Well, I have been living in America for a long time, darling, and there really hasn't been the opportunity to"— she paused, eyeing her daughter questioningly—"who's been telling you all this?"

"Rory. He's Jonas's son."

Claire nodded slowly. "Right, and where did you meet him?"

"He came into the greenhouse this morning and Pavel got us to do some planting for him in the garden, and then this afternoon, I went to meet him and his sister in the woods and we played on their rope swing. It's really cool, Mom, because you go right out over a ditch that's filled with water, and if you let go, then you are splattered!" She slapped her hands together to accentuate the force of body hitting water.

"That sounds like fun," Claire replied flatly.

"And I was going to meet them there

tomorrow afternoon . . . if that's okay with you?"

Claire hesitated momentarily before smiling at her daughter. "I don't see why not. We can do things together another time." She got to her feet. "Now, come on, time for sleep."

"I saw his father too," Violet said, avoiding her mother's attempt to make her lie down.

"Did you now? And where was he?" Claire tried to make her voice sound light and interested although, in truth, her mind was racing.

"By the house. I only saw him from a distance, but he looked really nice."

Claire leaned over and plumped up Violet's pillow. "How about some sleep now?"

Violet lay down but continued talking. "Rory's mum said to his dad that it all happened a long time ago and he should sort it out with you."

Claire kissed her daughter on the forehead. "There's nothing really to sort out, darling."

"Good, that means you can speak to him, doesn't it?" She looked up at her mother. "Will you?"

"Is it very important to you that I do?"

"Yes, it is. I really like Rory and Asrun and I want our families to be friends."

Claire shook her head, finding herself trapped by the youthful insistence of her daughter. "In that case, I will make a point of speaking to him."

"When?"

"When the opportunity arises, Violet," she said, walking over to the door and opening it. "Now go to sleep."

"Love you, Mom," Violet called out, her voice already muffled by the pillow.

"I love you too, darling."

Claire closed the door and walked over to the top of the stairs. She stopped and folded her arms and looked back at Violet's bedroom door. Her first reaction had been to tell Violet that she didn't want her to play with those children, but then that would be pointless. No, actually, it would have been stupidly selfish. It was difficult enough for her being an only child, as she herself knew only too well. Violet needed someone of her own age to play with, just as she had needed . . . Jonas.

Dammit, why did it still rankle so much just to think of his name? It had been so long ago. She didn't need this now. She was here for Leo, not to patch up the consequences of some silly childhood relationship.

She began walking down the stairs.

When the opportunity arises, she had said to Violet. She hoped it never would.

28

❧

Alloa—August 2006

Jonas ascended the back stairs quietly and stood in the hall, listening for any sound in the house. There was a low hum of voices coming from the kitchen, so he made his way over to the door and tentatively peered in, being ready to withdraw hastily if there was someone there he did not wish to see. He breathed out with relief when he saw that it was only Agnes and Gabriela, both sitting at the kitchen table with steaming mugs of tea in front of them. He gave a brief knock and entered.

Agnes turned her head stiffly to look at him. "Well, here's a stranger then. Where have you been hiding yourself away these past few weeks?"

"I've had a lot of work on. The strawberry picking's been non-stop because of this good weather, and there's always a flush of new cars going out of the showroom in August."

Agnes chucked back her head and glanced knowingly at Gabriela. "Aye, I'm sure those will be the reasons."

Jonas smiled thinly at the housekeeper. Agnes was no fool. She knew exactly why he had not been coming to the house, so he did not pursue her remark. "Is it just you two here?" he asked.

"Aye, you're safe enough, lad," Agnes replied with a small laugh, "the coast is clear. Art's away at the golf course this morning and Claire and Violet have taken themselves off to Edinburgh for the day." She eyed him knowingly. "But you'll no doubt be aware of that for yourself."

Jonas nodded. "Rory did say something about it."

"That's what I'd be thinking. The three of them are getting on well enough with each other, are they not?"

"Seems so."

"It's that good for the wee girl to have someone to play with. She'd be having a real scunner of a time if not."

"Why so?"

"Och, just because her father's away working or playing at his golf all the time and Claire's thinking she has to be with Leo every hour of the day."

"How is Leo?"

"He's doing fine, fair getting the hang of that wheelchair contraption of his, I would say."

Jonas smiled and leaned a shoulder against the doorpost. "And his mind?"

"Well, there seems to be real improvement on that front as well. The doctor has had him on some new tablets for the past couple of weeks and we're thinking he's quite a bit more on the ball." She glanced across at Gabriela. "Isn't that right, lass?"

The young Czech girl grinned at Jonas and nodded her agreement.

"Is he up and about?" Jonas asked.

"Aye, Gabriela has just taken a cup of coffee through to him in the sitting room."

"I might go and see him, then."

"You should do," Agnes replied. "He's been wondering where you've been."

When Jonas entered the sitting room, his eyes were automatically drawn to the chair in which Leo customarily sat. It was empty. He moved to one side of the room to avoid the blinding glare of the mid-morning sun and saw the old man by the window at the far end of the room. He was sitting in his wheelchair, hunched over the table, as if studying something with great scrutiny. Jonas approached him and Leo looked up when his shadow fell upon the large sheet of paper that was spread out on the table. A broad smile broke out on the old man's face.

"Jonas, dear boy, this is a nice surprise. How are you?"

"I'm well. More to the point, how about yourself?"

"Not so bad at all." He gestured to a chair. "Grab a seat."

Jonas pulled out the chair and sat down. "So, how's the hip doing?"

"Getting better all the time. The only drawback is that I get visited by this brutal woman physiotherapist every three days, who puts me through hell, and the bloody thing is agony after that. I'm beginning to think she's a closet sadist."

"Maybe it's a case of no pain, no gain."

Leo laughed. "Were those not the words of the Grand Inquisitor?"

Jonas smiled at the old man. It had been nearly three weeks since he had last seen him, and the change in his appearance was remarkable. His face seemed fuller, a healthy flush having replaced the pallor on his cheeks, and below the bushy eyebrows that were raised in expression his blue eyes once more sparkled with vitality. Even his dress was in keeping with the old Leo, a smart shirt and tie with a V-necked sweater worn beneath his tweed jacket. But what struck Jonas more than anything was the quite unexpected improvement in the alacrity of his mind, demonstrated by his last sharp retort.

Leo reached over and slapped a hand on Jonas's knee. "I've missed your visits, my boy. How's Liv and the children?"

"They're well."

"And I hear little Violet has been having a whale of a time with Rory and Asrun."

"They get on well. She's a nice kid."

Leo smiled. "Very much like her mother at that age, wouldn't you say?"

Jonas scratched a fingernail up and

down his cheek. "There are certainly simi-
larities." He wanted to halt that subject right
there and leaned forward on the table, di-
verting attention to the sheet of paper that
was spread out in front of Leo. It was an
architect's drawing of some large-scale development. "What's this you've got here?"

"It's Art Barrington's plans for the house.
He wants to turn it into a conference centre and, my word, what a huge undertaking it is." He began pointing to various
parts of the drawings. "This here, in the
eastern wing of the house, is the main
conference room, with two smaller ones
adjoining. There are partition walls that
can be opened up to merge it all into one
big space. And this here is the dining area,
with the kitchen behind, where the butler's
pantry and the old scullery are at present.
And then the hall is going to have a bar
and seating area in that corner where local businessmen can come for their lunchtime meetings. And this block here is going
to house a swimming pool and fitness
gym, and then outside, Art's got a small
nine-hole pitch and putt mapped out for
those who want to swing a golf club during
their leisure time." Leo scratched his cheek

thoughtfully. "I must say, some of the holes look dangerously close to the house. I think it might be advisable for Art to nego-tiate a maintenance contract with a local glazier!" He laughed, sitting back in his chair. "Rather impressive, don't you think?"

Jonas felt his face prickle with unease. Because of his recent workload, he had completely forgotten about these plans. He had initially learned about them from a note Leo had given him a month before when the old boy had returned from hospi-tal. Jonas craned his head round to have a closer look at the drawings. "So he's go-ing ahead with it after all, is he?"

Leo frowned at him. "Did you know about this?"

"Yes, you told me about it, but it had slipped my mind," Jonas replied as he studied the drawings.

Leo chuckled. "Well, it's very gratifying to know I'm not the only one who forgets things." He pored over the plan once more, pressing a finger on a small square half-way up the sheet. "The idea is they build a small house for me right there, on the site of the farthest greenhouse. Rather fun, don't you think?"

"Hmm," Jonas replied distantly, not really looking where Leo's finger was pointing, being more interested in the scale of the development that lay below the old man's arm. He studied particularly the new building that was to house the swimming pool and fitness gym, as it appeared to extend out to the north, almost to the point where his own property bounded with Leo's. He leaned back in his chair and stared out of the window, the old man's continued absorption in the plans giving him precious time to think.

It was on the day that Leo had given him the note that he had discovered those discrepancies in Leo's financial statements. He had immediately sat down and written a few cursory notes in formulation of a basic plan of action, but since then he had been so taken up with the farm and the car dealership, he hadn't a clue where they were or what he had written. But if there was ever a time to implement that plan, then this was it.

He had a good five minutes to get his brain in gear before Leo turned to him with a smile on his face.

"All very exciting, wouldn't you say?"

"Looks pretty impressive," Jonas replied. "You wouldn't happen to have any idea what the timescale is on this?"

Leo clasped his hands together. "Not sure on that account, but Art's got a meeting with the town hall this afternoon to show them his business plan. He's hoping that'll help get the project fast-tracked through the planning department."

"Have these drawings already been lodged?"

"I think that's happening today as well."

Jonas nodded. He hadn't expected it to be so far advanced.

"Leo, has anyone spoken to Marcus and Charity about all this?"

Leo's face became serious. "I wouldn't have thought so. They've all been swanning off on holidays abroad until quite recently."

"Well, if you don't mind me saying, as an executor of the estate, I think it would only be right for Art to contact Marcus to tell him about all this and to negotiate a price for the house. After all, they will be the main beneficiaries from the proceeds of the sale and they have already shown an interest in putting the place on the market."

Leo turned and stared sternly at Jonas. "I'm not quite sure why you're saying this, my boy. The house is still mine, you know."

Jonas held up his hands. "Believe me, Leo, I've only got your interests at heart. No matter who buys this property, you want to maximize your gain from the sale. If it went on the open market, as Marcus intends, then it would most likely get a great deal more than if you fixed a price with Art."

Leo rubbed his thumb hard against the palm of his hand. "I'm not at all sure about this. Marcus is in property development. He'd probably try to hoodwink Art."

Jonas laughed quietly. "Art's a successful businessman too. I'm sure they'll come to an arrangement that's agreeable to both."

Leo was silent for a moment, his eyes fixed on the plan in front of him. "Okay, so what are you suggesting?"

"If I were you, I would insist that Art fixes up a meeting with Marcus in London as soon as possible. Then he can show him the plans and negotiate a sale." He leaned forward, resting his elbows on his knees, and eyed the old man. "It is the fairest way, Leo, and guarantees you the best price. Just say to Art that his going to London is a condition that is non-negotiable."

"And when are you thinking he should go?"

"Well, if this gets fast-tracked through the planners, it would be best for him to go straightaway."

"Today?"

"Why not? The sooner, the better." Jonas reached over and patted the old man's arm. "Do you want me to write all this down for you?"

Leo sat upright in his chair and gave him an affronted look. "My mind may be a bit frazzled, but you can trust me to remember something for a day."

Jonas smiled at him. "That's good, I'm glad. And one more thing, Leo; I want you to tell Art all this was my idea, right?"

Leo frowned at him before nodding. "If you say so."

Jonas glanced at his watch. "I must get going. I've got a shift change coming up at the farm." He got to his feet and put his hand on Leo's shoulder. "It's great to see you looking so well." He walked across the room to the door.

"Talking of trust," Leo called out, "I trust you, Jonas."

"I know," Jonas replied, looking back at the hunched figure of the old man, "and I won't abuse it. It means a lot to me."

Closing the door behind him, Jonas glanced quickly in the direction of the kitchen before walking over to the far end of the hall. He took a mobile phone from the breast pocket of his shirt, found the number he was wanting and pressed the phone to his ear. "Hullo, is Gordon Mitchell in? It's Jonas Fairweather." While his call was being connected, he looked round once more to reassure himself that there was no one within earshot. "Gordon, hi, how are you? . . . good stuff . . . Listen, Gordon, I'll make this quick. Can you see me in about ten minutes? I want to get some plans drawn up for a development at Croich House . . . yes, but I can explain that when we meet . . . I would say about forty houses . . . okay, I'll be straight there. See you in a moment."

Jonas slipped the phone back into his pocket and made his way silently over to the back stairs.

Art was whistling as he drove back to the house. He never whistled unless things were going absolutely right for him, and at this moment in time, they could not be going better. The business plan and the drawings that he had just presented to the town hall had been received with as much enthusiasm as had been shown by the many companies he had visited over the past month. Without exception, every one of them had welcomed the idea of the conference centre, saying that it would be a guaranteed success and would fill a huge void in the marketplace, not only locally but farther afield as well. And the whole project had been a delight to research. Three-quarters of the chief executives with whom he had met were, like him, avid golfers, and more than happy to get the opportunity to talk business over a round of golf. In the past four weeks he had played, amongst many others, the Old Course at St. Andrews, the King's Course at Gleneagles and even the hallowed turf of Muirfield. And now, with the town hall having given the promised nudge to the planning department to approve the plans at the next meeting, it was time to move on with getting quotes from contracting firms—the next stage in turning his dream into reality.

He was still whistling when he got out of the car at the front of the house and ran up the steps and opened the front door. He put his briefcase down on the pine table and immediately walked across to the door of the sitting room. He wanted Leo to be the first recipient of the good news.

Five minutes later he reappeared, shutting the door quietly behind him, and went to stand in silent thought in the hall. He turned when he heard someone coming out of the kitchen. It was Agnes, slowly making her way to the sitting room with Leo's afternoon tea on a tray.

"You're back, then," she said. "Will you be wanting some tea yourself?"

"No, thanks," Art replied distantly as the housekeeper walked past him. "Say, what are these pills the doctor's given Leo? They've . . . changed him."

Agnes smiled. "Aye, they've certainly made a difference. He still has his bad days, though, gets in a fair muddle with things."

Art shook his head. "Not today, I tell you. He's as sharp as a razor." He moved quickly to the door and opened it for Agnes.

"Well, isn't that a good thing to hear," Agnes replied as she entered the room.

Art pulled his wallet from the back pocket of his trousers and walked over to the telephone that sat on the old oak sideboard below the staircase. He dialled a number and waited. "Yes, could you give me the number for British Airways Reservations?"

Claire sat back in the taxi as it made its way to the house from the station. Violet had already succumbed to their long day in Edinburgh, falling asleep the moment they had got into the taxi, her head leaning heavily against her mother's arm. Claire looked out of the window as they drove through Alloa and turned into the housing estate that bordered Leo's property. She remembered the first time she'd come here—a quick calculation in her head made it twenty-five years ago—when some of these houses weren't even finished. Now the development spread out way beyond the original boundary, line upon line of tightly packed dwellings that fronted onto roads that stretched out beyond sight. Claire realized now, more than ever before, that Leo's property and Jonas's farm were standing isolated in the centre of this urban encroachment, the final green bastion against the ever-growing tide of bricks and mortar. Its only hope of long-term protection was the success of Art's plan.

Violet woke just as the taxi came through the dense cover of rhododendrons on the drive. Yawning loudly, she stretched her arms above her head and looked blearily out of the window to get herself orientated. Seeing where they were, she turned eagerly to her mother.

"Can I go and play with Rory and Asrun?" she asked, her voice slurred with fatigue.

"I think you should give it a miss for now, darling," Claire replied. "It's been a pretty long day for both of us."

Violet groaned, disappointed, and slumped back in the seat, but she made no further attempt to reason with her mother. As the taxi approached the circular front lawn, Violet looked towards the house. "Where's Daddy going?"

Claire followed her gaze and saw Art

coming down the steps with a small overnight bag in his hand. He opened the back
door of his car and threw it in, and then
stood waiting as their taxi approached him.
By the time Claire had paid the driver, Violet had jumped out, given her father a quick
greeting and disappeared into the house.

Art approached the taxi and opened the
door for Claire.

"Hi there, how's it all gone today?" she
asked, handing him a bundle of shopping
bags before getting out herself. She
reached up and gave him a kiss on the
cheek.

"Really good until about two hours ago."

Claire frowned. "What's happened?"
She glanced towards the car. "Are you going somewhere?"

"London."

"Why?"

Art sighed deeply. "At the insistence of
your stepfather. He wants me to meet up
with Marcus in person and show him the
plans for the conference centre and negotiate a price for the property."

"Why on earth would he want you to do
that? Wouldn't it be simpler just to phone
Marcus and send him the plans?"

"Believe me, that's what I was hoping to do. I've got enough on my plate without having to do this, but the old boy was adamant. He even said the continuance of the plan depended on my doing as he requested."

Claire shook her head. "That's really strange. It sounds as if he's got himself into a bit of a tizzy about the whole thing. It's probably just part of his dementia."

"Ha!" Art exclaimed. "Don't you believe it! The man's right on the ball. He's already called Marcus and fixed up our meeting for tomorrow morning, so there's no way of getting out of it." He waggled a forefinger at Claire. "But, hey, all this wasn't his idea, you know."

"What do you mean?"

"Your friend Jonas Fairweather came to visit Leo this morning and just happened to see the drawings for the conference centre on the table. When Leo explained what they were, Jonas said that, in his role as an executor of the estate, he thought it only fair that I should meet with Marcus in person and show him the plans and negotiate a price on the property."

"Why on earth would he suggest that?"

Claire gasped. "He can't stand Marcus. He would never consider 'fairness' in relation to him. Do you think Jonas might be playing some sort of game?"

Art shrugged. "I'm not sure, but even if he is, I don't think it would have much consequence on what we've got planned." He walked over to the car and opened the driver's door. "It's almost signed, sealed and delivered already."

"When will you be back?"

"Tomorrow afternoon. I'm catching the midday flight back to Edinburgh."

Claire approached him and put a cautionary hand on his arm. "Watch out for Marcus, Art. I suspect he's pretty sharp . . . and probably quite dangerous in these kinds of dealings."

Art leaned over and gave her a kiss on the forehead before handing her back the shopping bags. "Then we'll be a good match for each other, won't we?" he said before getting into the car and setting off at speed down the drive.

Claire remained outside the house for a time, her eyes fixed on the point where Art's car had disappeared amongst the rhododendrons. There was something not right about the way in which Jonas had forced this issue. She knew that Leo had been avoiding all contact with both Marcus and Charity since their attempts to reintroduce the idea of moving him into a home, and now he was considering how fairly Marcus was being treated over the sale of the house and insisting that Art should meet him in person. It just didn't make sense.

She slowly crossed the gravel and began to climb the steps, now pretty well convinced that Marcus and Charity were not the only two whose motives were untrustworthy. She had a suspicion that Jonas might be taking advantage of his long friendship with Leo to further his own ends, but she couldn't work out what that could be.

Maybe the time had finally come to confront him.

29

The forecast on the television the previous evening had shown that the weather would break the next day. Too late for the farmers, the weather forecaster had quipped, but it would be good for the gardens, and he advised gardeners to take advantage of it and get their water butts filled up because it was only going to last a couple of days.

"You can almost see the grass greening up in front of your eyes," Claire heard Agnes say to Gabriela that morning as she entered the kitchen. The old housekeeper was standing over by the sink, staring out of the window, as she scrubbed slowly at a dirty saucepan. She trilled out a laugh. "Aye, but a bit of rain doesn't stop those two enjoying themselves."

Claire walked over to the window to see what Agnes was talking about.

"For heaven's sakes!" she exclaimed when she saw Violet, dressed in only a pair of shorts and T-shirt, kicking a football with Rory on the lawn. While waiting for the ball to come to her, Violet stood with her arms clasped around her for warmth, her hair plastered against her face. "Agnes, why did you let her go out there? She'll catch her death."

The housekeeper fixed her with a hardened look. "It's not for me to say what she's to do and what she's not, my girl. Anyway, a bit of rain never did anyone any harm."

"Well, I'm going to get her in," Claire said, turning on her heel and walking quickly back towards the door.

"You can always take her out a raincoat," Agnes called out, never taking her eyes away from the pair playing on the lawn.

"No, she's coming in," Claire replied adamantly as she left the room.

Laying the saucepan on the draining

board, Agnes turned and looked towards
the door. "Oh my wordie, I wonder what's
going on with her this morning?" she said
quietly to Gabriela. "It doesn't sound very
much like it's the rain she's objecting to."

Claire grabbed the umbrella, that she
had seen many times lying unused on the
pine table in the hall, and made her way
over to the back stairs. She didn't want to
get soaking-wet herself, so her thought was
that the back door might give the quickest
access to that part of the garden. As she
descended the stairs, she happened to
glance out of the window into the courtyard
and saw a car parked with its nose facing
the back of the house. It was a low-slung
machine, dark blue with gold-spoked
wheels and a large rear spoiler spanning
its boot. She stopped, realizing that it could
only belong to one person. That had to be
the reason why Rory was over here so
early. She went quietly to the bottom of the
stairs and listened, hearing along the unlit
passageway the sound of a filing cabinet
drawer being closed with force. She took in
a deep breath and walked steadfastly along
the passage and threw open the door of
Leo's office.

Jonas looked up in surprise as she entered. He was standing behind the desk with a pile of papers in his hand. Good, Claire thought to herself, he's looking embarrassed.

"Hi, Claire, long time no see." There was a distinct edge of trepidation in his voice.

"It's raining, you know," Claire said sharply.

Jonas smiled at her and put the papers down on the desk. "Yes, I had noticed."

"Violet and Rory are out on the lawn, getting soaking wet."

"Are they? Dammit, I told Rory to stay in the greenhouse with Pavel." He came out from behind the desk and walked towards her. "I'll go out now and tell them to get inside."

Claire did not move away from the door. Leaning the umbrella against the filing cabinet, she crossed her arms and let out a nervous breath. "Before you do that, I'd like to know what you're doing, Jonas."

Jonas glanced behind him at the desk. "I'm helping Leo out with his paperwork. I've done it for the past year."

"No, I mean what was behind your idea

of getting Art to go down to London to meet with Marcus?"

Jonas pushed his hands into the pockets of his jeans and shrugged his shoulders. "Nothing, other than I thought it was the right thing to do. Leo agreed with me."

"I know he did," Claire replied bluntly, "at your insistence."

Jonas shook his head. "I'm sorry, Claire, I think I'm missing the point here."

"Oh, it's quite simple. I'm not sure what your game is yet, Jonas, but you really have managed to inveigle your way into Leo's life, haven't you? Not only the executor of his estate, but here you are, going through all his papers."

There was anger in Jonas's eyes, but he controlled it in his voice. "I do it, Claire, because he is incapable of doing it for himself and there happens to be no one else around, family or otherwise, who can give it the time."

Claire felt her face go red. He was right. That was a stupid thing to say, and she knew well enough that the vehemence with which she had said it had come not from any great concern for Leo or Art, but because of this unbidden anger that kept welling up within her over something that had happened a long time ago.

She looked down at her feet and began scuffing her shoe against the stone floor. Damn and blast you, Jonas Fairweather, she thought, why do you have to have that look on your face? I know it only too well. It was just the same when I told you to stop skipping school and get on with your work. Why the hell do I have to find it so . . . captivating?

Jonas swept a hand over his head. "Listen, Claire," he said quietly. "Leo trusts me, and that's all that matters to me. If you feel that you can't, then I'm sorry—"

"Have you ever given me any reason to?" Claire cut in, looking up at him and wishing that her voice didn't sound so shaky.

Jonas stood looking at her for a moment before turning and picking up his key ring and the papers from the desk. Claire stood aside as he opened up one of the filing cabinet drawers and shoved the papers carelessly into a folder. He shut and locked the cabinet with one of the keys, and then held up two of them firmly between thumb and forefinger, allowing the others to dangle below. "These are the keys for the filing cabinet and the back door. Do you want them back?"

Claire stared at them trance-like before shaking her head.

Jonas nodded. "I'm taking Rory back home now, so I'll tell Violet to come inside." He walked out of the office but then reappeared in the doorway a moment later. "Is Art meeting with Marcus today?" he asked.

"Yes, he is," Claire replied.

"At what time?"

"He didn't say."

Jonas leaned a hand against the doorpost. "It might be worth ringing him and telling him that he shouldn't be bidding more than two hundred and fifty thousand for this place."

"Don't you think that's really for Art and me to decide?" she said.

Jonas shrugged. "Okay, but just remember I said it." He spun the key ring on his finger and left.

Claire stood looking out into the dark passageway, hearing the back door open and close again. She walked over to the desk and leaned against it, her arms crossed.

He was right. Leo did trust him implicitly, and she didn't want to place a barrier between herself and her stepfather by airing her disquiet at Jonas's motives in front of him. But then Jonas would understand that, wouldn't he, which left him in prime position to take advantage of his friendship with the old man and use it to feather his own nest.

Maybe, then, Marcus was not the most dangerous figure in the overall equation.

30

Jonas sat in the Subaru in the courtyard, the driver's door left wide open. He stared straight ahead, overcome by the dull ache of sadness that had been brought about by Claire's hostility. He knew that it was inevitable she would feel that way when they eventually did meet and he knew he deserved it, and that was the reason hitherto he had done his utmost to avoid coming into contact with her. Not just today, but for the past sixteen years.

It should never have happened. He knew that. Claire had been the most important person in his life, but he had never felt he could tell her the true feelings he had for her, because that would have been hopeless, a hiding to nothing. He was just the son of a farmer who had happened to fall in love with the stepdaughter of his father's landlord. God, it now sounded all so old-fashioned, so feudal, but back then it did matter, and the whole situation was made impossible by the vitriolic attitudes of both Marcus and Charity towards him. It was they who made him feel like an uneducated lout, they who had called him hurtful and debasing names out of earshot of Leo, and that was why he had always kept clear of the house during holiday times. If he and Claire had come together under those circumstances, how could he ever have imagined trying to fit into that family?

And so he had lost himself in the dream of becoming a champion rally driver. It was the one thing he knew he was good at, but the true prize he wished for himself was not the glory of victory, the euphoria of adulation and recognition. What drove him to succeed was the fact that he saw it as the one lifeline thrown to him to escape the farm, to get away from Croich and the perpetual resentment of Marcus and Charity, to have a future that was financially secure—and to take Claire away with him.

The memories of what had happened that late December night were still all too clearly etched in his mind. How his whole life had been changed, complete happiness turned to devastating loss in no more than two hours. They had been together all evening in the workshop, chatting and laughing with each other as he worked on his car, and then she had announced that she was leaving and he had turned to say goodbye. He usually just stuck his head straight back into the bowels of the engine, but on that occasion he had stood looking at her. She was dressed in her Doc Marten boots, thick black tights and skirt and big floppy jersey, her weird dyed hair sticking out from under her woolly hat. But it was the huge grin on her dark plum-coloured mouth, the deep twinkle in her eyes caught by the single bare bulb that was hanging from the rafter, that made his heart leap and he knew, there and then, that he would have to tell her. He walked with her to the door, and he was ready to put his grease-stained arms around her and tell her he loved her and had done so ever since they first met. But then, as he stood inches from her, spinning the ring spanner around on his finger, he had thought to himself, Leave it for now, leave it until you get yourself the sponsorship and you're ready to fly away from here forever. Then telling how you feel for her will be all the more sweet.

Oh yes, there lived on that same sense of yearning that had lain deep within him for so many years after: to have frozen time at that point, to have grasped that opportunity when it had been offered to him; but circumstances and his own stupidity had set their destinies on separate paths thereafter, never to be redressed. And then he had met Liv and she had eventually been able to convince him that he was not to blame for what had happened that night. He had learned to love again, to respect himself again, and the feelings he had for Claire had faded in the contentment of his marriage.

But they were back now, not as an uncontrollable impulse to rekindle unrequited love, but as a longing to bury the past and repair their shattered friendship.

But that would have to wait. What he had

to do was bound to set distrust and even hatred in Claire's mind. Still, he could think of no other course of action to redress the clandestine dishonesty of Marcus and Charity and, ultimately, the irrevocable disruption they had caused in his own life.

Heavy raindrops on the roof of his car signalled another heavy shower looming and reminded Jonas that the two children were still out in the garden. He got out and ran round the side of the house to call them in before they had the chance to get soaked once more.

31

London—August 2006

The Kerr-Jamiesons' annual summer party, held in the extensive gardens of their house in Holland Park, had become a highlight in the calendar of London's social gatherings. It was always held in the last week of August, a time when those who attended had returned bronzed and refreshed from their summer holidays and were gearing themselves up to sending their children back to their various public schools in the home counties and beyond. Even if one did nothing else in the year, to be seen at the Kerr-Jamieson party was enough to mark one's place amongst the accepted elite of West London society.

Charity did not mind that their invitation for this year's party—a first for Mr. and Mrs. Thomson—had come slightly by default, or, to be more exact, through careful manipulation. Their house in Blythe Road, Hammersmith, was, after all, not a million miles away from Holland Park. With her son James being at the same school as Patrick Kerr-Jamieson, it seemed only right to Charity that she should phone up his mother Jessica and suggest that she could quite easily take the two boys back together to start the summer term at Marlborough College. And then, when Charity had gone round to pick the boy up, she had made sure she arrived a good half an hour early, knowing that Patrick would still be mouldering around the house trying to get the last cricket shirt stuffed into his suitcase, and had accepted Jessica's offer to come in and wait. Over a cup of coffee in their sumptuously appointed kitchen, Charity managed to slip in a question on how plans were going for this year's party, and after a lengthy discourse on the subject, it was only left for Jessica to say, "Oh, my dear, but you must come. I'll send you an invitation."

Thereafter, Charity had offered her services to ferry James and Patrick back and forth to school throughout the summer term, just to keep her name foremost in Jessica's mind. It never really concerned her too much that it was a constant source of embarrassment for James to be seen getting into the same car as Patrick, who was two years his junior and was known throughout the school as being a real loser. That was immaterial in the light of things.

When the invitation came through, all hard white card and black embossed italic lettering, Charity and her husband, Harry, synchronized their diaries and he had been given no option other than to cancel a weekend away in Somerset with his company's cricket team. Charity was delighted that the date of the party fell exactly three days after their return from holidaying in the south of France. Anticipating the captivating glory of an all-over tan, she bought herself a new dress from Fenwick in Bond Street, back-less and with a low-cut front, which would show off her Mediterranean glow to full effect.

"Harry, are you ready?" she called out as she put the finishing touches to her make-up in front of the dressing-table mirror.

Harry appeared at the door of the bedroom. "I've called the cab. He should be here in five minutes."

Charity looked aghast at the dark pinstriped suit that her husband was wearing. "Why have you got that on? You're not going to the office, for heaven's sakes. This is a garden party. People will just laugh at you if you wear that."

"Thanks a bunch," Harry said, looking down at his suit and giving a cursory flick to a speck of white dust on its lapel. "What would you rather I wear?"

"What about those nice dark blue chinos I've just bought for you from Boden?" Charity replied, turning to the mirror and pursing her mouth to apply her lipstick. "And your white linen jacket?"

Harry laughed quietly. "No, thanks, I'm fine as I am."

Charity got up from her stool and walked seductively towards him, her tight dress swishing against her plump body as she moved. "Oh, come on, darling," she purred, pushing herself against him. "Do it for Chary." She gave him a saucy wink. "I'll make it worth your while later."

"Oh, well, I suppose one has to take every chance," Harry murmured as he walked over to the wardrobe, taking off his jacket.

"I hope that wasn't a jibe at what happened on holiday," Charity said as she swept her make-up off the table into her handbag. "I was very ill, you know, and certainly not in the mood for . . . that."

"I reckon it was just too much sun," Harry replied as he pushed his legs into his new trousers. He surveyed the row of shirts that were stacked neatly on the shelf. "Okay, so if you're going to dress me tonight, what shirt do you want me to wear?"

Walking over to the wardrobe, Charity pulled one out at random and handed it to him before leaving the room.

Harry stood looking at the shirt. "This is pink," he called out after her.

"It'll offset the blue trousers and the white jacket perfectly" came back Charity's voice from somewhere on the staircase, "and I wouldn't bother with a tie. It's still very warm outside."

Harry sighed deeply and began undoing the buttons of the shirt. "For crying out loud," he muttered, "she's going to have me looking like a Greek millionaire."

"Do you notice anything?" Harry said as they passed through the blind-shaded conservatory and stood, champagne glasses already in hand, at the top of the stone steps outside the Kerr-Jamiesons' white-walled Regency house, looking out over the clusters of guests gathered on the lawn.

"What's that?" Charity asked distractedly, interested only in searching out people that she knew.

"Every one of the men is wearing a dark suit," Harry said through gritted teeth.

"Don't worry, I think you look great," Charity replied without sparing him a glance as she tottered on her high heels down the steps. "Jane, darling, how wonderful to see you!"

Everything that evening fulfilled Charity's expectations. Jessica Kerr-Jamieson's attention to detail was exquisite, from the

pink-lined marquee to the white wrought-
iron tables and chairs placed strategically
in far-off corners to afford different views
of the house's beautifully tended garden.
Moët et Chandon champagne and sparkling repartee between like-minded guests
flowed incessantly throughout the evening,
and at every opportunity Charity would
seek out Jessica to compliment her on
such a wonderful party. Spotting her imminent approach, Charity's strategy was
to take her leave immediately of the person with whom she was speaking, either
with a laugh or an intimate brush of her
hand, just to show that she knew people,
and regale her hostess with phrases of
pandering approbation, such as "Where
on earth did you find . . . ?" or "Do tell me
who your marvellous caterers are?"

She didn't care how much she monopo-
lized Jessica's company, just as long as
she made sure that there was no earthly
reason why that treasured hard-backed invitation should not be pushed through the
letter box of their house in Blythe Road
same time, next year.

People had begun to drift away from the
party when Charity, searching out another

suitable person to talk to, happened to glance towards a group of men gathered around one of the wrought-iron tables. She started in amazement when she recognized her brother, leaning over and chatting to a rotund gentleman, wearing a Marylebone Cricket Club bow tie, seated at the table. She walked over to Marcus and put her hand on his arm.

Her brother looked round at her, and then gave the man a smiling farewell before turning his attention to Charity.

"I'm surprised to see you here," she said.

"Why?" Marcus asked, taking her by the arm and guiding her towards a secluded spot over by the marquee. "I come every year."

"How do you know the Kerr-Jamiesons?" she asked indignantly.

"Ronnie was an old business partner of mine," Marcus replied, casting a look around him as if making sure there was no one in earshot. He turned back to Charity, ignoring her look of sudden deflation. "Listen, never mind that," he said, rubbing a hand agitatedly at his forehead, "where the hell have you been?"

"What do you mean?"

"I've been trying to get hold of you for the past three days."

"Well, I've only just got back from France."

"Didn't you get my email?"

"I haven't checked them yet."

"What about your mobile, then? I left at least five messages for you."

"Ah, well, now that's a dreadful bore because it's somewhere at the bottom of the Med. It fell off the side of the yacht when I was sunbathing." Charity realized now that there was real concern etched on her brother's face. "What's the matter with you?"

"It's about the house."

"Which house?"

"Oh, come on, Charity, get your bloody mind in gear. I'm talking about Croich."

"What about it?"

Marcus sighed uncertainly and scratched at the back of his head. "I had a meeting in my office the other day with Art Barrington."

"Art Barrington? Do you mean angel Claire's husband?"

"None other."

"What did he want?"

Marcus fixed his eyes on his sister. "He's got plans to turn Croich into a vast conference centre and, by the looks of things, the whole project is pretty far advanced."

Charity looked aghast. "He can't do that! He's got no right! What did you say to him?"

"Well, after the initial shock, I told him it was really up to you and me what became of the house, to which he replied he thought we had no interest in the place."

"For heaven's sakes, neither of us want to live there, but of course we have an interest in the place. It's part of our inheritance."

Marcus shrugged. "Not until Dad pops off the mortal coil, I'm afraid, and it does look as if the old devil has given his unconditional blessing to this project."

Charity took a step towards her brother. "But what about our own plans for the place, Marcus? I mean, why have we not been told about all this before?"

Marcus twisted his mouth. "We haven't exactly been open about what we've been up to either, have we?"

"No," Charity replied quietly, feeling a

flush of guilt rise to her cheeks. "And now I don't suppose we can wait until Dad dies to get the house, because of Art Barrington's wretched plans."

"We couldn't wait anyway. We've gone too far to let that happen."

Charity paused for a moment before shaking her short blonde curls. "Dammit, Marcus, we are desperate for the money. Harry's business is not going well, and we have a standard of living we want to keep up." She glanced around at the assembled company to indicate to Marcus what she meant. "What we've got so far is not enough. If we can't go through with our own project, then we're sunk."

"Don't worry," Marcus replied, "We've still got a controlling hand in all this."

"What do you mean?"

"Dad's obviously incapable of handling the sale himself, so he's left it up to me to negotiate the price. I know how much we can get for that place fully developed, and Barrington hasn't come anywhere near that figure in his offer."

"How much was that?"

"Well, he had a phone call half-way through the meeting and went outside my office to take it, and I took the opportunity to have a quick look at his notes. There was a figure of four hundred thousand written down, but when we started discussing price on his return, he was talking somewhere around the two-hundred-and-fifty-thousand mark."

Charity blew out a derisive breath. "That's nothing. He's obviously got no idea."

"Exactly, so what I'm proposing we do is keep Barrington dangling on a line. I'm almost there getting the financial package together, and when that Czech couple head back home in mid-September, then there'll be nothing standing in our way of getting Dad moved into a home. We'll lodge our plans with the planning department and our consortium will pay a hell of a lot more money for Croich than Barrington has offered."

Charity looked worriedly at her brother. "Dad'll be needing the money."

Marcus shook his head. "Oh, don't start on about that again. We've just been using the capital prudently. Everything will get sorted at the end, I promise you, and no one will ever be the wiser. And remember, it all eventually does come back to us and it'll be one hell of a lot of money."

Charity's face lightened, a thin smile of contentment edging her mouth. "And angel Claire and her husband will have to return home empty-handed."

Marcus nodded thoughtfully. "Yes, they will . . . in every way."

Charity laughed. "I like that bit the best." She looked over Marcus's shoulder to see Harry approaching them. "Here we go, looks like someone wants to leave." She sighed disappointedly.

Glancing behind him, Marcus gave Harry's dress a quick appraisal before turning back to Charity. "I'm surprised he hasn't felt like leaving earlier. Whatever possessed him to wear such extraordinary clothes?"

32

Alloa—September 2006

Jonas slowed his car to a halt half-way down the wooded lane at a point where he could see through the bushes to the front of the house, yet still be concealed if anyone chanced to go past on the drive. He felt guilty about having to involve Rory so much in this ongoing subterfuge, but the boy had become his ears and eyes in keeping him informed as to what was happening in the house. It wouldn't have been necessary if he had been able to take Claire into his confidence when they met in Leo's office three weeks before, but he had to play this one out by himself. He had been able to give her a brief warning about the value of the house, and at that stage he could do no more.

He cast an eye down at the pile of papers that sat on the passenger seat beside him. His plans were all there, an impressive forty-house complex that his architect friend had managed to lift off another development and superimpose directly onto Croich's policies. Yet despite his pleasure at their apparent authenticity, his stomach still fluttered with trepidation. He only hoped that Leo was going to be strong enough to take this all in. He had put off telling him about what he'd discovered up until that point, but now, with the plans firmly lodged with the town planning office, he knew that he could put it off no longer.

He reached over to the passenger seat and sorted through the papers, pulling out the brown envelope with the London address on it. He read it through and then tapped the edge of the envelope on his hand. He knew that the moment he put it into the letter box, the game would be on and he'd be letting himself in for the biggest speculative gamble he had ever taken in his life. If it worked, though, as he believed it would, then . . .

He glanced at his wristwatch. This was about the time that Rory said they'd be leaving. He ducked his head to peer through the dense foliage and saw Violet and Claire getting into the car at the front of the house. Good lad, Rory, he thought to himself, as next he saw Art quickly descend the steps and jump into the car. A moment later it began to move and Jonas sat back in his seat and looked straight ahead down the lane until he saw their car flash past. He left it for five minutes before reaching down to the ignition key and starting up the Subaru.

Art parked the car outside the town hall and turned to smile apprehensively at Claire. "This is it, then," he said, opening up the door. "Let's pray it's all gone through planning."

She gave his arm a reassuring squeeze. "Good luck."

Art got out and Claire watched as he walked over to the steps and took them two at a time.

"Are we going to be here for long, Mom?" Violet piped up from the back seat.

"I hope not, darling," she replied as Art disappeared into the building. "The quicker Daddy's out, the more likely it is that everything's gone all right."

Art pushed open the double doors of the planning office and went over to the unmanned reception desk. He was about to ring the bell for attention when he caught the eye of a young clerk seated in front of a computer screen at the far end of the room. Swinging round in his seat, he got up and approached the desk.

"Can I help you?" he asked sombrely.

"Yes, I'd like to find out about the progress of some plans I've submitted."

"Name of the project?"

"Croich House."

The clerk turned without a word and went over to a row of filing cabinets close to where he had been sitting. He opened one drawer, thumbed through some files, and then shut it and tried the one below. He eventually pulled out a brown file and came back to Art and spun it onto the desk.

"Is this the one?" he asked.

Opening the file, Art looked at the

folded-up plan and groaned. "Isn't there usually a stamp on here if it's gone through planning?"

The clerk picked up the brown folder and turned it over and pointed to a date stamped on the back. "It's hardly likely to have gone forward yet. It was only submitted a week ago."

Art bit at his lip to suppress his fury, knowing from experience that if he came out with a remark now, the young clerk would see to it that his application went to the bottom of the pile.

"I actually put these in over four weeks ago," he said in a measured voice as he opened up the plan. He laid it out on the desk and stared at it in bemusement. These weren't his plans. This was for a huge housing development. "Hey, I think you've got the wrong folder. These aren't mine."

The clerk once more studied the folder in his hand. "It says 'Croich Development' on here." He twisted his head round to look at the plans on the desk and placed his finger on the bottom left-hand corner. "And there," he said in a smug voice. "These are definitely the plans."

Art never looked up, his gaze fixed on the name below where the clerk had been pointing. "What the hell?" he murmured. "Jeez, that good-for-nothing . . ."

"What's that you're saying?" the clerk asked indignantly.

"Sorry, I wasn't talking to you," Art replied, shutting his eyes and pinching hard on the bridge of his nose. "Listen, do me a favour, would you? There were some other plans submitted for Croich. Could you just find out where they are?"

Claire's colour drained rapidly from her face as she stared open-mouthed in shock through the windscreen. Her whole body felt numb in disbelief at the news.

"Aren't you going to say anything?" Art asked her.

Claire shook her head. "I don't know what to say." She turned to look at Art. "What does he think he's going to achieve by doing this? Leo's already agreed to sell the house to us."

Art rubbed both hands hard against his face. "I know, I can't work it out either. He's clearly trying to delay our plans from going through, but, as you say, for what reason?

He knows we're the ones going to buy the place, and that's solid. The only way he can change that is by going to speak to . . ." He stopped talking and Claire saw the look of horror slide across his features.

"What's the matter, Art?"

"When was the last time you were away from the house?"

"I don't know, maybe about a week and a half ago."

Art flicked his fingers and pointed at her. "Exactly!" he exclaimed, hurriedly turning on the ignition and reversing with little care out of the parking space. "Those plans were only lodged a week ago. Jonas won't have wanted to go see Leo until he knew for certain we'd all be out of the house."

"You mean . . ."

"He'll be there right now," he said, pulling the car out onto the street and putting his foot down hard on the accelerator. "Let's just hope we get back in time."

"Does that mean we're not going swimming?" Violet called out disappointedly.

"Yeah, I'm afraid so, honey," Art said as he swerved past a slow-moving car and received a loud blast on the horn for his efforts.

"I could have guessed!" Violet moaned, crossing her arms grumpily and slumping back in her seat.

Walking slowly from the front steps of the house to his car, Jonas opened the door and got in and sat for a moment, his hands held tightly to the top of his head. The revelation that Leo had made during their meeting had been almost as shocking as the news that he himself had given to the old man. As it transpired, Leo had known all these years the true reason why his relationship with Claire had ended so abruptly. The more now Jonas considered this, the more he came to realize that it had been nothing short of an extraordinary act of benevolence and understanding on Leo's part that he and his father had been allowed to stay on at the farm after all that had happened.

He started the engine and then slapped the leather-clad steering wheel with his hand. Now, if anything had strengthened his resolve in seeing this thing through, it had been the sight of that ashen-faced old man, whose whole world had just been shattered, turning to him with a smile and saying, "Jonas, my boy, I've known that forever, and I tell you now that I don't hold you to blame at all. Never have. I'm afraid I always half-expected something like that would happen."

Jonas slipped the car into gear and drove off slowly down the drive. He was still churning over in his mind what the appalling consequences might have been, had Leo taken a different view on matters, when he reached the point where the lane led off to the right. He turned in and had driven no more than ten yards when he saw in his rear-view mirror a car flash past, heading at speed towards the house. He muttered an oath to himself for having been so distracted and gunned the engine, eager to get away from the place as fast as possible.

*

"We're too late, I think," Claire said quietly.

"What do you mean?" Art asked as he drove towards the circular lawn and swung the car hard to the right.

"I've just seen Jonas's car going up the lane to the farm."

"Jesus!" Art exclaimed, accelerating to a speed that nearly had the car slewing round the final curve of the lawn. He slammed on the brakes in front of the house, churning up gravel before finally coming to a halt. Throwing open the door, he got out and ran up the steps, taking them in three long strides.

Claire turned round and gave Violet's knee a pat. "Sorry about this, darling. I promise you I'll take you swimming this afternoon."

They got out of the car and Claire walked with her arm around her daughter's shoulders. They had reached the front door when it opened abruptly and Art stood aside to let them in. "Leo doesn't want to say anything until you're here."

"Jonas has been, then."

"The old boy hasn't said as much, but from the look on his face I'd say there's no question of it."

As Claire entered the hall, Leo came out of the sitting room with Pavel pushing him in his wheelchair. The change in his appearance since they had left the house no more than an hour before was only to clear to see. He was slumped low in the wheelchair, his head bowed as he stared vacantly into his lap, and the look on his colourless face read total devastation.

Claire watched Violet scuttle off into the kitchen before going over and kneeling down beside him. "Leo, are you all right?"

Leo looked up at her and smiled. "I'm feeling rather tired. I'm going to bed."

"What did Jonas say to you?"

A tear fell from the old man's watery eyes and he brushed it away with the back of a liver-spotted hand. "Nothing that you'd want to hear, my dear, I assure you."

"Did he tell you he'd put in his own plans for the development of the house?"

Leo nodded. "He did."

"Did you ask him why?"

Leo did not reply but once more dropped his eyes to his lap.

Art stood behind Claire and rubbed a hand at the back of his neck. "Oh, this is bad news."

Leo looked up with a sudden jolt and glared at him. "Art, my boy, if you think that's bad news, you should have been party to what I've just had to listen to."

Claire laid a hand on her stepfather's arm. "Leo, tell me what Jonas . . ."

She stopped when Leo held up his hand.

"At this point, I've only got a couple of

things to say," he said before letting out a laboured breath. "I have just this minute given instructions to John Venables to put Croich up for public auction at the end of September—"

"But Leo," Art cut in, "Claire and I have everything resting on this deal going through. If you put the property up for auction, then Jonas has a chance of getting in on the—"

He was interrupted by Leo thumping his fist hard on the leather arm rest of his wheelchair, the noise echoing around the hall. "I trust Jonas Fairweather more than anyone. I hate this all happening, but he will see us right." As he spat out the last word, he looked round sharply at Claire and, in that instant, she could see that there was still strength in the old man. She watched as his gaze lifted to Art. "Now, I understand that Jonas gave you a ballpark figure for the house."

Art did not reply immediately, but stood biting at his top lip. "Yeah, he did. Two hundred and fifty thousand pounds."

"Then it would be my advice to take that into careful consideration when you are bidding for the place." Leo turned slowly in his chair and nodded to Pavel, who had been standing uneasily behind him throughout the interchange. "And now, if you don't mind, I have had quite enough excitement for one day."

Art and Claire watched as Pavel pushed the wheelchair to the far side of the hall and manoeuvred it through the door to Leo's invalid bedroom.

"What the hell . . ." Art said with a slow shake of his head.

"I don't know," Claire murmured, her eyes still fixed on the door. "It just doesn't seem to make sense." She put a hand on Art's arm. "I'm so sorry, my love, this could mean the end of your project."

Art laughed. "Don't you believe it! I'll match that guy pound for pound in the auction."

"But Leo said—"

"I couldn't give a damn what Leo said. This place is worth a hell of a lot more than two hundred and fifty thousand."

"But wasn't that the price you offered Marcus?"

Art smiled at her. "Yeah, sure it was, but I can work leeway on that figure." His face went serious. "You know, we sure as hell can't have any contact with Jonas after all this happening."

Claire looked at him quizzically. "But we don't anyway."

"I mean contact with any of his family."

Claire nodded slowly, understanding now what he was saying. "You mean Violet."

Art nodded. "Exactly. No more playing with her friend Rory. I reckon he's been the go-between."

"I don't think so, Art."

He smiled sadly at her. "I'm sorry, but how else would Jonas have known we were going to be out of the house today?"

Claire was saved from answering the question by the sound of Art's phone ringing in his pocket. He took it out and walked over to the front door. Claire turned and went towards the kitchen, already trying to work out how best she could break the news to Violet, conscious that by a quirk of fate, she was now to be instrumental in breaking off yet another friendship between her own family and the Fairweathers.

Ten minutes later, Art put his head round the side of the door of the kitchen. "Claire, can I have a word with you out here?"

Claire sighed quietly to herself. She had been chatting with Agnes since entering the kitchen and had just got the opportunity to broach the subject of Rory with Violet. She got up from the table and walked out into the hall. Art was pacing up and down, biting pensively at a fingernail.

"Is everything all right?" Claire asked.

Art raised his hands in desperation. "It doesn't rain, but it pours."

"What's happened?"

"That was my accountant in New York on the phone. There's a problem with last year's accounts for the restaurant and the IRS want to do an audit."

"Do you think you owe them money?"

"No, I doubt it. It's probably just an anomaly that's come up with our revenues being so much more since we expanded."

Claire crossed her arms. "When will you have to go?"

"Right away, dammit. There's a meeting fixed up the day after tomorrow."

Claire shook her head. "I see what you mean now about raining and pouring. What do you want to do about the project?"

"Well, planning's delayed now, thanks

to Jonas, but I've done enough canvass-
ing with the town hall to think they'll probably favour our plan."

"Will you be back for the auction?"

"I can't guarantee it, depends on how
long the audit takes. But I was thinking
you'd probably want to stick around for a
while, especially to work out what the hell
is going to happen to Leo if it comes to the
worst and Jonas gets the house. So, if you
could be here for the auction, that'd be
great and I could just be on the other end of
a phone. Do you reckon you could handle
that?"

Claire bit at her bottom lip. "That means
I'd be bidding against Jonas."

"Yeah, it would. Is that okay?"

"I suppose."

"That's great." Art paused, scratching at
the side of his face. "Listen, there's another thing we've completely lost focus on.
My accountant said that he thought we'd
probably be coming back next week to get
Violet ready to go back to school."

Claire clasped her hand to her mouth.
"Oh my goodness, I'd completely forgotten about that."

"I know, too much going on."

"What shall we do?"

"I guess the only thing we can do under the circumstances is for Violet to come back with me." He gave her arm a reassuring pat. "I'm sure she'll be just fine, though, and Pilar can help to get her things together for school." He paused. "Anyway, maybe it's for the best she's away from here now, considering this whole thing with Rory. You didn't say anything about it to her yet, did you?"

"No, I was just about to when you came into the kitchen."

"Well, we don't have to make any excuses now."

Claire crossed her arms to stem the nervous shudder that suddenly ran through her. "Oh, I don't like this happening at all. I feel as if I'm being abandoned in the lion's den."

Art came over and put his arms around her and gave her a tight hug. "Yes, I can understand that exactly and I'm sorry. I wish there could be another way." He gave her a kiss. "I promise I'll keep in touch every day, and if this IRS business gets finished with before the auction, then I'll be over here like a shot."

Claire nodded, easing herself out of Art's embrace. "Come on, I think we'd better tell Violet."

33

London—September 2006

Charity took off her apron, revealing the neat little suit that she had chosen to wear for James's return to school, and walked out into the narrow hallway of their house in Blythe Road. She dithered for a moment in front of the vast trunk that blocked her path to the bottom of the stairs before deciding she wouldn't even attempt to step across it in case she laddered her tights.

"James?" she called out loudly.

"Yeah?" A morose, deep-toned voice sounded back from upstairs.

"We should go now. I said we'd be round at the Kerr-Jamiesons at four o'clock."

Her son appeared at the top of the stairs and began ambling slowly down towards his mother, a sneer of disdain on his face. "Why the hell do we always have to take that geek back with us?"

"Because it makes sense, that's why. It saves on petrol."

James snorted. "Yeah, it saves petrol for the Kerr-Jamiesons, don't you mean?"

"Well, just think of it as a friendly gesture," Charity said with a little smile. She stood away from the trunk, her hands raised delicately in the air. "Now, can you manage to put that in the car yourself? I don't want to damage my nails."

James groaned and stepped over the trunk and leaned down to take hold of the handle. Charity wrinkled her nose in disgust as she went back into the kitchen.

"And, for goodness' sakes, do pull up your jeans. I can see your bottom again. I don't know why you insist on not wearing a belt with them."

The shrill ringing of the telephone drowned out James's reply. With an irritable sigh, Charity went over to the kitchen table and threw aside the newspaper that had been covering the hands-free receiver. She answered the call with a clipped hullo.

"Hi, it's Marcus."

Charity picked up the car keys which were lying on her new central work station and threw them randomly through the open door into the hall. "Oh, Marcus, is this important? I'm just about to take James—"

"Of course it's important!" Marcus replied heatedly. "Do I ever call you when it's not!"

"All right," Charity said huffily. "You don't have to be like that. What do you want?"

"Listen, the shit has hit the fan. We've got a major problem with Croich."

"What's happened?"

"That bloody Jonas Fairweather has gone and submitted his own plans for a development of forty houses on the property."

"What?" Charity exclaimed incredulously. "How do you know this?"

"I received a copy of them today in the post. I don't know who sent them. There was no covering letter."

"But that's . . ." She let out a shrill laugh. "But that is ridiculous. I know Dad in his rank stupidity made Jonas an executor of his estate, but he hasn't a hope in hell of getting his greasy little mitts on the property. We'll make sure of that."

"I'm afraid that's only the start of it."

The smile dropped from her face. "What do you mean?"

"About five minutes ago, I received an email from Dad's solicitor, John Venables."

"Saying?"

"Saying that the whole property is going to be sold by private auction on the twenty-fourth of September."

Charity froze at the news and she stared blankly out of the window before her bottom lip began to quiver uncontrollably. "But . . . Dad can't do that! It's so unfair! It means that the house is as good as being put on the open market."

"You've got it in one," Marcus replied dully. "We're going to be pitching against both Barrington and Fairweather."

Charity clenched her teeth. "I'm going to phone Dad right now and ask him what the hell he thinks he's doing."

"You won't have any luck. I've just tried and got that Czech girl. She said Dad has had one of his bad days and he's headed off to bed."

"Well, serves him right, the demented

old fool." At this point, Charity's face crumpled and she began to sob. "Marcus, what are we going to do? If we can't get the house . . . then we're completely ruined. We won't be able to afford a thing." She pulled a hanky from the sleeve of her jacket and dabbed carefully above her cheekbone, hoping that this unwarranted grief wasn't going to make her eyeliner run.

"Come on, it's not all over yet," Marcus replied, his voice now at least registering a modicum of sympathy. "Actually, I've given it a bit of thought and maybe this will work to our advantage."

"Why do you say that?" Charity asked, momentarily calmed by her brother's positive response.

"Because I reckon it'll put Barrington out of the equation. He only offered two hundred and fifty thousand, remember. Our financial package is secure, so we can go way over that figure if necessary. He'll be forced out of the bidding and we'll simply blow him away."

This news brought a thin smile to Charity's unhappy face. "But what about that dreadful Jonas?"

"Well, he may be rich, but to be quite

honest, if he's acting alone, which I think he is, I don't think he'll get near us."

"How can you be sure he is acting alone?"

"Because it's taken me about two years to put this financial package together and I'm in the property development business and I live in London. I think he's just taken action since finding out that Barrington was after the place, so I doubt he'll have had either the time or the contacts to get a serious bid together."

"Do you think we might get it, then?" Charity asked meekly.

"Yes, I'm pretty confident that we will, and, of course, another thing that might help our cause is that we bid blind at the auction."

"What does that mean?"

"We'll just do it over the phone. Fair-weather will only know then that he's bidding against a London-based consortium, and that should put the frighteners on him."

Charity breathed out a long sigh of relief. "Oh, thank goodness for that! When you first started telling me about it, I thought we were completely . . ." She paused, her back straightening in indignation. "Actually, why on earth could you not have said all that before, instead of making me snivel away here?"

"I was thinking on my feet, Charity."

"Well, maybe next time give it a bit more thought before you call. I think you've probably ruined my eye make-up, which means I'm going to have to do it all over again, and I'm late as it is in taking James back to school."

Marcus laughed disparagingly. "Just remember, Charity, that it's only through my efforts that you're going to be able to keep your son at that school!"

34

Alloa—September 2006

Leo never ventured out of his bedroom for three days following the departure of Art and Violet. He remained in bed, turning his face away from the door whenever anybody entered the room. When he did eventually summon Pavel to help him get into his wheelchair, he was taken through to the sitting room, where he sat at the table in the bay window, staring blankly at the trees at the far end of the lawn. Claire tried on more than one occasion to coax gently out of her stepfather what it was that Jonas had said to him, but he would divulge nothing, simply turning to her with a smile and saying exactly the same thing—how she must miss Art and Violet and that it wouldn't be long before she could return to New York to be with them. She could never understand his certainty in saying this, knowing that Pavel and Gabriela were due to return to Czechoslovakia the following week and, as yet, no arrangements had been made to replace them. It was beyond consideration that she should allow Agnes to remain in sole charge, and her constant quandary was about what would happen to Leo if Jonas were to be successful in buying the house.

The result of the complete downturn of activity in the house was that Claire, for the first time since she could remember, began to feel the hollow pangs of loneliness. She was missing Art and Violet so much, and sitting in silence with Leo did little to assuage this feeling. She did not want to be constantly in the company of Agnes and Gabriela in the kitchen, nor did she want to leave the house, especially with Leo's state of mind being so unpredictable. So she would potter around, going into rooms that she had hardly entered since her childhood and putting them in order as best she could

and, where possible, giving them a superfi-
cial clean. Some were past redemption,
being so full of junk that her only course of
action was to simply close the door and
leave them well alone. Thus it was that the
main focus of her day became the long-
awaited telephone call with Art and Violet
each evening, when she would keep them
talking long after Art had said his initial
goodbye.

Her spirits, however, were given a considerable lift the following week when Leo
decided to join them in the kitchen for the
farewell meal that Agnes had cooked for
Pavel and Gabriela. There seemed to be
an inexplicable yet distinct improvement in
his mood and almost an air of excitement
in his conversation at table, and he even
took it upon himself to propose a lengthy
toast to the young Czech couple, during
which he managed to make them both
flush with embarrassment when he said
that he hoped to be invited to their wedding. As they were due to depart early the
next morning, the meal ended at nine
o'clock amidst much laughter and fond
farewells, and when Pavel eventually manoeuvred Leo's wheelchair away from the

table, the old man slipped him an envelope, saying that what it contained was small recompense for their friendship and all the work they had done. It was a touching moment, and Claire smiled when she saw the young man wipe away a tear that fell below his small round spectacles before he pushed Leo away.

The next morning, Claire was woken by the scrunch of gravel as Pavel and Gabriela's taxi arrived outside the house. A quick glance at the alarm clock told her it was seven o'clock. She lay on her back and listened to the sound of their departure, the footsteps in the hall and the moving of heavy baggage to the front door. She was slightly bewildered when she heard a second vehicle pull up, but then she thought that she must have dreamt about the other in anticipation of its arrival. She heard no voices, just the sound of feet on the gravel, the laboured loading up of the taxi, the slamming of doors, and then the revving of the engine as they left. When there was no sound other than the sporadic twittering of birds, Claire turned onto her side, pulling the duvet snugly about her, and went back to sleep.

It was nine-fifteen when she eventually appeared in the kitchen, finding Agnes already busying herself in emptying the dishwasher of the plates and cutlery from the evening before. Claire made them both a cup of tea before taking a carton of yoghurt from the fridge, an orange from the fruit bowl, and sitting down at the table with the old housekeeper. It was apparent that Agnes was quite tearful at the departure of the young couple from the house, so Claire commiserated at length with her about what a miss they were going to be and how nice they were and how the house was now going to seem very empty with them and Art and Violet all gone.

It was Agnes who brought their conversation to an abrupt close when she glanced at the clock above the cooker and then began struggling to her feet.

"Here, my girl, look at the time! It's half past ten! I was completely forgetting Leo now with Pavel away. We'll be needing to get him up and about."

"Don't you worry about it," Claire said, draining her tea and getting to her feet, "I'll go and see to him. He'll probably have benefited from a lie-in after all that excitement last night."

Claire made her way out into the hall and across to Leo's bedroom. She pushed open the door and walked down the corridor, at this point not hearing any sound coming from his room. She turned the doorknob carefully and peered in, expecting to see him still lying fast asleep in his bed. Letting out a small cry of surprise, she entered and moved immediately through to check the small ensuite bathroom.

"That's extraordinary," she said out loud, because Leo was not there, neither was his wheelchair.

She hurried into the hall, making straight for the sitting room. Walking its length, she glanced behind sofas and chairs in case Leo had collapsed behind them. Her pace quickened considerably as she left the room and returned to the kitchen.

"Agnes, I can't find Leo."

The housekeeper froze in her action of drying a saucepan. "What d'you mean you can't find him? Is he not in his bedroom?"

"No, nor in the sitting room."

"Well, surely he can't be that far away,"

she said, putting the saucepan down on the table and making for the door. "He's not able to use the stairs, so he's not likely to be anywhere else but on this floor."

Five minutes later, they met in the hall, their faces both expressing the same bewilderment and worry.

"I have no understanding of this," Agnes said in a shaky voice. "You don't suppose he's tried to . . ."

Their eyes simultaneously turned to the front door and they both rushed towards it, Claire beating Agnes by at least four strides. She threw it open, half-expecting to see Leo lying in a crumpled heap at the bottom of the steps with the mangled remains of his wheelchair on top of him. She stood stock-still in the doorway, her hand covering her mouth, as it began to dawn on her that what she had heard that morning was no fleeting dream. It was not Leo and the wheelchair in front of the house, but a low-slung, dark-blue car with gold-spoked wheels and a rear spoiler spanning its boot.

"Now I wonder why that's there," Agnes said as she peered past Claire. "He's meant to be taking the young 'uns to the airport."

Claire turned to her. "Did you know he was?"

"Aye, of course. You'll remember that it was Jonas who fixed for the young 'uns to come and work here. He's always dashing back and forth to the airport with his workers."

Claire glanced back at the car. "So how . . . ?"

"Maybe . . ." Agnes paused. "Maybe . . . he's taken a bigger vehicle."

Claire saw the uneasy smile on the housekeeper's face and understood it immediately. "You mean one that can take a wheelchair, don't you?"

"That's what I'm thinking," Agnes replied quietly.

"Oh, for heaven's sakes!" Claire exclaimed, slamming the front door shut. "What is he up to? Why is he being so . . . damned *devious*?"

And as she stormed off into the sitting room, Agnes was left to puzzle whom she was actually talking about.

Claire was never far from the front door for the rest of the day. If she heard a car pull up on the gravel, she would rush across the hall, fixing a thunderous scowl on her face, and throw the door wide. This not only resulted in the postman jumping back in shock and nearly falling down the steps, but also in the hasty withdrawal of a double-glazing salesman, who must have thought he'd come across his Nirvana when first arriving at the multi-windowed house.

It was a quarter past eight in the evening, and the sun had sunk low enough to touch the treetops at the far end of the lawn, when Claire, standing at the kitchen window, saw the dark blue minibus drive slowly up the drive. She hastily finished off what she was doing and ran through to the hall and stood in the open doorway, her arms crossed and her face fixed in a frown, as the vehicle made its final approach and came to a halt at the bottom of the steps. Leo, who was sitting in the back seat, caught sight of her and gave her a broad grin and a wave. She did not return it but walked slowly down the steps as the taxi driver got out and slid the door open for him.

"For goodness' sakes, Leo, where have you been?" she asked angrily.

"Oh, my dear, we've had the most wonderful time. Now, come on, take that moody face off because I'm absolutely fine." He manoeuvred himself around on his backside so that his feet were sticking sideways out of the taxi. "I know I should have told you I was going, but it gets so tedious having everything done for you, and I just wanted to do something for myself, and I know you would have probably tried to stop me." He laughed, his blue eyes twinkling teasingly. "I'm right, aren't I?"

Claire was saved from giving an answer by the slamming of the vehicle's rear door and the appearance of Jonas, pushing Leo's wheelchair. He said nothing but smiled at her before manhandling the old man into it.

"So, I shall tell you what we did today," Leo said as Jonas settled him into the wheelchair. "First we went to the airport with Pavel and Gabriela where we got them checked in, and then we had a very good cup of coffee at one of those stall places. Golly, that place has got bigger since I was last there." Claire glanced at Jonas as he paid the taxi driver. "And then

Jonas and I jumped back into the taxi and headed off into Edinburgh and we had a wonderful morning going round the Botanical Gardens. Such a fantastic array of plants they have there." As the taxi departed, Jonas manoeuvred the wheelchair backwards across the gravel and began bumping it up the steps. "Be a good girl and push from the front, would you? And then, we drove right out into East Lothian and had the most delicious lunch in a little place called . . . what was it again, Jonas?"

"Dirleton," Jonas replied as he strained to pull the wheelchair up the last step.

"That's right, Dirleton. Charming village. And then, you'll never guess what we did."

"I can't begin to," Claire said tetchily.

"Well, we went to this marvellous new residence near Dunbar. It's an old mansion house that's been converted quite beautifully, and it has the most breathtaking gardens, not at all unlike this place, actually, and we met all these delightful people who work there, and the rooms are quite splendid with the most eye-catching views across the fields and right out to the North Sea."

Claire frowned and looked up at Jonas, but he purposely kept his eyes averted by choosing to continue pulling the wheelchair across the hall towards the sitting room.

"And the long and the short of it is that they've offered me a room there at the end of September, and I've accepted it. So what do you think of that, then?" Now positioned by the table in front of the sitting room window, Leo thumped once on the armrests of his wheelchair. "Now, what I *really* want is a good strong whisky. Haven't had one since God knows when, but I feel like celebrating in style." He stuck his thumb up in the air. "Jonas, would you do the honours? Ice and water, please, and you'll find a bottle in one of the cupboards in the dining room."

Claire waited until Jonas had left the room before putting her hand on her stepfather's shoulder. "Leo, why are you doing this?" she asked quietly, glancing towards the door. "You don't have to. Art and I will make sure we're the ones who buy Croich and then you can have your cottage and we'll make sure you're looked after."

Leo shook his head forcefully. "No, I

want to get shot of this place. Had enough of it. Time to move on."

"But, Leo . . ."

"I'm feeling very positive about all this, Claire, much more so than I have done in the past week, I can tell you. It's given me the direction I've been needing."

"Why did you not discuss it . . ."

She did not want to say any more because Jonas had returned, walking steadily across the room with a brimming glass in his hand. He handed it to Leo.

"Well, cheers, then," Leo said, holding up the glass to them. "Here's to the future." He took a healthy swig and then placed it on the table in front of him. "Now, I want to be left in peace, if you don't mind. It's been a long day and I need a bit of time by myself." He turned to Claire and nodded at her. "Meantime, my dear, I want you to go with Jonas because . . ."

"I'm not going anywhere with Jonas."

"Yes, you are, my girl, because he's got quite a lot to tell you."

Claire shook her head resolutely, looking directly at her stepfather to avoid catching Jonas's eye. "Leo, I'm sorry, but I'm not going."

Leo sat up rigid in the wheelchair and glared at her, his bushy eyebrows set so hard that they almost met in the middle. "Claire, you will go with Jonas. I have never asked much of you, but on this, I absolutely *insist.*"

His tone was so strong that Claire took an involuntary step back. She could not remember Leo ever talking to her like that. She even found herself looking towards Jonas to avoid her stepfather's angry expression, but Jonas did little other than shrug his shoulders.

"All right," Claire replied, "but we won't be long. I'll see you when I can get back and we can talk some more about all this."

Leo took a sip of his whisky. "I'll be in bed when you get back, and if I'm not . . ." he turned and smiled at her ". . . then you shouldn't be here."

Claire bent down and gave him no more that a dutiful peck on the side of the head. She walked past Jonas without looking at him and he followed her out into the hall.

"Where are we going?" she asked with little interest.

"For a drive," Jonas replied.

"I want to get my handbag, then. It's upstairs in my bedroom."

"Okay, I'll wait in the car."

Claire made her way up the stairs and walked along the corridor to her room. Closing the door behind her, she leaned against it and held her hands hard against her face. Why was Leo making her do this? What was he trying to achieve? Maybe to avoid going in that blasted car with him, she should go straight downstairs and tell Leo now about all his subterfuge and plotting, about his plans to build forty houses on the property, and that was the *real* reason why Jonas had taken him off today to inveigle him into reserving a place at that residence. But then again, Leo had been so adamant that she should go with Jonas, and she really didn't want to go against his wishes and risk precipitating him into another mental decline. There was no option open to her other than to do what he asked.

She walked over to the dressing table by the window, sat on the stool and looked at herself in the mirror. She pushed her short dark hair behind her ears and leaned forward to study her face more closely, gently flicking a finger at a small black smudge below her left eye. She stopped suddenly mid-action. Why on earth was she trying to make herself presentable for him? There was simply no need for that.

She got up, took her handbag from the bed, let out a long, steadying breath and left the room.

35

Not a word passed between them as they drove through the outskirts of Alloa and headed up towards the hills. Conversation, at any rate, would have been difficult because the noise emanating from the twin exhaust pipes was almost ear-splitting inside the black leather confines of the car, especially when Jonas began moving fast through the gears as he powered the machine around the tight bends of the country road. Claire had an inkling that he was doing this on purpose, just to get some sort of reaction out of her, trying to force her to say something, but she simply braced herself in her seat, clenching a hand to the double-strapped safety harness, and stared resolutely ahead as the bright beams of the car's halogen headlights swung mesmerizingly to and fro in front of her.

They had driven for about fifteen minutes when Jonas suddenly braked and pulled the car over to the right, bringing it to a halt in front of a wooden gate. He unbuckled his safety harness and got out and Claire watched as he walked over to the gate, moving to one side to allow the headlights to play on the large padlock that secured it. He turned the key, slipped out the heavy chain and pushed the gate open. The headlights now picked out the dirt-track road that lay beyond the gate, and she felt a knot of apprehension grip her stomach as he made his way back to the car and got in.

"Where are you taking me?" she asked uneasily.

He looked round and smiled as he did up the buckle on his safety harness. "Don't you know where we are?"

Claire's eyes darted around like a frightened rabbit. "No, I do not, and I'm really not liking this. I want to get out." She began fumbling with her own buckle, but Jonas laid his hand gently over hers to stop her.

"Come on, nothing's going to happen," he said before pushing the car into gear and rolling it slowly through the gate. He stopped and flicked a switch on the dashboard and the headlights broadened and intensified, casting out a beam that now lit up the dense cover of fir trees on either side of them. He pushed another button above his head that shone a thin shaft of light onto Claire's knees and then reached over to the glove compartment in front of her and opened it. He took out a few creased and dirt-spattered sheets of paper and dropped them in her lap. Claire studied them for a moment and then turned to him, her eyes wide with surprise.

"That's my handwriting," she said incredulously. "These are my navigating notes."

"I know they are," he replied, revving up the engine. "I kept them for you."

Claire peered through the windscreen. "Is this the road?"

"Yes, and it's exactly as it always was. Nothing's changed." He smiled at her. "Shall we give it a go, then, just for old times' sake?"

"No, we will not!" Claire exclaimed, throwing the sheets onto the dashboard and crossing her arms. "That is just the stupidest suggestion! We did all that ages ago, and what's more, I hardly go in a car nowadays. Anyway, look, it's pitch-dark. I only did it a couple of times and that was in the daylight."

Jonas laughed. "What a lot of excuses!" He paused, jerking his head to the side. "Actually, it's going to be a new experience for me as well."

Claire glared at him. "Listen, Jonas, we are not going to go up that road and that's final. Now just turn the car around and let's go back home. I've had enough of this."

Jonas slumped back in his seat. "Oh, well, if you don't want to do it"—he suddenly slammed the car into gear and pressed his foot hard against the floor— "then I'll just have to do it myself!"

The car's wheels kicked up a shower of dirt and loose stones before taking grip and shooting forward at a speed that sucked Claire back into the folds of the winged rally seat.

"For God's sakes, don't do this!" she yelled frantically above the screaming

noise of the engine. "We haven't got hel-
mets! You'll kill us both!"

"Help me, then," Jonas yelled back,
grabbing the sheets of paper off the dashboard and throwing them into her lap. He
quickly put his hand back on the steering
wheel in time to slew the car round the
first corner. "I can't do this without you."

"Just stop the car then!"

"No!"

Another corner came at them, a hard
right-hander, and Jonas nearly lost control, the back wheels sliding precariously
near the edge of the road. Claire's head
was thrown to the side, the only part of her
body that wasn't firmly anchored into the
seat, and she clenched her fists tight, understanding now exactly what was meant
by a "white-knuckle" ride, and then the
headlights picked out a drainage pipe pro-
truding from the bank on the right-hand side
and, in that instance, Claire knew where
they were. She looked down at the sheets
of paper and hurriedly went through them.

"Right, a hundred yards and—"

Her call was too late. Jonas swung the
car to the left round a ninety-degree bend
and the car's wheels juddered in defiance

of the gravity pull that had them nearly in the ditch.

"Go from now, Claire," Jonas yelled. "Come on, you were the best navigator I ever had."

Claire looked round at him, amazed at what he had just said.

"Call, for Christ's sakes."

Claire looked down at her notes. "Fifty yards, right-hander, forty degrees!"

And then the years rolled back and it all came to her naturally. It didn't matter that it was pitch-dark. She hardly had to look up from her notes, knowing instinctively when to call out her next instruction. Her brain raced, her eyes widened with the exhilaration of the drive and she felt once more like that girl in her late teens, sitting next to the boy who meant everything to her. She glanced round at Jonas, seeing the smile on his face and the strong hands that never stopped moving on the steering wheel, his left darting back and forth to the gear stick. And then Jonas slammed his foot to the floor, the brakes locked, and she was thrown forward, her straps cutting into her shoulders, and the car came to an abrupt standstill. She turned to look ahead and the headlights seemed to shine away to infinity down a narrow firebreak between the trees, picking out the dim outline of a distant hillside. She peered out the side window and swallowed hard when she realized that the car had come to rest only feet away from a near-vertical drop.

"Oh my God," she said quietly.

"You missed that corner," Jonas replied nonchalantly. "Mind you, you were doing a pretty good job up until then."

She turned to him, unsmiling. "That really was the stupidest thing ever to do."

"No, it wasn't . . . not until that point. You see, Claire, I put my trust in you. I'd never have been able to drive at that speed if I couldn't rely totally on the person sitting beside me."

"Ah, right, so it was my fault you nearly got us both killed."

Jonas's only reply was to smile at her and shake his head. He put the car into reverse gear and swung it round so it was heading down the road again. "Come on, let's go and get something to eat."

"You've got to be joking!" Claire exclaimed in disbelief. "Just take me home, will you?"

"Can't, I'm afraid," Jonas replied as he drove slowly down the road. "Leo was insistent that we talk. You should know, he was pretty vehement with you about it back at the house. Anyway, I've booked a table, so we may as well make use of it."

Claire turned to him. "Does your wife know about this?"

Jonas nodded. "Yes, she does, and she knows all about you, because I told her."

"She sounds a very understanding person," Claire replied with more than a hint of cynicism in her tone.

Jonas turned and smiled at her. "You're right, she is. Liv is a very beautiful person and she doesn't mind me taking you out because that's the way she is. If I get back at midnight tonight, she'll just wake up and smile at me. If it's two o'clock in the morning, she'll no doubt frown, but tomorrow morning she'll once again smile at me."

Claire blushed, realizing that what she had said was wrong. It was as if the time warp, created in her mind by the reckless drive up the road, was yet to wear off, the remark befitting more the spiteful jealousy of a shunned teenage girl. "I'm sorry," she

mumbled in embarrassment, "that was un-
necessary."

"Yes, it was rather," Jonas said as he
unbuckled his seat harness to get out and
shut the gate. "You should come round to
the house sometime to meet Liv. I reckon
you'd both get on really well together."

It took them ten minutes of sedate driving to get to the restaurant. It was an old
whitewashed coaching inn, set in the centre of a village that consisted only of a main
street and through which cars drove at a
speed that far exceeded the thirty-miles-
an-hour limit. From the moment they entered the low oak-beamed establishment,
it was quite apparent that Jonas was a
regular, being greeted by the landlord with
a good deal of joking laughter and mascu-
line backslapping. The man led them down
a narrow corridor, past the bustling public
bar, and into a long room at the back of
the inn, lit only by flickering candles that
sat in the centre of each of the eight small
square tables and lined the stone mantelpiece above the wide unlit fireplace. There
were only two other couples in the restaurant, and each acknowledged Jonas with
a wave or a nod of the head as they made

their way to the table at the far end of the room.

When the landlord asked them for their drinks order, Claire realized that her greatest need was for a large glass of red wine, so Jonas ordered up a bottle of Rioja without even bothering to consult the wine list. They sat opposite each other without speaking, awkwardly glancing around the restaurant, and it was then that Claire noticed a strange unease come over Jonas. When he caught her eye, his expression seemed to read both apprehension and regret, but it vanished immediately, replaced with a broad smile the moment the landlord returned to their table to pour a small amount of wine into his glass. Jonas took a sip, nodded his approval, and the man poured wine into both their glasses.

Claire took a long drink from her glass. "Oh my goodness, I needed that," she murmured, putting the glass down on the table. She shook her head. "That was one of the most irresponsible things I've ever known anyone to do. We were only inches away from . . . I don't know what."

"We were fine," Jonas replied dismissively. "Okay, so it's true I've never driven that road before at night, but I do know the feel of every car I drive. I know what it's doing and what it's capable of doing, regardless of whether I'm driving at twenty or a hundred miles an hour."

"Rather like what those macho car magazines say about having a good woman."

Jonas looked surprised. "No, actually, I hadn't even thought to say that." He laughed, relieved that at last Claire seemed to be showing a glimmer of humour. "But I suppose it's quite an apt analogy."

Claire, however, did not react to this. She sipped her wine and put the glass on the table. "And, no doubt, in your motorracing world, you managed to have your fair share of those."

The smile slid from his face, once again replaced by the gaunt look of apprehension. "Yes, again you're right," he said, running a finger hard against the rim of his wine glass. "And that's what completely changed my life. I had one too many."

"What do you mean by that?"

He leaned back in his chair, pressing his hands to his face before pulling them hard across his dark hair. "Look, Claire, this is really not easy for me to say. In fact, it's probably the most difficult thing I have ever done in my life." He paused for a moment, keeping his eyes averted from her, and Claire could tell, in that instance, that he was summoning up every last vestige of courage to continue. "But after I've told you, you will understand everything about why our friendship ended."

Claire stared at him, feeling an extraordinary sense of panic well up in her. She wasn't expecting this. She wasn't prepared for this. She glanced around, wondering where she could go just for a moment, just to . . .

Jonas leaned forward on the table, now looking directly at her. "I . . . well, Charity and I . . ." He rocked his hand to and fro and let his words trail off, leaving it to Claire to understand what he was getting at.

Because Claire's mind had been elsewhere, both the action and words took time to penetrate, as if picking up the sound of a high-flying plane's roaring jets long after it had come into view. She frowned in total incomprehension at what he had just implied, her mouth trying to form words that just wouldn't come out.

Eventually, she just let out a short, incredulous laugh. "You did . . . what?"

"Do I need to spell it out?"

Claire shook her head. "Are you being serious?"

Jonas held up his hands. "Why would I admit to it if I wasn't being serious?"

"But you didn't even . . . like her."

"It was not a planned event, Claire," Jonas replied.

Claire was stunned. "I'm sorry, I don't believe what I'm hearing here. When . . . did this happen?"

"When do you think? It was during a Christmas holidays, wasn't it?"

Claire felt herself beginning to tremble as the lid on the hidden vault of memories that lay buried within her creaked wide open, and she felt a lump forming in her throat as she thought back on the most dismal time of her life.

"That was when you stopped talking to me," she said quietly.

Jonas did not reply, but rubbed a finger hard against his mouth.

Claire leaned down and picked up her handbag. "I think I want to go now," she said, pushing back her chair. "I've heard enough."

Jonas raised a hand to stop her. "No, please, not yet. It wasn't my idea, all this. It was Leo who asked me to tell you."

She stared at him open-mouthed, the shock at this news checking her departure. "Leo knew about this?"

"I had no idea he did until a couple of weeks ago. He'd kept it to himself all these years, yet never took any action over it."

Claire resumed her seat. "How . . . did he find out?"

"I told my father and he, in turn, told Leo. He went round to see Leo just after the holidays had finished to say he wanted to give up the tenancy of the farm. My father was completely devastated by what had happened and he didn't believe we had any right to remain there."

"But he did."

"Yes, but only because Leo refused to let him go."

The landlord once again interrupted their conversation, coming to stand at their table with a pencil hovering expectantly above his order pad. Jonas glanced pleadingly at

Claire and, with a resigned shake of her head, she picked up the menu and ordered a medium-rare fillet steak. It was the first thing she saw.

Jonas visibly relaxed when she had placed her order. "Make that two," he said, handing back the menus to the landlord. He watched the man leave before leaning his elbows on the table. "I was young and I was stupid, Claire, and what I did was unforgivable, but I never realized at that stage that I was just being used as a pawn in an evil little game that didn't even involve my father and me."

Claire shut her eyes and sighed. "Okay, I think you'd better explain all this."

Jonas took a large gulp of his wine and put the glass down with such force that Claire was surprised it didn't shatter in his hand. "Well," he began, "I was working on my car in the workshop late on at night." He laughed, but his face only told sadness. "I remember my father had given me twin Weber carburettors as a Christmas present and I wanted to get them fitted as soon as possible so that you and I could get the car up onto that road to try it out. Anyway, you had been with me most of the evening and had left only about half an hour before. I was head down under the bonnet when I heard the door open and I turned round, expecting to see my father"—he shook his head—"but it was Charity. Dammit, I had no idea what she was doing there, and I certainly didn't want her around, so I just said hullo and then got on with what I was doing. The next thing I knew she'd come over to stand next to me, and then she began pressing her body against me. She said she'd always fancied a bit of rough and was I up for it? I felt confused and frightened by the way she was behaving, because she had shown nothing but disdain and contempt for me before that. And so I just pushed her away, pretty forcefully too, but that only seemed to encourage her and then she began to . . . show herself to me. The confusion in my mind just came out as . . . anger and I wanted to hurt her for everything she had done to you and for her . . . superior bloody attitude to me, so I wasn't for holding back and I took her right there in the filth of the workshop." He paused, taking another slug of wine before letting out a long breath to steady himself. "After we'd finished, it suddenly dawned on me what I had done . . . and what it would mean to my relationship with you, and I felt mucky and soiled and"—he rubbed a hand across his face—"and devastated. I just left her where she was and went over to the washroom at the back of the workshop. As I opened the door, I thought I heard her leave, so I went in and scrubbed myself, hoping that in some way it would help get rid of the guilt and the fear that I felt. It was only when I came out of the washroom that I realized the sound that I'd heard had not been Charity leaving, but Marcus entering. They were both standing leaning against the car, smiling at me." Jonas poured more wine into his glass and took another gulp. "Marcus asked me if I had enjoyed myself, and I tell you, that made me more frightened than I'd ever been in my life. I said I didn't know what he was talking about, but that made them smile at each other even more, and then it dawned on me that the sick bastard had been there all along, watching everything that I had done to his sister . . . and she to me." He studied Claire's face concernedly. "Are you all right?"

Claire shook her head and got quickly to her feet, her hand covering her mouth. "The ladies' room," she mumbled, "where is it?"

Jonas sprang to his feet and guided her quickly to the door at the back of the restaurant. She went in and he stood outside, casting uneasy smiles at those others in the restaurant, who had turned to see the cause for such sudden and urgent activity around their table.

Five minutes later Claire re-appeared, her face almost green and her eyes puffed from crying.

"Are you all right?" he asked.

She nodded.

"Listen, maybe this wasn't such a good idea after all. I'll take you home. I can cancel the orders."

"No," Claire replied, wiping her eyes with a tissue. "I want to hear it out." She snuffled out a laugh. "Actually, I feel quite hungry now."

Jonas put a steadying hand on her elbow as they made their way back to the table. She didn't shrug it away. He saw her seated before going back to his own chair.

"I want to hear it all."

Jonas nodded slowly. "Okay, then." He paused for a moment, gathering his thoughts. "So Marcus said that what he'd just witnessed was a classic case of statutory rape. Of course, this threw me into a complete panic and I told him it hadn't happened like that at all, but he just said it would be my word against theirs and I wouldn't have a leg to stand on if it came to legal proceedings. I had this vision of myself up in court and heading off to prison, and then Marcus threw me the lifeline. He said that we could keep it to ourselves, but there were conditions attached. I was never to go near the house again, but more importantly, I was never to see or have any contact with you ever again." He paused, holding out his hands in a hopeless gesture. "What was I to do? Dammit, I wasn't even nineteen yet. I was young, unworldly and very frightened. I always had been frightened of those two. Charity only had a year on me, but she and her brother always seemed so much cleverer, so much more grown-up. If they were to tell Leo about what had happened, there was little doubt he'd have us chucked out of the farm. That meant my father losing his livelihood, and

I'd have lost the trust and friendship of Leo, the one man whom I really looked up to. So I agreed like a shot, and once they'd got that out of me, they left . . . and that was the last time I saw them." He paused, biting his lip. "And then, the following morning, you came round . . . and that was it. I got rid of you as they wanted."

The landlord, at that point, came over to their table with their food, and the interruption gave Claire time to try to gather her thoughts. She was still trying to take it all in when the man had returned to his place behind the bar.

"I don't understand all this," she said eventually. "I mean, why would they do such an appalling thing?"

Jonas stared at her. "My word, you have no idea, do you?" He picked up his knife and fork and cut into his steak. "Marcus and Charity were both consumed with jealousy. They were jealous of everything you had, everything they believed you had taken from them. They despised the love you were given by your mother, but more especially the love you got from Leo, their own father. They wanted everything that you had, and they knew that the one possession

you valued above all others was your friendship with me, and that's what they came to
realize as being the weak point at which
they could strike. Through me, they could
bust everything apart . . . and they suc-
ceeded."

Claire toyed with her steak and then laid
down her knife and fork and leaned forward on the table, covering her face with
her hands. "My God, I never thought that
anyone could hate me that much."

Jonas shrugged his shoulders. "Welcome to my world, Claire." He took a mouthful of food and paused while he finished it.
"A few days after it happened, I decided I
had to tell my father about it. It was the only
time I can ever remember him hitting me. It
wasn't just a slap, either. He used his fists,
both blows to my face. He knocked me
down on the kitchen floor and then he put
his hand out to help me up and I saw that
he was crying. When I was back up on my
feet, he just clung onto me, sobbing on my
shoulder. I have never felt so wretched in all
my life. I had let him down and I'd betrayed
everyone." Jonas took another drink of his
wine. "And then Leo told me the other day
that Dad went round to see him a couple of

days later to tell him what had happened, and Leo said that the fault was his own, not my father's or mine, that it had always been a slow-fused bomb waiting to blow. However, he had never envisaged anything like this taking place. He told my father that the last thing he wanted was for him to leave the farm, and then he said that you and I should be kept separate for the time being, and that he would arrange for you to go off and travel. Everything, he hoped, would be settled by the time you returned. But then you went off to Australia and you never came back."

Claire cut at a corner of her steak. She had yet to eat any of it. She was remembering now the pain and loss she had felt during her travels, the complete emptiness in being separated from this man who now sat opposite her.

"Did it not hurt you?" she asked, almost bitterly.

Jonas stared at her and shook his head. "Claire, on the day you went away, I watched you leave. I stood in the bushes at the far end of the lawn and saw the car drive away. And when I walked back to the farm, I felt . . . God, I'm not great at expressing my feelings . . . but I felt as though I'd had my heart cut out."

Surprisingly, Claire felt not one iota of compassion for him. She just felt glad that he had suffered, that even in that one instance he had gone through the same sense of misery and deprivation that had lasted in her for all of a year. At last she took a mouthful of food, fixing her eyes on her plate as she ate it.

"So how does this all fit in with what you're up to now?" she asked.

Jonas looked puzzled. "I'm sorry?"

"You're getting your own back, aren't you? Not just against Marcus and Charity, but against the whole family. That's the real issue, isn't it, Jonas? You don't just blame them for what happened, you want to get even with all of us."

"I suppose it depends on how you view it."

"I view it like this, Jonas. I was devastated by what you did to me but I've got over that. You have not, and your . . . hurt, or whatever you want to call it, is manifesting itself in revenge, and you've worked out a pretty good plan to achieve that, haven't you? You've got yourself into Leo's

confidence, you're an executor of his estate, and now you're pushing him into that
home, so that you can buy Croich and
build your bloody houses."

Jonas rubbed a finger against his chin
and slowly nodded his head. "Claire, when
we were up on that road earlier, I put my
trust in you. You were the one calling the
tune. Now you've got to put your trust in
me."

"In that case, I'll ask you one question,
Jonas. Are you still going ahead with trying
to purchase the house?"

Jonas paused, linking his hands together.
"Yes, I am."

Claire threw her napkin onto the table.
"That's what I thought." She picked up her
handbag from the floor and got to her feet.
"I think we've talked enough, Jonas. I
would like to go home now."

She turned and strode the length of the
restaurant, the one small pleasure she
had extracted from the evening being that
he was going to have to pay for the over-
priced steak that she had barely touched.

36

Claire planned not to speak to Leo about what Jonas had told her. She felt that she just could not bring herself to do so. When she got back to the house that night, after a drive that was filled with as much tension as when she and Jonas had set out, she had gone straight to bed and had just lain there, unable to sleep. It was neither rage nor regret that had kept her awake, but an overpowering sense of guilt that it had all been her fault, that Leo had been made to suffer so unbearably because of her. He had had to undergo the inexplicable hardship of going against his own children, admitting their faults, and taking the side of a young man whom he knew to have had loveless sex with his daughter. Oh yes, Claire had suffered during those now-distant holidays, and she had not held back over the next few months in demonstrating to her mother and to Leo just how miserable and distraught she was. But in no way could it ever have matched Leo's complete devastation in learning the true facts of what took place. And he had never told anyone.

When she went to see him the following morning, she stood outside the door of the sitting room for a full minute, staring round the silent hallway, trying to work out how best she could avoid talking about what had happened. Realizing then that it didn't just depend on her, she took in a deep breath and entered.

"Ah, good morning," Leo said, turning from his customary position by the window. He said nothing more, but as Claire approached him he opened his arms and she leaned over his wheelchair to receive a long hug and a kiss on the forehead.

"That was a very hard thing for you to have to learn, wasn't it?" he said.

Claire clasped her arms tightly around his neck. "Leo, I don't know what I can say—"

"Nothing," he cut in. "I decided long ago it wasn't worth talking about. I have never been very good at dwelling on bad things."

"I'm so sorry."

"Don't be," he said, patting her back. "It was nothing at all to do with you. If anything, it was my own love for you and your mother that proved to be the catalyst for all that took place—and that, my girl, was something I was never prepared to forfeit."

She gave him a kiss on his wrinkled brow. "You are a wonderful man, you know."

"Well, it's kind of you to say so, but I have a much lower opinion of myself."

"You've absolutely no reason to."

Leo pushed her gently away. "Oh, my dear, you only know the half of it. I have been very foolish and neglectful of my duties towards you and I can't forgive myself for that."

Claire stared at him questioningly. "In what way?"

Leo held up a shaky hand. "I think it's best if we left these matters for now. I'm praying that we'll have everything sorted out in the next few weeks."

Claire stood upright and eyed him with concern, wondering if the pressure of all that he had had to disclose over the past twenty-four hours wasn't taking its toll on his own fragile state of mind. Why would he think that all would be sorted out in the next few weeks? With the house going to auction in ten days' time, Leo might not even be living here anymore. Or maybe there was more in what he had just said? His reference to "we" certainly seemed to imply that he knew that she and Art were going to get the house and that there would be no reason for him to move away. It could be then that Jonas had had second thoughts about bidding for the house after all. She had never heard the telephone ring that morning, but that didn't mean that Leo hadn't called him to find out how the evening had gone and Jonas had let it be known to him then.

She had turned to gaze out the window as she thought this through and now looked back at Leo, preparing to question him further, but he had closed his eyes, his chin slumped forward on his chest.

She wondered if he really was asleep or whether this wasn't his way of avoiding any further discourse on the matter. Either way, she decided to let him be and walked quietly from the room.

At lunchtime the phone rang and Claire's immediate thought was that it could be no one else but Jonas calling. Since speaking with Leo, she had been going over in her mind what Jonas had disclosed to her the previous evening and what might have been the subsequent discussion between him and Leo. She hurried from the kitchen into the hall, wishing to answer the call alone, and having stood for a moment with her hand hovering over the receiver, she willed herself to pick it up.

"Hullo?" she asked tentatively.

"Hi, it's me."

She felt a wave of relief pass over her when she heard Art's soft American twang.

"Darling, how are you?"

"Good. You were a long time in answering."

"I was, erm . . . well, I had to come through from the kitchen. How's Violet?"

"She's good. Pilar has just taken her off to school and then she's got a birthday party this afternoon." He chuckled. "We had high drama in the household this morning while she decided what she was going to wear, and I'm taking that as quite an alarming indication that our little girl is growing up fast."

Claire laughed, although, in truth, she felt more like crying, his words having brought on a sudden rush of homesickness. "I'm missing you both so much," she said.

"Angel, the feeling is reciprocated, I can tell you."

"How have you got on with the IRS?" Claire asked, wanting to change the subject before she broke down into an emotional heap.

"Well, it's taken every waking moment to sort out, but I think we're there now. Thankfully, it was just an anomaly thrown up by the extra revenue after the expansion." He paused. "The only thing is I still don't think I'll be getting over for the auction, Claire."

"I thought that might be the case," she replied despondently.

"Hey, but the good news is that I'm not liable for anything to Uncle Sam, so we're still in with a chance of getting hold of Croich."

"Yes, I suppose that's right," Claire said, not wishing to mention anything about the turn of events since his departure.

"I've just been on the phone to John Venables and he says that he's put the sale of the property in the hands of a real estate agent in Perth. They'll be doing all the advertising as well as the auction it-self. I've found it on their website and John said it's also been in the national papers during the past week. You haven't picked that up, have you?"

"No, I'm afraid not. I've been trying to get the house in order, so there hasn't been much time for reading papers."

Art paused. "Hey, angel, I realize this must be so hard for you. I've really left you high and dry, haven't I? I do know how much that house means to you, and on top of that, you're going to have to deal with the auction by yourself. I really am sorry."

Claire smiled. "It's okay, I'll cope. It makes me feel better, though, that you un-derstand."

"Of course I do, and I tell you, we'll go for broke in trying to get that place. In the meantime, though, I'm afraid you may have to gear yourself up to showing interested parties around the house."

Claire gasped. "Oh my goodness, I hadn't even considered that. Won't it all be handled by the realtors?"

"I'm not sure, but I'm calling Venables this afternoon, so I'll ask him." Art laughed. "Of course we don't want too many folks showing interest. The fewer bidders, the better—and talking of which, John Venables is not too pleased with the way Jonas has been behaving—you know, submitting his own plans for the house. John thinks it's decidedly underhanded. Not that that'll help us in any way to get the place, but at least it looks as if he's on our side."

"That's good," Claire replied, again not wishing to tell him what she had surmised from her conversation with Leo that morning.

"I really want that house, Claire, for you and for Leo."

"I know, my love."

"And I'll be on the other end of the phone to guide you through the bidding. Just make sure you charge up that mobile phone, okay?"

"I'll do that."

"It won't be long now. Just over a week to the auction, and then, no matter what the outcome, you fly straight back here. We'll get Leo sorted soon after that. How is he, by the way?"

"He's . . . going to be all right . . . I think."

"Sure he is. You wait, in a year we'll have him settled into that little condo over by the greenhouse and the man will be as happy as a clam."

Claire bit at her bottom lip. "I'd better go, Art. Agnes will have lunch on the table."

"Okay. I love you, angel."

"I know, and I love you too. Give a kiss to Violet from me."

"Consider it done."

Claire put down the receiver and walked back to the kitchen, now wishing that the day of the auction would hurry up and arrive. She wanted the uncertainty of the future dispelled both from their lives and from Leo's as soon as possible.

37

The weather broke during that week for only the second time since Claire had been in Scotland, and it rained as if the heavens had been storing it up for the past two months. A marquee had been erected on the lawn for the auction and Claire had watched from the kitchen window as the riggers, shrouded in waterproof gear, had struggled against the elements to put up the sodden canvas canopy, their constant passage from the driveway to the erection site turning the green turf into a muddy quagmire, despite the rubber matting they had laid down to prevent such an occurrence. Claire continued with her ineffectual tidying of the house, but it was only to keep her mind occupied as the day of the auction loomed. The presence of the marquee, however, made her feel as if she were living under the shadow of the guillotine.

The auction was not due to start until midday, but by half past ten cars had already started to arrive, being diverted along the lane at the far end of the lawn for parking in one of Jonas's fields. Luckily the rain had died out, but still, threatening clouds hung low in the sky, making the day so dark that the headlights of the cars shone out as if it were night-time. People now traipsed across the lawn to the marquee while some of the earlier arrivals were already standing outside it in clusters, drinking coffee from polystyrene mugs and pointing to different aspects of the house as they discussed it.

At half past eleven, Art called Claire on the mobile phone, just to make sure they had contact. He reassured her that he would be there to help her all the way, but Claire could tell from his voice that he was as nervous as she felt. Leo had already told her that he had no wish to be present in the marquee during the proceedings. He didn't want to have to make small talk with anyone about the whys and wherefores of the sale, and anyway it was too damned cold to be sitting around out there in a wheelchair. So Claire put on an old quilted jacket that she had found in the cloakroom and left the house by the front door, clutching tightly to the mobile phone as she dug her hands into the deep cosy pockets.

The marquee was already crammed with people, the noise of their chat almost deafening as they gathered around the trestle tables where the staff of the catering company gave out hot drinks and frantically made up more sandwiches to replenish the fast-emptying plates. As Claire pushed her way through the crowd towards the auctioneer's plinth at the far end, she found that she did not recognize one person there and was relieved when she saw John Venables approach her.

"Hullo, Claire," he said, giving her a single kiss on her cheek. He eyed her concernedly. "How are you?"

"Fine," she said, looking around at the

milling hordes. "Who are all these people? I didn't realize there'd be so much interest. I haven't shown one person round the house."

John smiled. "I'm pretty sure none of them are here to take part in the bidding, more likely just out of interest. It's very rare for any property to be sold by public auction in Scotland. I think they've just come to fill themselves up with what's on offer and watch proceedings."

"I hope so," Claire replied distractedly as she pushed herself up on her toes to gaze towards the plinth. "Have you seen Jonas Fairweather by any chance?"

"Yes, he and his wife were over by the coffee stall a moment ago."

"Ah," Claire said, dropping back heavily onto her feet. "He'll be bidding, then."

"I've heard nothing to the contrary," John replied. "Have you got reason to believe he might not?"

Claire smiled at him. "More wishful thinking, really."

John put a hand on her arm. "Are you going to be in touch with Art during the auction?"

Claire drew the mobile out of her pocket and held it up for him to see.

"Right, well, I shall be standing next to you just in case you need a bit of support nearer at hand." He glanced at his wrist-watch. "We're about there, I think. Come on, we'd better get closer."

As John guided her to the end of the marquee, the mobile rang in her hand, making her start with surprise. She answered it.

"Is it time?" Art asked without any form of greeting.

"John seems to think so."

"Good, I'm glad he's with you. Are there many people?"

"Scores, but John doesn't think any of them will be bidding."

"Let's hope not. And what about Jonas?"

People had begun to drift back from the podium and Claire saw Jonas standing to one side next to a statuesque blonde woman. Both looked apprehensive, she thought, as the auctioneer, a burly middle-aged man in a dark suit, got up on the podium and placed a sheet of paper on the high desk in front of him. He glanced over his shoulder at the young clerk who stood behind him talking into a mobile phone. He gave a nod to the auctioneer, who acknowledged it before picking up his gavel and thumping it hard down on the desk.

As the man's voice boomed out over the speaker system, informing those gathered of the details of the sale, John Venables leaned his gaunt frame over to Claire's free ear. "Ah, I think I might have been wrong about there not being any other bidders."

"Why's that?" Claire asked.

"What?" Art cut in on the mobile phone.

"Hang on, Art, I'll tell you in a moment."

"The young man standing behind the auctioneer," continued John, "I think he might be on a phone bid. I'll see if I can't find out more about it." He left Claire and made his way over to the podium.

"Art?" Claire said into the mobile.

"What's going on?"

"John thinks there's another bidder. It's being done by phone."

"Dammit, that is not good." She heard him sigh. "We're in the lap of the gods now, angel."

"What do you want me to do?"

"Just bid from the start, and for goodness' sakes, keep telling me the price."

"Okay. What price are we going to?"

Art sighed again. "Oh, I don't know. I'll play it as it comes."

"Oh my God, he's started!" Claire exclaimed as John returned to stand beside her.

"London-based, I'm afraid," he said. "That's all I could ascertain."

It was the telephone bidder who came in first with a bid of two hundred and fifty thousand pounds. Claire glanced across at Jonas and saw him raise his hand to push the price up by a further twenty thousand.

"Jonas has already gone up to two hundred and seventy thousand," she said into the mobile.

"There you go then," Art replied. "The man cannot be trusted. Get in the bidding fast."

Claire put up her hand in time to push the price up to three hundred and thirty thousand, but Jonas and the telephone bidder had taken it on to three hundred and ninety before she had even dropped her hand to her side.

"Art, it's going so fast!"

"Just keep in there!"

She raised her hand again, securing a bid for four hundred and thirty thousand. She glanced across at Jonas, who was now glaring at her, a deep frown creasing his forehead. There was a lull in the bidding and then Jonas moved forward and said something to the auctioneer.

The man nodded and called out, "Thank you, sir, we have a bid now of six hundred thousand pounds."

"Did you hear that, Art?" Claire said into the mobile.

"Yeah, I did. Who was it?"

"Jonas."

"The conniving bastard!" He paused. "Okay, Claire, seven hundred and fifty thousand tops. I'm sorry, darling, that's all I can do."

Claire was silent. There was no need for her to raise her hand again. The price had gone through their limit and was still rising.

"We're through, Art," she said quietly. "It's just gone up to eight hundred and thirty."

"I don't believe it!" Art exclaimed. "Who the hell are these guys?"

The bidding had stopped momentarily and the auctioneer was surveying the room for fresh bids. He looked at Claire and she shook her head and then she glanced across to Jonas and his wife to find that both were looking in her direction. The blonde woman smiled at her and reached out and clutched her husband's hand tightly. Jonas now turned his gaze away from Claire and faced the auctioneer, his face hard in concentration.

All that could be heard now in the marquee was the voice of the auctioneer, the crowd standing deathly silent as the price rose higher and higher.

"What's it up to now?" Art asked, his voice still registering deep disappointment.

"It's gone through the million mark," Claire said quietly, "and it's still going."

Art laughed. "Well, at least we've been beaten by a country mile. Is Jonas still going?"

"Oh yes," Claire replied acerbically. "There's no stopping him."

And with that, Claire saw Jonas falter in his bidding, turning towards his wife and then glancing over at her. The auctioneer was levelling his gavel at Jonas, waiting for his bid. The price stood at one million four hundred and ten thousand. Jonas wiped a hand against his brow and then raised it. The auctioneer called out one million four hundred and thirty thousand and then turned to face the young man behind him. The moment seemed to go on forever as the clerk listened on the phone, and Claire saw Jonas stare down at the ground, scraping a foot hard against the turf. His wife placed a hand on his shoulder and bit hard on her lip as she stared, like everyone else in the marquee, at the young man.

He nodded.

The auctioneer spun round to face his audience. "One million five hundred thousand," his voice boomed out.

There was a loud exhaling of breath throughout the marquee and Jonas looked up at the man and shook his head.

"Jonas is out of it!" Claire said to Art.

"Ha!" Art exclaimed. "Good riddance to the man too."

Going once, going twice, and the auctioneer banged down his gavel and immediately the noise in the tent rose to a

volume far greater than it had been before.

"What did it go for?" Art asked.

Claire pressed the mobile hard against
her ear. "One and a half million."

Art laughed. "Well, that should please
Leo." He paused. "My God, I hadn't
thought . . . what's going to happen to him
now?"

"I think that's all sorted," Claire replied
sadly.

"In what way?"

Claire pressed a hand to her other ear.
"Art, I can hardly hear you. It's really noisy
in here. I'll call you later."

"Okay, and listen, I'm sorry we didn't get
the house. It would have been crazy to go
any higher."

"I know," Claire yelled into the phone,
"I'm beginning to think that it's probably all
for the best. I'll call later."

She pressed the button on the phone
and returned it to the pocket of her jacket.
She turned and smiled to John Venables,
who still remained standing silently beside
her. "Well, that's it, then."

"I'm afraid so," he said distantly as he

stared over her head to where Jonas and his wife were standing. "Am I imagining it, or does Jonas seem quite content with the outcome?"

Claire looked across to see Jonas giving his wife a long hug before putting his hands to her face and giving her a kiss on the mouth. A man approached him and said something and Jonas turned to him with a broad grin on his face. He laughed and then swept his head round and caught Claire's eye. She gave him her hardest glare, but he just smiled at her and gave her a wave.

"Why is he so happy?" Claire said to the tall solicitor. "He didn't get the house."

John Venables shook his head. "I've no idea. It's not the reaction I'd expect either."

The sound of rain drumming hard on the canvas roof of the marquee now rose above the cacophony of voices. People had started to gather at the open section, ready to leave, pulling coats over their heads and readying umbrellas, and Claire looked past them to see the rain teeming down outside.

"Would you like to go and find out who bought the house?" the solicitor asked.

"Not really," Claire replied. "It's finished with, not only for us but for the house as well. They can't have paid that much without having plans to develop everything."

"I fear that probably will be the case," John replied sadly.

Claire put her hand on his arm. "I have to thank you, John, for all your support, especially today."

John Venables smiled at her. "It's been my pleasure, I can assure you. I'm only sorry that you and Art were not successful."

Claire sighed. "I don't know. I'm beginning to think this outcome is just a sign for us all to move on." She pulled the quilted jacket tight around her. "I'm going to head back to the house. Leo will want to know what's happened. At least he's got a heap of money now."

"All right," John replied. "I'll be in touch tomorrow."

Claire walked over to the opening and stood for a moment, readying herself for the dash to the front door. Through the blanket of rain she surveyed the side aspect of the house, seeing the water cascading from the clogged drainpipes and running in wide streams down the ancient stone, staining it dark like tears of abject misery. The tall windows showed no inner light, being like visionless eyes set below the hooded brows of their cold carved lintels. It was as if the place had taken on a character of its own, melancholic in its reminiscences, accepting with quiet resignation the eventuality of its demise.

The Dragon Plant House. The name came into Claire's mind the moment she thought back to her childhood memories of the place. She remembered arriving there, driving in Leo's old Humber through the canopy of rhododendrons, leaving behind the urban sprawl and having revealed to her this unexpected oasis of calm and beauty, with its wide green lawns and tall broad-limbed trees, and the proud rectangular edifice that stood sentinel over all. She remembered days with her mother and Leo in the greenhouse, and the laughter between them and their uninhibited spontaneous embraces while they worked. And she remembered, above all, her days with Jonas, their silly childish game of Balloon Man and Monkey Girl, and the constant two-way treading of the path between the house and the farm. She remembered the

countless evenings spent in the workshop,
he leaning over as he dug deep into his
car's engine while she chatted to him, handing him wrenches and other mechanical
instruments for which she had never found
out the names.

The workshop. Another image came to
mind, that of Jonas and Charity, and it was
one that broke her away from the nostalgic reverie. It was something she never
wished to imagine. It was all over, all finished with, and she now fully understood
why Leo wished it all to end. Happy memories had been blighted, and were therefore best banished from mind.

She hunched her shoulders and left the
marquee at a run, feeling her feet sink into
the sodden turf as the rain fell remorse-
lessly, penetrating her jacket and plaster-
ing her short dark hair against her head
and face.

Having discarded her wet jacket and shoes
in the hall, Claire entered the sitting room,
rubbing a hand through her sodden hair,
and was brought immediately to a standstill by the sight of Leo standing by the
window, leaning heavily on the sill.

"Leo, what are you doing?" she exclaimed, walking quickly to the far end of the room.

He looked round stiffly at her. "Damned good, eh? Just thought I'd see what I was like on the old pins."

She grasped his arm tightly, but her hand was shrugged away. "Don't fuss, Claire, I can manage." He slowly made his way back to the wheelchair, leaning heavily on the table as he went, and flumped back down into the chair with a great exhalation of breath.

"There you go. Well on the way to recovery, don't you think?" He turned to Claire, his triumphant smile sliding quickly from his face. "All right, let's be having it. What's the outcome?"

"We didn't get it, I'm afraid."

"Right—and Jonas?"

"He didn't get it either."

Leo paused. "So, what was the price?"

"One and a half million pounds."

He shut his eyes tight and rubbed a hand across his mouth. "Oh dear, oh dear. Well, I suppose it can't be helped." He turned to Claire. "You know, sometimes I do get awfully confused with events that have just taken place, but when it comes to certain things from way back, I'm still pretty sharp." He paused. "Can you remember what you and I used to call this house?"

Claire smiled. "Funnily enough, I was thinking about it all of five minutes ago. The Dragon Plant House."

Leo nodded. "That's exactly right, and I said to you that maybe it would change the house into a fire-eating monster that gobbled up people."

She laughed. "Ah yes, but only if they were evil and nasty."

"That's what you said," Leo replied distantly, turning to stare out of the window. "The very words." He was silent for a moment, linking his hands and rubbing them together. "Listen, my dear, I think it's time you went back home. You've been here long enough." He looked round again. "I want you to go back to Art and Violet."

Claire approached him and leaned over to put her arms around his neck. "Will you be all right, Leo?"

He reached up a hand and gave her arm a reassuring pat. "Of course I will. It's important that we all look to the future now."

She kissed him on the side of the head, keeping her face close for a moment to breathe in the nostalgic smell of ancient tweed. "I'll miss you, my darling man."

He moved his head to one side, detaching himself from her embrace. "Oh, I expect you to come back. I doubt I'd survive very long if I didn't see you quite often."

Claire laughed and stood up, wiping a single renegade tear from her cheek. "Of course I'll be back, and I promise it'll be on a more regular basis."

"Good," he said, manoeuvring his wheelchair round and pushing it towards the door. "Come on then, we've got things to do. You call Art and start your packing, while I break the news to old Agnes." He laughed. "I'm not sure if she's going to break down in tears of utter desperation or jump up and down in sheer delight, waving her hands in the air, yelling, 'At last I'm free!'" He stopped short of the door to allow Claire to open it for him. "The funny thing is," he said as he pushed himself out into the hall, "I rather suspect it might well be the latter."

38

New York—December 2006

Art never even waited for Claire's return from Scotland before he began looking for another investment. He was a business-man, after all, and there was no use in being retrospective over their failure to pur-chase Croich. By the time he was due to pick up Claire from Newark Airport, he had already sourced three failing restaurant businesses that were up for sale in mid-town, all within easy reach of their home in Gramercy Park but none of which en-croached on their present establishment's catchment area in the East Village.

He and Claire eventually settled on the

smallest of the three, a former pizzeria on East Thirty-eighth Street between Third and Lexington. Art had wanted to go bigger, but Claire had reasoned that the kitchen had been recently upgraded to full Health Department standards and that they would be better off spending capital in simulating the interior decor of their existing restaurant. They struck a deal with the owners only five days after Claire had stepped off the plane and the workmen moved in immediately, the plan being to have Barrington's Midtown up and running by Christmas. They made it with just two days to spare.

Art and Claire had hosted the initial evening, when with only ten tables they had managed sixty covers, but thereafter it was decided that Luisa, whom they had now brought in as a partner, should move up from Tompkins Square to manage the place while they continued to run the original restaurant until a suitable candidate could be found to take over from her.

Claire was quite happy for her days to be fully occupied once more. She had left Scotland with a troubled mind, bidding farewell to the house for the last time and leaving so many things hanging in limbo. She had, however, managed to gather together her mother's few possessions, leaving it to John Venables to arrange their shipment to New York, and she was thankfully away before Marcus and Charity came up from London to pick over those sparse pieces of furniture that were worth keeping, the rest being destined for the local auction house or the council dump. And then, on the day that they exchanged contracts on the new restaurant, her spirits were given a boost when she received a phone call from Leo, happily ensconced in his new home in East Lothian. She had listened without speaking, but with a smile broadening on her face, as he told her of the views from his bedroom window and the excellent quality of the food and the friendliness of the staff. He had only ended the call when one of the residents came into his room to invite him to make up a four at bridge. "Bloody hopeless at the game" were his parting words, "but, quite honestly, no one seems to mind." After that, nothing really mattered any more, and Claire put all thoughts of Scotland to the back of her mind and concentrated her whole being on the refurbishment of the new premises.

The restaurants were closed for two days over the Christmas break, and the Barrington family headed out to Long Island to stay with friends. It was during an unseasonably warm walk after Christmas lunch on Westhampton Beach when Claire's phone rang. Glancing at the screen, she saw who was calling her and immediately thought about leaving it to go to voicemail. But then she decided that it was Christmas after all and detached herself from the rest of the group and made her way up towards the dunes.

"Hullo, Charity. Happy Christmas to you."

"I suppose you think that's funny," Charity replied, and Claire immediately heard the distinct note of hysteria in her voice. "You know damned well it's the most miserable Christmas I have ever had."

Claire bit at her lip fiercely as she gazed out at the waves breaking idly on the beach. "Listen, Charity, I'm having a very nice walk on the beach with my family and some friends, so I'd be grateful if you'd hurry up and say what you have to say."

"Oh, I will, don't worry. You knew about this all along, didn't you? You planned the whole thing. Well, you bitch, you'll be bloody satisfied now."

"Hang on a minute. First of all, don't you dare call me a bitch, and secondly, I have absolutely no idea what you're talking about."

"Oh, don't try and pull the wool over my eyes, my girl, you know damned well what I'm talking about. I cannot believe you could be so filled with hate to do such a thing to Marcus and me." Charity now began to cry in deep gulping sobs that came over the phone so loudly that Claire winced at the noise. "Marcus and I are left with nothing, nothing, do you hear?"

Claire shook her head. "Oh, for goodness' sakes, Charity, what the hell are you on about?"

"I hate you, I always have, and I never want to see you again!"

Claire laughed. "Well, I'm not sure if that's going to have an everlasting effect on my life." She was beginning to enjoy this and waited for Charity to continue her tirade, but then the line went dead. She folded up the phone and slipped it into her pocket and looked round to see that Art and Violet had left their friends and were running up the beach towards her.

"Who was that?" Art asked, puffed from the exertion.

"Charity."

"Oh, God, what the hell did she want? Don't tell me she was wishing you a happy Christmas."

"No, far from it."

"Are you all right?" Art asked concernedly.

Claire grinned broadly at him and placed an arm around Violet's shoulders. "Yes, actually, I think I'm more than all right." She linked her arm through his and together they walked off down the beach to rejoin the others.

39

New York—January 2007

Three days into January and the weather continued to be so mild that pink blossoms started to appear on the two cherry trees opposite the restaurant in Tompkins Square. It was an incongruous sight when set alongside the bright Christmas lights that adorned the tall fir tree at the park's central point. Art and Claire even retrieved tables and chairs from the store and put them out on the pavement, and many customers chose to sit out for lunch and then well into the afternoon, long after the warming rays of the winter sun had slipped away behind the buildings. Both restaurants continued to be fully booked, so they were given no respite after the Christmas break, and their lives settled back into the same hectic pattern that had existed for them both over the past seventeen years. They relished it, as did Violet, who now spent most afternoons at a lively after-school social club, and it was only at weekends that she waited for the familiar late-morning nudge from Pilar to get her out of bed before going off to spend the day with friends.

At ten that evening, Claire began to feel the familiar aching tiredness in her legs and practiced her customary routine of walking over to the lectern by the entrance door and leaning on it while she slipped off her shoes and made a show of checking through the bookings. She ran her finger down the list, relieved that all but three of the names were crossed off. She did not look up when the door opened, hoping that Art would notice that she was in rest-mode and come forward to welcome the new arrivals.

"Excuse me, we have a reservation for two at ten o'clock." The voice was female, the accent lilting, almost as if she were singing her words.

Claire still did not look up, but brought her finger to rest on the first of the unticked-off names. "Is it Brewster?"

"No." Claire felt the woman brush against her and she was enveloped by a waft of expensive scent. A slim finger with subtle pink nail varnish pressed onto the page. "That's us there. Fairweather."

"Oh, sorry," Claire said, and then the name suddenly registered with her—and then the accent. She looked up slowly at the tall, strikingly blonde woman whom she had last seen at the auction in Scotland.

The woman smiled at her and held out her hand. "Hullo, Claire, we never got the chance to meet. I'm Liv."

"Yes, of course, hullo," Claire said, forcing a smile onto her face and hearing not one hint of friendliness in her own voice. She glanced behind Liv to see Jonas, looking quite uneasy, standing with his hands pushed into the pockets of his jacket.

Claire was momentarily frozen, completely taken aback in seeing them both here in New York, and she was therefore relieved when she heard Art's exclamation of surprise behind her.

"For heaven's sakes, this is a bit unexpected!" He walked round behind Claire and shook hands with Jonas, who then introduced him to Liv. "Are you eating with us tonight?"

"We have made a reservation," Liv said.

"Great!" Art said, smiling broadly at Claire, although his eyes told her that these two were the last people he wanted as guests in the restaurant that evening. "I can't understand why we never picked this one up."

Claire glanced down at the register. "I think it must have been one of the staff who took the booking."

"No matter," Art said, clapping his hands together, "welcome to Barrington's. Have you been over here for New Year?"

Liv turned to catch her husband's eye and shook her head. "No, we only arrived today."

"In that case, you must both be pretty tired and hungry," Art said, taking two menus from the slot at the back of the lectern, "so let's get you eating as soon as possible." He was about to lead them to a vacant table at the far end of the restaurant when Jonas reached out a hand to stop him.

"Actually, Liv hasn't really explained yet. We've come over here to see you two."

Claire glanced round at Art and saw that his face expressed the same puzzlement as she now felt.

"I was wondering," Jonas continued, "if we could go somewhere to have a chat."

Claire swallowed hard. "Well, I'm afraid I don't think that's possible right now. We are very busy and we haven't—"

She was cut short by Jonas handing her an unsealed envelope that he had taken from the inside pocket of his jacket. She stared at it for a moment before slipping in her hand and sliding out a photograph. It was of Leo, sitting in an armchair, with a beaming grin on his face and giving the thumbs-up with both hands. The happiness that radiated from the image was infectious and Claire felt her mouth crease into a smile. She looked up at Jonas. "He looks really well."

"He is," Jonas replied. "Now read the back."

Claire flipped over the photograph and

recognized immediately Leo's scrawling handwriting. It read, "I love you very much, my darling girl. This is for you, from your dotty old stepfather, Leo."

She pushed the photograph back into the envelope and smiled at Jonas. "Thank you." She laughed. "Mind you, it might have been cheaper all round if you'd just mailed it to me."

Jonas brought another envelope out of his pocket and handed it to Claire. "What Leo was referring to was not the photograph. It was this."

The envelope this time was sealed, and was embossed in the top left corner with the name of John Venables' legal practice. Claire stared at both Jonas and Liv, but their faces gave away no reckoning of what it might contain. She slowly slid her finger along the top of the envelope and pulled out the single slip of paper inside, reading the name of the Clydesdale Bank as it appeared. She stood transfixed as she took in what was written on it.

"My God," she said, looking up at Jonas in open-mouthed amazement.

"What is it?" Art asked.

"It's a cheque—for half a million pounds," she said quietly.

Art came forward and took it from her inert fingers.

"Where did it come from?" Claire asked.

Jonas shrugged. "It's what's due to you, mostly from your father."

"But his investment for me never amounted to that much money."

Jonas laughed. "Well, your investment gathered . . . rather unusual interest."

Claire's mind suddenly turned to the extraordinary conversation she had had with Charity on Christmas Day. "Has this anything to do with Marcus and Charity?"

Jonas's silent glance at Liv was all the confirmation she needed.

"What's been going on, Jonas?" Claire asked.

"That's what I wanted to explain." He looked around the restaurant. "Could we not go somewhere for just half an hour? I promise you it won't take any longer than that and then Liv and I will get out of your way."

It was Art who spoke. "Listen, Jonas, if you and Liv have come all the way over

here to give us a cheque of this . . . mag-
nitude, then the least we can do is give
you our time." He glanced around the restaurant. "There's no table for four free at
the moment. Do you mind talking in the office?"

"Anywhere's good," Jonas replied.

Art turned to Claire. "I'll sort things out
here and then join you in a moment."

Claire held up a hand. "No, you go with
them. I have a feeling that what Jonas has
to say might entail something that I already know about." She turned to Jonas.
"Am I right?"

Jonas nodded. "It has some bearing on
the matter."

Art gave Claire a questioning frown before throwing up his hands. "All right, then,
you'd better follow me."

As Art led them through the arch towards
the office, Claire watched them go and then
stood in a daze, trying to take in what had
just happened in the past few minutes. She
had never expected, nor even wanted, to
see Jonas again, and here he was with his
wife in New York. And if that wasn't a big-
enough shock, the sheer size of the cheque
that he had presented to her had simply

taken her breath away. More than three quarters of a million dollars! She herself had never in her life owned anything outright, it was all part of the business and, as such, really belonged to Art. But now, she was . . . wealthy.

"Excuse me."

She turned to find one of the customers standing behind her. He had been sitting with his wife at the table next to where the Fairweathers were due to be seated.

"I wonder if I could get the bill."

Claire shook her head to get herself back to reality. "I'm so sorry, I was miles away. Of course, I'll have it brought right over."

She walked over to the bar, where one of the young waiters was opening up a bottle of wine.

"Michael, table eight needs the bill."

"Okay, I'll get it to them," the young man replied.

"And listen, Art and I have to be in the office for the next half an hour, but you should be able to cope now. Things are beginning to quieten down."

"Sure thing," he replied before hurrying off with the wine.

Claire stood at the bar for a moment, a grin spreading across her face as she envisaged once more the cheque with her name and that incredible amount written upon it. She turned to the icebox and took out a bottle of champagne, but then had second thoughts and returned it. Let's hear first what Jonas has to say for himself, she thought.

When she entered the office, there was a pause in conversation. Art, who was leaning against the filing cabinet, stared at Jonas with a look of incredulity on his face. He turned to Claire and shook his head. "Jeez, angel, that's some weird family you were brought up with."

Claire simply nodded in reply and pulled a chair over from the corner of the room and sat down next to Liv.

"So you never saw Claire again after that . . . incident in the workshop?" Art asked.

Jonas sat on the edge of the desk, his arms crossed. "No, I didn't, and I wasn't around the place for much longer after that, either. I'd always hoped I might make it as a rally driver, but I never made the grade, so I eventually got a job working as a mechanic for one of the Formula One racing teams. That took me away for about eight years before I made a bit of money, and then Liv and I came back to Croich and bought the farm off Leo."

"Were you still quite resentful of what had happened to you?" Art asked.

Jonas grinned and caught Claire's eye. "I wasn't coming back to seek revenge, if that's what you mean. Life had moved on, and I was quite content with my lot. I'd made some money and I was married to Liv, and by that time, Rory was born." The smile faded from his face. "But then my father died suddenly and I began to wonder if he had ever truly forgiven me for what had happened. I guess that did sort of bring things back to mind."

"Were you still seeing Leo?"

"On a regular basis. My relationship with him never faltered. Even when I was away travelling the world, we were always in touch with each other. He was probably the greatest influence in my life. Anyway, when he began to get a bit . . . confused, I started going over to the house every two days or so to sort out his bills, and it was then that I began to notice . . . irregularities in his affairs."

Art frowned. "What sort of irregularities?"

"Well, I'll come to that," Jonas replied. He paused, biting on the side of his lip. "As I said, my initial plan was just to help him out with his mail, but when I first went into his office, it was abundantly clear that what he was in most need of was a full-time filing clerk. I don't think anything had been filed away for about a year, so I asked him if he had any objections to my dealing with this and he was more than delighted to give me carte blanche. So I set about the task, and it was during the course of cataloguing his bank statements and portfolios of investments that I realized Leo was still quite a wealthy man. Okay, he had sold the farm to me and most of that money went into the house, but he still had considerable share capital. Now, despite Leo's complete disorganization, one of these portfolios had been kept separate from the rest. It was in Leo's name, but written on the folder in his own handwriting was 'This is for Claire. Inheritance from her father, the late David Barclay.' There was no way of knowing this, other than the words on the folder."

Art nodded. "Yes, we knew about that. John Venables mentioned it on the day we went through Daphne's will. We just decided to leave it be and use it if and when we managed to purchase Croich."

Jonas smiled ruefully. "In retrospect, it's a pity you didn't take control of it at that point."

"Why do you say that?" Art asked.

Jonas paused again, scratching at the back of his head. "When I was made an executor of Leo's estate, I had a meeting with John Venables, who explained to me, amongst other things, that Leo had given both Marcus and Charity power of attorney over his affairs. Now, I never gave that a second thought until about twenty months later, sometime after he had been diagnosed with dementia. Actually, I seem to remember it was the day he returned from hospital after breaking his hip. I was down in his office and happened to be filing away some of his statements when I realized that his bank balance and the worth of his portfolios had started to diminish at an alarming rate, and I began to put two and two together."

Art looked at Claire, his eyes widening with sudden realization, and he let out a long slow whistle. "Oh my God."

"I'm sorry," Claire said, "what was happening?"

"I think that what Jonas is saying is that Marcus and Claire had invoked their power of attorney and were selling off Leo's shares."

Jonas nodded. "I didn't know what action to take. I didn't want to mention it to Leo because it was really none of my business. Maybe he had sanctioned it." He glanced at Claire. "But then I noticed that Claire's portfolio was beginning to be sold off as well . . . it was in Leo's name, after all . . . and that's when I realized Marcus and Charity had to be acting without Leo's knowledge."

"But they had no right to do that!" Claire exclaimed. "That was my father's money."

"I know it was," Jonas continued, "and that's why I decided I had to do something. Leo had told me that Marcus and Charity were keen for him to move out of the house, citing his dementia as the reason, but Leo knew that what they really wanted to do was to develop the property. It was a gold mine as far as they were concerned. Leo had given me a note saying you and Art had plans to turn the place into a conference centre, but I had forgotten about it until, one day, I came to visit Leo when you were both staying and I saw your proposed drawings for the place. That's when I started to formulate some kind of plan of action. The first thing I did was to suggest to Leo that Art should go down to London to have a meeting with Marcus to discuss his ideas and to negotiate a price."

"Why?" Art asked.

"I wanted it to be known. It was the best way to manipulate everybody. Firstly, I wanted Marcus to know that the house wasn't going to come directly to him and Charity, as he had believed."

"But why then did you suggest to me the ridiculously low price of two hundred and fifty thousand pounds for the house?" Claire asked.

"Because I wanted to get that figure fixed firmly in your minds, and at the same time gambling on the fact you'd let Marcus know that that amount would be your ballpark bid for the place." He smiled at Art. "You did let him know, didn't you?"

Art shrugged. "That's what I based my price on."

"Well, thank goodness you did," Jonas said, raising his eyebrows in relief. "So, while you were away in London, I moved onto the next stage and had an architect friend of mine put together some drawings for a fictitious development on the site of Croich. These were submitted to the planning office about three weeks after yours."

"Your plans were fictitious?" Art asked in amazement. "Do you mean you were never serious about developing the property?"

Jonas held up a hand. "I promise you, it will all come clear." He paused. "I then Googled Marcus Harrison, found the name and address of his company and sent him a copy of my plans with no covering letter. That made it clear to him that I too was interested in buying Croich and I knew it would be like a red rag to a bull. As we all know, Marcus and Charity hated anyone to have anything that they felt was rightfully theirs, especially if it was going to be myself . . . and you and Claire, of course.

That's the reason I couldn't tell you what I was doing. I needed to be sure he and Charity would take the bait. Then, about five days after my plans were submitted, I got my architect to ring the planning office to ask if there had been any other interest in the property. The clerk told him he had recently received an inquiry by phone from a London-based consortium. I knew then that Marcus had begun to take action, because no one else was aware that the house was for sale at that point."

Arts scratched slowly at his cheek. "But, wait a minute, you knew that Leo had agreed to sell the house to Claire and me."

"Yes, and I'm afraid I had to change all that. The difficulty was trying to see Leo by himself, because you two were constantly in the house. I'm afraid I had to rely on Rory to get the information from Violet about when you were going to be away."

"We thought that was the case," Claire said wryly. "It was on the day we were going to take Violet swimming."

"Exactly. That was when I came clean with Leo and told him about Marcus and Charity siphoning off all the money, including Claire's. It was not an easy thing to do because the poor old chap took it really hard, but he had to know. He was so ashamed and angry at what his children had done, he had no qualms about teaching them a real lesson and gave me a free hand in organizing the sale of the house by public auction."

"But why would you want to sell it that way?" Claire asked.

"Because I would never be able to judge the offers for the property in a closed-bid situation."

"So, despite your fictitious plans," Art said, "you really were after the property."

Jonas nodded. "Yes, in a way, I was. When it came to the auction, I was still hoping you'd both kept in mind my saying that the property wasn't worth more than two hundred and fifty thousand pounds. When you went all the way up to seven hundred and fifty thousand, I admit I was pretty worried that the whole thing was going to blow up in my face, but then you dropped out and that was when I had to start concentrating." He laughed. "It was, without doubt, the biggest financial gamble I have ever taken in my life."

"But you didn't get it," Claire said.

"No, the London consortium did."

Claire shook her head. "I really don't understand this, Jonas. Why did you go to such lengths to prevent Art and me getting the house? And why, after all Marcus and Charity had done to you, were you so pleased that they were the ones that managed to buy the place? I saw you after the auction. You weren't disappointed at all."

Claire felt Liv's hand on her arm. "Jonas did this whole thing for you and Leo, Claire," she said. "Of course he was not disappointed. On the contrary, he was very much relieved, because, you see, the place is worthless as a housing development because it is impossible for it to be developed."

"What do you mean?" Claire asked, glancing round at Jonas.

"I had known ever since I was a young boy that the whole property is undermined," Jonas said. "Our family hadn't always been in farming. My grandfather was a miner, and it was he who told my father there were old coal-mine shafts coming in from the direction of the farm. They swing in a perfect loop round the outer perimeter of the gardens and, for some extraordinary reason, never touched the house nor the outer suburbs of the town that lies a mere two hundred yards away. The planning office would have records of this, but I was pretty well convinced they'd be lost somewhere in the archives. Marcus was so focused on taking the house from under our noses that he never did his homework correctly." He grinned conspiratorially. "As it happens, those old coal-mining shafts came to light in the planning office sooner rather than later."

"How so?" Art asked.

"As soon as the sale was complete and John Venables had received the funds, I sort of reminded them."

Claire nodded slowly. "And Leo knew exactly what you were doing all the time, didn't he?"

"He gave me his full support after that meeting I'd had with him. And it was Leo himself who decided he wanted to move into a residential home after that. He was devastated at what Marcus and Charity had done. He just wanted to be rid of the place."

Art pushed himself away from the filing cabinet and swept a hand across his hair.

"So it was all rather an elaborate sting, wasn't it? You did get your revenge on Marcus and Charity, after all."

"I suppose initially there had been an element of that, but when Leo told me he had known forever what had happened between myself and Charity, that part really became quite insignificant. From then on, I did it for Leo and Claire, just as Liv said."

"So what happened to the proceeds of the sale?" Claire asked.

"Enough was put aside so that Leo could spend the rest of his days quite happily in his residence, a substantial amount went to his pet research project at Kew Gardens, you were repaid your father's inheritance, and the rest was split between Marcus, Charity and yourself."

"But what about them?" Claire asked tentatively. "Are they ruined?"

"Well, I did a bit of research after the sale and found out that fifty-one per cent of the Croich Development Company was owned by Marcus and Charity and the remaining forty-nine per cent by a group of Marcus's business acquaintances. I worked out that they would have just about been able to pay back their investors, but I'm afraid it's left them both with pretty large financial headaches."

"Hence my phone call from Charity," Claire murmured.

Art shook his head slowly, holding out his hands in complete bewilderment at what Jonas had just told them. He pushed himself away from the filing cabinet and approached Jonas with his hand outstretched. "Listen, I really don't know what to say to you—other than thanks. You put your neck on the line for both of us, and for Leo."

Jonas shook his hand. "Regardless of what you might think, it wasn't in my nature to do such a thing, but considering the circumstances, I'm afraid it had to be done."

Art nodded and let out a long breath of relief. "Well, I reckon the best thing we can do now is open up a very large bottle of champagne, don't you?" He went over to the door and opened it and then turned. "And, of course, dinner is certainly on the house tonight. It's the least we can do."

As he left the office, Liv uncrossed her long slim legs and got her to her feet. "I think I might go to the restroom before we have dinner." She smiled at both Jonas and Claire. "I think you two might have something to say to each other that is probably long overdue." She brushed a kiss on Jonas's cheek before leaving the office, closing the door behind her.

Claire pushed herself slowly out of the chair and stood with her arms crossed in front of Jonas. There was an awkward silence, neither of them looking at the other.

"Do you remember the Dragon Plant House?" she said eventually.

Jonas smiled. "Of course I do."

"What do you think will happen to the place now?"

Jonas pushed himself to his feet. "Oh, its life goes on. It was sold off pretty cheap to a young family from England. They're really nice people. The kids are good friends of Rory and Asrun, so they still spend a good deal of time around there. They're actually with them at the moment."

Claire smiled. "It's lovely to think of children careering about that place again." She sighed. "I still can't quite believe I've seen it for the last time. It really was so much part of my life."

Jonas shrugged. "There's no reason why you shouldn't see it again."

"What do you mean?"

"Well, Rory has never stopped talking about Violet since you left. He wanted to come over with us to see her, but we felt we were going to be here for such a short time, it wasn't worth it. So we came to a deal. I was to ask you and Art and Violet to come back to Croich and stay with us any time you want. He said it was the perfect place for you to be if you wanted to go and visit Leo."

Claire laughed quietly. "And what did you think of that idea?"

Jonas stepped forward and put his arms around her. "Oh, Claire, what do you think I feel? I cannot think of anything I'd like better. My whole reason for doing what I did was to try to rekindle our friendship, nothing more."

Claire pressed her face against his jacket. "I think you've done more than enough for that to happen." She reached up and gave him a kiss on the cheek. "You said you were to be trusted. Thank you a million times for everything you've done for me."

"It was my greatest pleasure," Jonas replied, pushing her gently away, and Claire could see the broad smile on his face and the blush in his cheeks. He laughed. "You know, I think that's the first time you've ever . . . kissed me."

"You think?"

"Well, isn't it?"

Claire laughed and pushed him towards the door. "Oh, Jonas, I know it is. Believe me, I know."

Acknowledgements

Thanks to Tom and Karyn in New York, Felicity and her great team in Oxford, Kirsty—of course, and a special thanks to Caroline at Little Brown whose intuitive editorial notes really sorted this book out.